PENGUIN MODE

MW01579686

Uncommon Danger

Eric Ambler (1909–98) was one of the most fascinating British writers of the late 1930s. These five thrillers, republished as Penguin Modern Classics for Ambler's centenary, retain a remarkable sense of the dread and terror that filled Europe as world war broke out. Some were made into films (not least Orson Welles' superb version of *Journey into Fear*), all were bestsellers, inventing a new, more realistic form of spy novel, where the main protagonist is not so much a hero as a victim, pursued by malevolent Fascist forces of overwhelming power. These are paranoid stories, but written at a time when paranoia was disturbingly close to common sense.

Thomas Jones is a journalist based in Italy. He has written for the *Guardian*, *Internazionale*, *National Geographic*, *New Statesman* and *Daily Telegraph*, and is currently a contributing editor at the *London Review of Books*.

ERIC AMBLER

Uncommon Danger

With an Introduction by Thomas Jones

PENGUIN BOOKS

To my Mother

PENGUIN CLASSICS

Published by the Penguin Group
Penguin Books Ltd, 80 Strand, London WC2R 0RL, England
Penguin Group (USA) Inc., 375 Hudson Street, New York, New York 10014, USA
Penguin Group (Canada), 90 Eglinton Avenue East, Suite 700, Toronto, Ontario, Canada M4P 2Y3
(a division of Pearson Penguin Canada Inc.)
Penguin Ireland, 25 St Stephen's Green, Dublin 2, Ireland
(a division of Penguin Books Ltd)
Penguin Group (Australia), 250 Camberwell Road,
Camberwell, Victoria 3124, Australia (a division of Pearson Australia Group Pty Ltd)
Penguin Books India Pvt Ltd, 11 Community Centre, Panchsheel Park, New Delhi – 110 017, India
Penguin Group (NZ), 67 Apollo Drive, Rosedale, North Shore 0632, New Zealand
(a division of Pearson New Zealand Ltd)
Penguin Books (South Africa) (Pty) Ltd, 24 Sturdee Avenue, Rosebank, Johannesburg 2196, South Africa

Penguin Books Ltd, Registered Offices: 80 Strand, London WC2R 0RL, England

www.penguin.com

First published by Hodder and Stoughton 1937
Published in Penguin Classics 2009

019

Set in Dante MT 10.5/13pt
Typeset by Palimpsest Book Production Limited, Grangemouth, Stirlingshire
Printed in England by Clays Ltd, Elcograf S.p.A.

978-0-141-19034-1

Introduction

For Graham Greene he was 'unquestionably our best thriller writer'. John le Carré once called him 'the source on which we all draw'. But Eric Ambler never intended to be a writer of thrillers. If his 1985 autobiography, the wrily entitled *Here Lies Eric Ambler*, is to be believed, his ambition as a young man was to be a playwright. Born in 1909 in south-east London, the eldest child of music-hall artists, at the age of sixteen he won a scholarship to study engineering at Northampton Polytechnic in Islington (now City University). He soon dropped out, and after the General Strike found a job as a trainee at the Edison Swan Electric Company. During a six-month secondment to the firm's cable works in Gloucestershire, he wrote the first two chapters of a realist novel, in the manner of Arnold Bennett, based on the life of his father. Returning to London, he was asked to compose a press release extolling the bogus virtues of a batch of dodgy bulbs for car headlights. They sold so quickly on the back of it that the company even thought about making more. As for Ambler, the experience may or may not have given him a taste for concocting plausible fictions with a pseudo-technical bent, but it certainly showed he had a talent for it. Before long he was working full time as an advertising copywriter.

Here Lies is almost coy in the way it slips mention of Ambler's first novel into the narrative: he gives his girlfriend a bound page proof in a cinema on the Kings Road just before the lights go down. *The Dark Frontier* (1936) began life as a parody of the contemporary British thriller. The problem with the genre, as Ambler saw it, was principally one of character. Whether 'power-crazed or coldly sane', the villains were wholly implausible, while the heroes were defined only by their 'abysmal stupidity combined with superhuman resourcefulness and unbreakable knuckle bones'. Julian Symons, in *Bloody Murder: From the Detective Story to the Crime Novel*, frames it slightly differently: 'After the First World War began, spy stories became unequivocally nationalist in tone and right-wing in political sympathy.'

In *The Dark Frontier* a mild-mannered academic is knocked on the head in a car accident shortly after picking up one of these novels in a West Country pub. He comes round convinced he is Conway Carruthers, secret agent, the thick-skulled, tough-knuckled hero of the book he's just been reading, and charges off to Eastern Europe to thwart the nuclear ambitions of a power-crazed countess. It's extremely silly, but also, as if despite itself, a fairly decent thriller, not merely mocking but beginning to improve on the shortcomings of the form. That contemporary readers were prepared to take it at face value is perhaps a sign of how severe those shortcomings were. The *Scotsman* called it a 'genuine thriller'.

By the time reviews of *The Dark Frontier* were coming out, Ambler was already deep into his next book, a straight – or at least non-parodic – thriller with the working title 'Background to Danger'. A short, fast-paced, intensely gripping novel, set over the course of a few days in November 1936, it was written, he later recalled, during 'the year in which Italy invaded Abyssinia, Civil War broke out in Spain and Hitler ordered the German Army to reoccupy the Rhineland. It was a year of yet more refugees and of marriages arranged to confer passports. It was also the year in which the League of Nations was at last seen plainly to be impotent. Those were the things that I was trying, in my own fictional terms, to write about.'

The protagonist of *Uncommon Danger*, as Hodder and Stoughton thought the novel should be called, is not a professional hero. Far from it. Kenton is a thirty-year-old cash-strapped freelance journalist, based in Berlin, working for whichever London papers will use his stories. He 'had never regarded himself as a particularly courageous man. Such scenes of physical violence as he had encountered in the course of his work had upset both his digestion and his mental processes.' He's no good with his fists, missing his target the one time in the novel he tries to punch someone, and has never fired a gun before in his life.

Many of the heroes of Ambler's later novels are in the same mould: a journalist, a teacher or an engineer rather than a professional spy, short of money, not straightforwardly a member of any one nation state (Kenton's father was from Belfast, his mother French), and ever so slightly disreputable. Some or all of this description could apply to Josef Vadassy in *Epitaph for a Spy* (1938), Steve Fraser in *The Night-Comers* (1956), Greg Nilsen in *Passage of Arms* (1959) or Michael Howell in *The Levanter* (1972). But Desmond d'Esterre Kenton – his given names occur only once in the novel, when he's reading the file the Russians have been keeping on him – is the prototype for them all.

We first meet him waiting in the cold at Nuremberg station in the middle of the night, trying to get to Vienna, because he's lost all his money and got into debt playing poker-dice; there's a man in the Austrian capital, a Jew he helped escape from Munich two years earlier, whom he thinks he might be able to borrow money from, though he'd really rather not have to ask. So when a fellow passenger offers him a substantial sum to smuggle an envelope over the frontier, he's all too willing to oblige. The story doesn't take long to get going. 'Kenton was one of those persons, of whom there are many, who find the contemplation of scenery very boring.' And Ambler isn't one to waste time with gratuitous passages of description. Kenton soon finds himself not only wanted by the Austrian police for a murder he didn't commit, but up against a particularly vicious thug called Stefan Saridza and entangled in a plot to install a Fascist government in Romania.

The reader already knows more about this plot than Kenton does, because in the prologue we witness a gathering of the senior conspirators: a meeting of the board of the Pan-Eurasian Petroleum Company in the City of London. The company, under the leadership of its loathsome chairman, Joseph Balterghen, wants greater access to the oilfields of Bessarabia, and sees regime change as a perfectly reasonable way to go about getting it – seventy years later, the scenario is anything but dated. None of the board members makes an appearance in the main body of the narrative. 'You see,' as one of the other characters explains to Kenton, 'your business man desires the end, but dislikes the means . . . That is why Saridza is necessary. For at some point or other in the amazingly complicated business structure of the world, there is always dirty work to be done.' This dark territory stalked by the likes of Saridza, the hinterland that Kenton stumbles into, between the secret decisions made in boardrooms and the global upheavals they effect, is ideal terrain for a thriller to explore.

Kenton learns about Saridza from Andreas Zaleshoff, the Soviet Union's man in Switzerland. But Kenton's own views on the might of capital aren't so very different: 'It was the power of Business, not the deliberations of statesmen, that shaped the destinies of nations,' he reflects. In *Uncommon Danger*, the representatives of Communism and what Zaleshoff calls 'moderate radicalism' but Kenton himself would probably think of as basic human decency are pitted against the agents of capital and Fascism: Balterghen, Saridza and their many cronies. There's no shortage of unsavoury foreigners in the novel, but they're more than matched by the unsavoury Englishmen. The most hateful character of all is Saridza's chief henchman, Captain Mailler. Stupid, sadistic, public school-educated, a former Black-and-Tan and one-time professional strikebreaker in the United States, 'wanted in New Orleans for the murder of a coloured woman', it's tempting to see him as a satirical portrait of the archetypal hero of the moribund thrillers that Ambler was so determined to supersede, unmasked and revealed for the cryptofascist brute he really is.

Kenton's alliance with Zaleshoff isn't always an easy one – the journalist is unimpressed by the spy's attempt to fob him off with the official Stalinist line on Trotskyite subversion, for example, and Zaleshoff is not unreasonably suspicious of Kenton's motives for helping him – but it's kept afloat by the undercurrent of sexual attraction between Kenton and Zaleshoff's sister. Tamara Prokovna isn't the token love interest, however, or some kind of damsel in distress: she's a vital character in her own right, intrinsic to the main plot, not to mention extremely handy behind the wheel of a supercharged Mercedes.

Ambler became less comfortable with his own relationship with Communism as the years went by. 'If the term fellow-travellers had been used in its present pejorative sense at the time I think that many of us could well have been described in that way,' he says in *Here Lies*. The tone of regret is disappointing – what does he have to apologize for? – but hardly surprising in a memoir written both at and in a more conservative age. The first novel he wrote after the Second World War, *Judgment on Deltchev* (1951), about a Stalinist show trial in Eastern Europe, provoked a flurry of hostile responses from former comrades. But some of those who were outraged by his perceived treachery must have been among those who left the Communist Party of Great Britain in droves five years later, after the Soviet tanks rolled into Hungary. Perhaps in this, as in so many other ways, Ambler was simply several years ahead of his time.

Thomas Jones

Contents

'Today, with Europe assuming the appearance of an armed camp in which an incident, unimportant in itself, would be sufficient to ignite a conflagration that would consume Europe and perhaps spread to other quarters of the globe: today, when national security in Europe and perhaps elsewhere, depends primarily upon the strength and effectiveness of a nation's armed forces, the question of supply of raw materials and particularly supply of petroleum is of the first importance.' – *World Petroleum*

PROLOGUE

In Gracechurch Street

One sunny morning in July, Mr Joseph Balterghen's blue Rolls-Royce oozed silently away from the pavement in Berkeley Square, slid across Piccadilly into St James's, and sped softly eastward towards the City of London.

Mr Balterghen was a small man and, as his Rolls-Royce was a very large car, the few persons waiting for buses on the north side of Trafalgar Square would have had to have craned their necks to see him. None of them troubled to do so. This was a pity, for, while Mr Balterghen was anything but pleasing to the eye, he was chairman of Pan-Eurasian Petroleum and of fifteen other companies and a director of thirty more, including one bank. In the words of those who write bank references, he was 'highly respectable'.

That the phrase had nothing to do with church attendances, ten o'clock bed-times and nicely rolled umbrellas was made obvious by his face. A disgruntled business associate had once described it as looking like 'a bunch of putty-coloured grapes with some of the crevices filled in'. He should have added that the grapes were also very shrivelled and that a black tooth-brush moustache sprouted surrealistically from the lower part of the bunch.

As his car glided down Northumberland Avenue, Mr Balterghen gnawed thoughtfully at his moustache. The chauffeur, catching a glimpse of this in the driving mirror, muttered 'the perisher's goin' to a board meetin',' opened out along the Embankment, and did not look in the driving mirror again until he pulled up outside the new offices of the Pan-Eurasian Petroleum Company in Gracechurch Street.

Inside the building, Mr Balterghen stopped gnawing his moustache, set his face in the impassive glare he reserved for business hours, and was shot up to the sixth floor in a chromium-plated lift. Then he went to his office.

To Mr Balterghen's second secretary, his master's office was an evergreen source of wonder. Blundell had been taken into Pan-Eurasian under Mr Balterghen's 'Recruiting-from-the-Universities' plan and was one of the few bewildered survivors of the subsequent 'Experience-not-Education' purge. 'Balterghen's room', he had once told his wife, 'is more like a harlot's parlour than an office. He's got a red Turkey carpet and stippled green walls, a Second Empire desk and a Chinese lacquer cabinet, a neo-Byzantine book-case and six baroque chairs plus a Drage-Aztec cocktail cabinet that flies apart and exposes all the bottles and things inside when you press the button. Even if you didn't know from experience what a complete wart the man is, that room would tell you.'

The first thing Mr Balterghen did on that sunny July morning was to operate his cocktail cabinet. From it, he took a large bottle of stomach powder and mixed himself a draught. Then he lit a cigar to take the taste away and rang the fifth bell on the Second Empire desk. After a short interval, Blundell came in.

'What time was the meeting called for, Blundell?'

Mr Balterghen spoke English as though he had a hot potato in his mouth.

'Eleven, Mr Balterghen.'

'It's five to now; are the other directors here?'

'All except Lord Welterfield.'

'We'll begin without his lordship.'

'Very well, Mr Balterghen. I'll tell Mr Wilson. Here are your notes.'

'Put them down there. Wait a minute. If a gentleman named Colonel Robinson calls for me about twelve forty-five, I don't want him shown in here to wait. Put him in a vacant office on the floor below. You understand? I don't want him shown up here.'

'Yes, Mr Balterghen.'

He went out.

At eleven-two precisely, the board of directors of Pan-Eurasian Petroleum began their meeting.

The agenda that day was tackled with a certain amount of gusto. All knew that there was only one really interesting item on it, but that titbit had been placed last. When Lord Welterfield arrived at a quarter to twelve his profuse apologies were acknowledged hurriedly. It did not, it was clear, matter whether Lord Welterfield was present or not.

'I see,' said Mr Balterghen at last, 'that the next item on the agenda concerns my Roumanian negotiations.'

He said it with an air of slight surprise that deceived nobody. The board settled itself in its chairs. The chairman continued.

'I don't think Lord Welterfield was present at the first meeting we held on this subject, so I think that I had better run over the few main points that were discussed then. You will remember that, in nineteen twenty-two, the Company obtained a drilling concession from the Roumanian Government. That concession covered a tract of land east of Jassi which was believed at the time to be rich oil country. You will also remember that the concession turned out to be a failure from the Company's point of view. In the years nineteen twenty-three and twenty-four only five thousand barrels were produced and early in nineteen twenty-five the most promising well ceased producing. Our geologists reported unfavourably on the prospects of striking commercially useful deposits and the concession was, to all intents and purposes, written off as a dead loss. At the time, this did not matter very much as our subsidiaries in Venezuela, Mexico and the Near East were producing profitably and, for that matter, still are.'

There was a murmur of agreement.

'But,' continued Mr Balterghen, 'the developments in the political situation in Europe during nineteen thirty-five and thirty-six have suggested that we should look once again in the direction of Roumania. The sanctions against Italy taught Mussolini one thing at least – that Italy could not safely depend for her supplies of oil on the Caribbean. Iran and Iraq were in the hands of the British. Russia was in the hands of the Soviets. The Italian fleet was oil-burning, the big Italian air force would be helpless faced with an oil shortage; so would the mechanized army. There was only one solution – Roumania. At the moment Italy is taking large quantities of Roumanian oil. She will take more. Her new armament programme – and I speak from personal knowledge – is based less on further increases in man-power than on the addition of submarines to her navy, heavy bombers to her air force, and a new kind of tank to her army. That is important, for in all three cases' – he tapped a stubby finger on the table – 'in all three cases diesel engines are being used.'

The meeting looked impressed. The chairman licked his lips and went on:

'I did not have to explain to you gentlemen that here was worthwhile business. Lord Welterfield will, I feel sure, see the point immediately. Two months ago we made representations to the Roumanian Government. We asked that the existing concessions should be revised. We told them that we were ready to pay and pay handsomely. All that we required was a fair share of the oil lands at present divided between our competitors. Our agents in Bucharest approached the right people. Steps were taken – their nature is unimportant to this meeting – to ensure a favourable reception of our proposals in Governmental circles. It was arranged that at the November session of the Roumanian Chamber of Deputies, a responsible leader would table our proposals for concession revision as a necessary reform – as, of course, it is.'

The meeting signified its approval of this sentiment.

'Ten days ago,' added Mr Balterghen calmly, 'I received news that at the November session, Concession Reform would be defeated.'

For a moment there was dead silence. Then everyone began to talk at once. The chairman held up his hand.

'I can appreciate your feelings, gentlemen,' he said amiably; 'they are much the same as were my own when I was informed. But allow me to give you the reasons for this set-back. I would like to say, at the outset, that no blame attaches to our agents in Roumania. They have done their work admirably. The failure has resulted from one thing and one thing only – a scurrilous article published in Bucharest.' He produced a battered newspaper from the folder in front of him and held it up. 'This is the sheet. It is called – I translate freely – *The Work People*, and it is published by the United Socialist Party of Roumania.'

'Reds!' said Lord Welterfield violently.

'Actually,' said Mr Balterghen, 'the United Socialists are not affiliated to the Communist International; but they are, I agree, very much of the Left.'

'Same thing,' snapped Lord Welterfield.

'However,' went on the chairman, 'I don't suppose any of you gentlemen read Roumanian. I do; so I propose to read to you one or two extracts from the article. It is entitled, "The Vultures Gather", and, after a rather wordy preamble on the subject of capitalist intrigue, it gets down to business. Who, it asks, are the directors of the Pan-Eurasian Petroleum Company? The question is rhetorical, for it goes on, I'm afraid, to give our names supplemented by a series of biographies which are such obvious lies that I will not trouble to translate them.'

'What,' said Lord Welterfield, incautiously, 'do the blackguards say about me?'

Mr Balterghen glanced at the paper.

'Lord Welterfield,' he read, 'colliery owner and millionaire. Famous for his patronage of sport. Less well-known as the man who employed *agents provocateurs* to provoke a riot in a colliery town during a strike, and for his numerous offences against the Factory Acts.'

'Lies!' shouted Lord Welterfield shrilly; 'it was never proved who employed the men. I absolutely deny it!'

The chairman sighed.

'Exactly, Lord Welterfield, we are agreed that the entire article is socialist propaganda. I assume, gentlemen, that we can take this portion as read?'

There were hasty murmurs of assent.

'Very well. It goes on: "There is a movement afoot to effect sweeping concession reforms. What exactly is meant by reform in this case? Simply, that the Government is asked to break its contracts with existing oil *concessionnaires* in order that the Pan-Eurasian Petroleum Company can have the lion's share of the increasing trade with Italy. Now there are three unsavoury aspects of this business. The first is that there has evidently been wholesale bribery in Governmental circles – there can be no other explanation of this sudden desire for revision. The second is the now familiar spectacle of foreign capitalist exploiters meddling with the destinies of the Roumanian people. The third is the obvious dangers of such a revision. The Pan-Eurasian Company probably has allies amongst the British and American interests already in our country; but what of the other nations? Nicholas Titulescu, manœuvred from office and poisoned by the Fascist Iron Guard, is no longer here to protect our interests. But the people must fight on without him. Our foreign alliances are too valuable to be jeopardized by corrupt officials and capitalist pawns . . ." The article,' continued Mr Balterghen, 'lapses here into mere abuse. The entire story is, of course, a flagrant distortion of the truth of the case. We are business men and we are anxious to do business with the Roumanian Government. We are not interested in politics.'

There were several 'hear-hears'.

'All the same,' went on the chairman, 'the article has caused us serious inconvenience. The paper was suppressed and its offices were destroyed by a band of youths armed with hand-grenades, but too late to prevent wide distribution of the article. The public prosecutor has been compelled to charge several of our friends in the Government with corrupt practices, public interest has been aroused and, though Concession Reform is tabled, it will not be supported.'

A stout man at the other end of the table cleared his throat loudly.

'Then we can't do anything so far as I can see.'

'On the contrary, Sir James,' said Mr Balterghen, 'we can do a great deal. I have, anticipating the confidence of the meeting, retained the services of a man with considerable experience in matters of this sort. He has worked for me before. His services will be expensive, but I think I can safely say that the results will warrant the expenditure.'

'What's he going to do?' wheezed the stout man facetiously, 'shoot the socialists down? Whiff of grape shot, eh?'

The meeting laughed heartily and felt a little better.

Mr Balterghen twisted his lips slightly. It was his way of smiling.

'Perhaps such extreme measures won't be necessary. The man in question could, I suppose, best be described as a propagandist.'

'Well,' said Lord Welterfield, 'as long as the fellow isn't a Red, he can call himself anything he likes as far as I'm concerned.'

'Then, gentlemen, I take it that I have your permission to deal with this man. I should like to make it clear, however, that, for the moment, I propose to keep the nature of the measures to be taken absolutely confidential.'

The meeting looked knowing, declared that it had every confidence in the chairman's judgement on the matter in hand and, after a few formalities, dispersed weightily to luncheon.

Mr Balterghen returned to his office. Blundell followed him in.

'Colonel Robinson is waiting in room 542, Mr Balterghen. Shall I show you the way?'

They went down in the lift and walked along a corridor.

'Here, sir.'

Mr Balterghen opened the door and went in. Blundell heard his employer say 'Ah, Stefan!' and noticed that Colonel Robinson's arm seemed to be a trifle stiff at the elbow as he shook hands. Then they began talking in a language he did not recognize. It sounded like a cross between Russian and Italian.

'Colonel Robinson my foot!' said Blundell to his wife that evening. 'If that fellow's name is Robinson then I'm Hitler. Salt, please.'

I

Linz Train

With a thick woollen scarf wound twice round his neck, his shoulders hunched and his hands thrust deep in his overcoat pockets, Kenton waited at Nuremberg for the Frankfurt-Linz train. An icy November wind blustered through the almost deserted station, swinging the enamel reflectors and causing mad shadows to dance on the platform. He shivered and, leaving his suitcase, started to walk up and down in the lee of a small station building.

A thin, intelligent-looking man, Kenton gave the impression of being older than his thirty years. It was, perhaps, the mouth. There was a pleasant quality of humour combined with discretion in the rather full lips. He looked more like an American than an Englishman, and was actually neither. His father had come from Belfast, his mother from a Breton family living in Lille.

As he paced the Nuremberg platform that night, his self-contempt increased with the numbness of his feet. It was not, he told himself, as if he enjoyed gambling. It bored him; but he had in him that unhappy quality of recklessness that decrees that when the possessor once starts to gamble he shall go on until all the money in his pocket has gone. It had happened to Kenton before; but as he had always been a sufferer from one of the two principal diseases of newspapermen, lack of money – the other is cirrhosis of the liver – it had not mattered much. Now, however, it was more serious, for, in his pocket that day, he had been carrying his entire fortune, four hundred-odd marks.

Kenton was accounted a good journalist. It was not that he possessed the miraculous nose for news that detects the visiting film star behind the dark glasses and dirty mackintosh. His qualifications were of a different order.

Most foreign news comes from the permanent correspondents of individual papers and the agency men. The free-lance abroad does not, as a rule, stand a very great chance against them. Kenton, however, had three important assets: the ability to learn foreign idiom quickly and to speak it with an un-English accent, a very sound knowledge of European politics, and a quick and shrewd judgement of news values. The first was the most valuable. The majority of English men and women working abroad speak the language of the country fluently. Very few speak it as it should be spoken. Kenton was one of those who did. That advantage made the difference between getting and not getting an occasional crumb of exclusive news.

It had been in search of such a crumb that he had come to Nuremberg. Some of the high Nazi officials were gathered together, and it had been rumoured that important decisions were to be made. Nobody had known what the decisions were about; but they were almost certain to be unpleasant and, therefore, News.

Ninety per cent of political reporting consists of waiting for conferences to end. The time is usually passed in a bar. At Nuremberg it was the Kaiserhof. When Kenton had arrived there had been several correspondents he knew already installed. Among them was the Havas Agency man, a Pole, whom he liked. It had been this Pole who had produced the poker-dice.

Kenton had lost steadily from the first.

Poker-dice is not a good game for those who don't know when to stop, for it combines the most dangerous aspects of poker with the simplicity of dice. Large amounts of money can thus be lost, and won, quickly and effortlessly.

By the time it had been learnt that the conference would issue no Press *communiqué* that day, but resume the sitting on the morrow, Kenton had had just five *Pfennige* left in his pocket. He had explained the situation to the other three players and, amid murmurs of regret and goodwill, drinks were called for. Over them, he had taken the opportunity to point out that the bankruptcy was merely temporary and that he possessed funds in Vienna. All that remained, he had added, was to get to Vienna. The Havas man had promptly volunteered a hundred marks. Feeling several sorts of worm, Kenton had accepted it as gracefully as possible, ordered and paid for another round of drinks, and left soon after for the station. There he had found that the only through train to Vienna that night carried first and second *luxe* only. If *mein Herr* wished to go third class there was a slow train that went as far as Linz in Upper Austria, where he could change for Vienna. He had resigned himself to waiting for the Linz train.

He had been waiting for three-quarters of an hour when the Night Orient Express from Ostend came in, flecked with melting snow. Behind the steamy windows of the coaches, braided waiters hurried towards the first-class restaurant car. He heard the clatter of dishes and the clink of glasses. From where he stood out of the wind he could see a destination board on the side of one of the sleeping-cars – Wien, Buda-Pesth, Belgrade, Sofia, Istanbul. The Orient Express looked warm and luxurious inside and he was glad when it moved out. At that moment it seemed to epitomize all the security and comfort – bodily, financial and gastronomic – that he craved. He wallowed in self-pity.

It would not have been so bad if his jaunty claim to funds in Vienna had been founded on fact; but it was not. He had no money whatever in Vienna. He was going there with the faint hope that a Jewish instrument maker he knew would lend him some. Kenton had been able to help him get his family out of Munich in the bad days of 1934 and the instrument maker had been grateful. But, for all Kenton knew, his old friend might have left Vienna. Or he might have no money to lend. That, Kenton told himself, would be far worse. He would have to explain that it didn't matter at all really, and the little man would feel miserable. Jews were sensitive about such things. Still, it was his one chance, and in any case, he couldn't be worse off in Vienna than he was in Nuremberg.

He dug his fists into his overcoat pockets. After all, he had been broke before – not always through his own folly either – and invariably something had turned up to help him. Sometimes it had been a good news story, sometimes an unexpected cheque from his New York agent for second rights on a long-forgotten article. Once he had been at the Sofia railway station when the King of the Bulgars had left for a destination unknown. The chance remark of a ticket inspector to a German commercial traveller had sent him scurrying to the telephone with the first news of a projected meeting between Boris and Carol. Perhaps Hitler would be on the Linz train on his way to meet the leader of the Austrian Social Democrats. The idea entertained him and he amused himself by sketching in the events that might render that fantastic encounter feasible. By the time the Linz train arrived he was feeling almost cheerful.

It was practically empty and he had a compartment to himself. The seats were hard, but not so hard as Nuremberg platform. He slung his suitcase on to the rack, wedged himself into a corner and went to sleep.

The cold woke him as the train was pulling out of Ratisbon. Another passenger had entered the compartment and opened the window an inch. The stream of icy air mixed with smoke from the engine completed what lack of food and the hardness of the seat had started. Suddenly, he was wide awake, cold, stiff, hungry and wretched. All the artificial optimism he had so painstakingly acquired had gone. For the first time he was conscious of the true seriousness of his position.

If Rosen wasn't in Vienna, what exactly was his next move? He could, of course, wire home to a paper for money; but they would probably refuse him. His contributions were of necessity spasmodic, and if he preferred running round as a free-lance abroad to a nice steady job doing police-court news in London, that was his own affair. Gloomily, he searched his mind for information on the subject of the Consular Service. What were the qualifications for becoming a 'Distressed British Citizen'? An English sailor he had once met had spoken contemptuously of a 'cargo of D.B.C.s' loaded at Cape Town. He saw himself consigned, with a label round his neck, carriage paid from Vienna to London. Looking round for something else to think about, he glanced at his fellow passenger.

Kenton had travelled on Continental trains long enough to regard anyone who wanted a window open, even the merest fraction, with some suspicion. The author of this window-opening outrage was small and very dark. His face was narrow and he had the kind of jowl that should be shaved twice a day, but isn't. He wore a dirty starched collar with a huge grey-flowered tie and a crumpled dark-striped suit. On his knees rested a limp American cloth attaché-case from which he was extracting paper bags containing sausage and bread. A bottle of Vichy water stood propped against the back of the seat beside him.

His eyes, dark brown and lustrous, met Kenton's. He waved a piece of sausage at the open window.

'Please?'

Kenton nodded. The other filled his mouth with sausage.

'Good. I prefer to travel *à l'anglais.*'

He munched. A thought seemed to strike him. He indicated the attaché-case.

'Please, you will acept some sausage?'

The automatic refusal that rose to Kenton's lips died there. He was hungry.

'It's very good of you. Thank you.'

He was passed a piece of sausage and a hunk of bread. The sausage was impregnated with garlic and he enjoyed it. His companion plied him with more. Kenton accepted it gratefully. The brown-eyed man crammed some bread into his mouth, saturated it with a draught of Vichy, and began to talk about his stomach.

'Doctors are fools. You would not think to look at me, to see me eating with you now, that two years ago the doctors told me that I must have an operation for ulcers of the duodenum. It is true. I have a stomach of iron' – he thumped it to prove the point and gurgitated violently – 'but it is thanks to no doctors. I tell you they are fools. They wish only to put you to the knife, to cut and probe and pry. But I said no. No prying and probing into me, my friends; I have a better way. They ask me what it is, but I laugh. I am not one to be tricked into telling such things to prying doctors. But you are no doctor and I will tell you. *Pasta* is the secret. Nothing but *pasta*. I ate nothing but *pasta* for six months and I am cured. I am no prying Italian, but I tell you *pasta* is good for the stomach.

Maccheroni, *fettucine*, *tagliatelle*, *spaghetti*, they are all the same; all are *pasta* and all good for the stomach.'

He continued in praise of flour and water, and Kenton's face must have revealed his wandering attention, for the owner of the iron stomach broke off suddenly and announced that he would sleep.

'Please to wake me,' he added, 'when we approach the frontier.'

He took off his hat, replaced it with a copy of the *Völkischer Beobachter* to protect his head from the smuts and, curling up on the seat, seemed to go to sleep. Kenton went outside to smoke.

It was ten-thirty by his watch and he estimated that another hour should see him at Passau. As he crushed out his cigarette he noticed that he was no longer alone in the corridor. A few compartments down a man was leaning on the rail, gazing out at the distant lights of a Bavarian village. Kenton had the impression that the man had that second turned his head and had been watching him. Then the man started walking towards him. Kenton noticed that he glanced in each compartment as he passed it and that he had small dull eyes set like pebbles in a puffy, unwholesome-looking face. As he came up, Kenton flattened himself against the window to allow the other to pass, but the man did not do so. Glancing behind him, Kenton saw that he was gazing into the compartment at his sleeping fellow traveller. Then, with a muttered '*Verzeihung*,' he walked back and disappeared into the next coach. Kenton dismissed him from his mind and returned to the compartment.

The newspaper had slipped from the little man's head. His eyes were closed. He looked sound asleep. But as Kenton passed him he saw that the man's forehead was shining with sweat.

Kenton sat and watched him for a bit, then he saw the brown eyes open slowly and flicker towards him.

'Has he gone?'

'Who?' said Kenton.

'He – the man in the corridor.'

'Yes.'

The other sat up and, after fumbling in his pocket, brought out a large and dirty handkerchief. He wiped his forehead and the palms of his hands. Then he looked at Kenton.

'You are, perhaps, an American?'

'No, English.'

'Ah, yes. You will understand – it was not your speech but your clothes that made me think . . .'

His voice trailed off into inaudibility. Suddenly he leapt to the switch and plunged the compartment into darkness. Kenton, not quite sure what was happening, stayed in his corner. If he were sharing a compartment with a madman, a negative attitude was probably safer. The next moment his blood froze as he felt the man sit on the seat beside him. He could hear him breathing heavily.

'Please do not be alarmed, *mein Herr.*'

The voice was strained, as if its owner had been running. Then he began to speak, slowly at first, then quickly and breathlessly.

'I am a German,' he began.

Kenton said 'Yes,' but disbelieved him. He had been trying to place the man's accent.

'I am a German, a Jew. My father was a Gentile, but my mother was a Jewess. Because of her I am persecuted and robbed. You do not know what it is to be a German with a Jewess for a mother. They have ruined my business. I am a metallurgist. You say perhaps this man does not look like a metallurgist, but you are wrong. I am a metallurgist. I have worked at Essen and at Düsseldorf in the foundries. I had my own business, my own factory – small, you understand; but you are English and will know that it is the small factory that is sometimes good. Now that is over. I have a little money. I wish to leave the country of my father and my Jewess mother and start again a small business. I wish to take my money, but these Nazi brutes say no. It is forbidden that I take my own money where I wish. I think perhaps I take it secretly by a quiet way across the frontier. All goes well. I meet a good English friend, we eat together, we hold conversation as gentlemen. Then I see this Nazi spy and he sees me. Now I know. They will search me at the frontier, strip me, send me to a concentration camp, where I shall be whipped. You saw this spy. He stopped and looked at me. You saw? He recognized me. I saw it in his face. In my pocket here I have ten thousand marks in good German securities – all I have in the world. Unless you will consent to help me they will take them from me at Passau.'

He paused and Kenton could see that he was wiping his forehead again.

The man was lying; of that he had no doubt. Metallurgist and Jew he might be. German he certainly was not. For one thing, his German was not as good as Kenton's own; for another, any German business man would know that, as at that time all German bonds were 'blocked' and not negotiable abroad, the only way to get money out of Germany was in hard cash. Again, there was the story of the Nazi spy. From what he knew of the Nazis, Kenton could not imagine them taking the trouble to send spies to peep at non-Aryan metallurgists in third-class compartments. If they had wanted the man, he would not have been allowed to board the train at Ratisbon. All the same, the whole thing was a little puzzling. The man in the corridor had certainly behaved oddly, and Brown-Eyes' fright was obviously linked in some way with his appearance. Kenton began to scent a story of some sort.

'I don't see how I can help you,' he said.

The other leant towards him. Kenton could feel his breath on his cheek.

'You could take my securities past the frontier for me.'

'And if I, too, am searched?'

'You are an Englishman. They would not dare. There is no risk. It is a little thing for you.'

Kenton was not so sure about that, but let it pass.

'I am afraid I cannot take the responsibility.'

'But I will pay you, *mein Herr* . . .' He stopped, rummaged quickly in his pocket and drew Kenton into the light from the corridor. He had a wallet in his hand. 'Look! . . . I will pay you one, two, three hundred marks to take my securities out of Germany for me.'

At that moment Kenton ceased for a time to be an impartial recorder of events and became a participator. Three hundred marks!

A hundred owing to the Havas man left two hundred. Two hundred! Enough to get back to Berlin with plenty to spare. Brown-Eyes might be anything but what he claimed, and he, Kenton, might be heading straight for a German prison, but it was worth the risk – for three hundred marks.

He hedged a little at first and allowed the man to press and finally persuade him. Tears of emotion oozed from the brown eyes as he handed Kenton one hundred and fifty marks in advance. The balance was to be paid when the securities were handed back. They were, their owner hastened to explain, in his name, Herman Sachs, and of no value to anyone else.

'*Mein Herr,*' he went on, laying his hands on Kenton's arm, 'I am trusting you with my poor savings. You will not betray me?'

His lustrous brown eyes were infinitely sad and appealing, but his fingers gripped with surprising force.

Kenton protested his good faith, Herr Sachs' grip relaxed, and with a cautious glance at the corridor he handed over a long, bulging envelope. Kenton could feel a bundle of stiff papers rolled up inside it. He put the envelope in his pocket.

Sachs drew a deep breath and relapsed into his seat exhaling loudly.

Kenton found this exhibition of relief a trifle disconcerting. With a growing dislike of the man he could not quite explain, he watched Sachs light a short black cigar and open a large and battered composite suitcase. He seemed to have forgotten Kenton's existence.

From where Kenton sat he could see into the suitcase. It was stuffed to bursting-point with soiled linen. But Sachs seemed to know his way about it. He dived straight into one corner of the case. When his hand reappeared it held a heavy-calibre automatic. He slipped it easily into a holster under his left arm.

There was, thought Kenton, more to Herr Sachs than met the eye.

They went through the customs formalities separately.

Sachs hurried off first. Kenton, with a hollow feeling in the region of the solar plexus, the envelope lodged down his right sock and his German banknotes tucked in his left shoe, followed at a discreet distance.

Waiting his turn at the German 'control', Kenton saw Sachs passed through with only the usual currency interrogation. The 'German' was neither searched nor detained. Kenton gave himself full marks for prophecy as he saw his doubts of Sachs' story confirmed. He also caught a glimpse of the 'Nazi spy' crossing a lighted yard on his way to the Austrian customs.

His own examination was casual enough, but he was profoundly relieved when it was over. Returning to the train, he found an anxious Sachs.

'Ah, here you are! You have it safely? Good. No, no, no, please!' as Kenton produced the envelope. 'Please put it away. It is not yet safe. Put it in your pocket.' He glanced furtively towards the corridor. 'He is on the train, the spy. There is still danger.'

At that Kenton lost his temper. He was cold, depressed and disliking Herr Sachs and his affairs intensely. His ordeal at the customs had unnerved him; he found this talk of spies and danger offensively melodramatic. Moreover, he had decided that the securities consisted of either (*a*) drugs, (*b*) stolen bearer bonds, (*c*) a report on white slave traffic possibilities in Westphalia, or (*d*) something else equally incriminating. Furthermore, he mistrusted Sachs. Whatever dingy game the man was up to, he, Kenton, was not going to be involved any longer.

'I'm afraid,' he said, 'that I must ask you to take your securities back. I contracted to bring them across the frontier. I have done so. And now, I think, you owe me one hundred and fifty marks.'

Sachs did not speak for a moment. His brown eyes had become slightly opaque. Then he leant forward and touched the journalist on the knee.

'Herr Kenton,' he said quickly, 'please put that envelope back in your pocket. I will increase my offer. Another three hundred marks if you will take my securities on to the Hotel Josef at Linz.'

Kenton had opened his mouth to refuse. Then that same streak of recklessness that had already proved so expensive that day asserted itself again. Six hundred marks! Well, he might as well be hanged for a sheep as a lamb.

'All right,' he said.

But even as he spoke the words, he knew that all was not right, and that this time his weakness had led him into danger.

2

Zaleshoff and Tamara

The offices of the firm of *Kiessling und Pieper Maschinen G.m.b.H. Zürich* are difficult to find. They are reached by walking along a narrow passage leading off a quiet street near Zürich station, unlocking a battered but very sturdy door, and climbing five flights of bare wooden stairs. At the top of these stairs is another door with the name of the firm painted upon it. An arrow points to a bell marked '*Bitte schellen,*' 'Please ring,' but this does not work. There is another bell which does work, but that is operated by inserting a key in the lock, and few know about it. The firm of Kiessling and Pieper does not encourage business.

Although the firm still retains its original name, Kiessling and Pieper themselves have long since severed their connection with it. Herr Kiessling died in 1910, Herr Pieper in 1924. The firm has not prospered since: chiefly because its subsequent proprietors have always had more important business on their hands than the disposal for profit of vertical borers, milling machines and turret lathes. Drab brown photographs of such things still decorate the office walls; but they remain as the firm's sole surviving connection with the trade it professes.

One afternoon in late November the proprietor of Kiessling and Pieper sat at his desk staring thoughtfully at one of those brown photographs. It portrayed an all-geared head, straight bed S.S. and S.C. lathe by Schutte and Eberhardt, but Andreas Prokovitch Zaleshoff did not know that.

The unofficial representative of the USSR in Switzerland was a broad-shouldered man of about thirty-eight, with brown, curly hair that shot up at an angle of forty-five degrees from his forehead. His clean-shaven face was ugly, but not unpleasantly so. 'Knobbly' would have been an unkind description; 'rugged' would have been a trifle too romantic. His nose was large and pugnacious, and he had a habit of shooting out his lower jaw when he wished to be emphatic. His eyes were of a surprising blue and very shrewd. Now, they moved from unseeing contemplation of the screw-cutting lathe to a sheet of paper on the desk, stayed there for a moment, then glanced towards the door leading to the outer office.

'Tamara, come here,' he called.

A few moments later a girl came into the room.

Tamara Prokovna Zaleshoff was not, by ordinary standards, beautiful. Her face was an idealized version of her brother's. The complexion was perfect and the proportions were good, but the bone structure was a little too masculine. Her hands were exquisite.

'Have you decoded the letters?'

'Yes, Andreas; there were only two.'

No correspondence came direct to Kiessling and Pieper. Those who had dealings with the firm at that time always addressed their communications to a Fräulein Rosa Neumann, care of the poste restante. Twice a day Tamara became Rosa Neumann and collected them. It was then her business to translate into sense the jumbled strings of letters and numbers, and enter the results in an innocent-looking book marked with the German equivalent of 'Bought Ledger' before passing them on to her brother. Most of the messages were dull and the routine bored her exceedingly.

She took off her coat and hung it behind the door. Then she looked at her brother curiously.

'What is it, Andreas?'

'While you were out collecting the letters, Tamara, Petroff telephoned from Berlin.'

'Petroff! What did he want?'

'He says that he was notified by Moscow last night that Borovansky has turned traitor.'

'Borovansky?'

'Yes, they found out at headquarters that he'd taken photographs of all B2 mobilization instructions and was on his way to Germany.

Petroff says that Borovansky took the train to Ratisbon this afternoon and that he bought a through ticket to Linz. It looks as though he delivers the photographs there.'

'Has he got them on him?'

'Yes, in the inside pocket of his coat.'

'But can nothing be done to stop him?'

Zaleshoff smiled wanly.

'Yes, Tamara, plenty; but not yet. Petroff has put Ortega on the job.'

'Ortega?'

'That Spaniard of Petroff's. The fellow uses a knife, I believe. Petroff, who is not, to my mind, fastidious, admits that the man is an obscenity, but says that he is very useful.'

'Can he be trusted?'

'That is one of his virtues in Petroff's eyes. Ortega is wanted for murder – he slit a woman's throat in Lisbon two years ago – and Petroff would put the police on to him if necessary.'

Tamara looked thoughtful.

'I never liked Borovansky very much.'

Zaleshoff shook his head.

'Neither did I. I always thought they trusted him too much. But they said he was useful because he had worked for years in German factories and knew the Germans well. Silly nonsense! Borovansky could work all his life in a country and not even learn to speak the language like a native, much less think like one. Besides, I'd sooner be served by a fool I could trust than an expert who might betray me.'

He lit a large pipe and then put it down.

'It's no use, Tamara,' he said irritably. 'I cannot – I will not smoke a pipe. It makes me sick.'

'It is better than those interminable cigarettes. You must try.'

Zaleshoff picked up the pipe impatiently, but he merely tapped the stem against his strong white teeth. His attention seemed suddenly to have wandered. The girl watched him for a minute.

'Just how serious is this affair, Andreas?' she said at last.

For a moment she thought he had not heard her. Then he shrugged.

'Nobody quite knows – yet. You see the difficulty, Tamara? Borovansky only took photographs of the stuff and it might be put about that they are forgeries. But we have so little to work on. If we knew even who was paying him, we could move. You see, those B2 instructions aren't just ordinary military information. If it were gunnery reports, or fortification details, it would probably find its way to the bureau at Brussels and we should know where we stood. But it isn't. I feel in my bones that there is a political end to this business, and I don't like it. If Borovansky wanted something to sell there are so many more marketable things he might and could have stolen. Why, Tamara, must he photograph these specific instructions? Why? That is what I ask.'

'Either because he hadn't time to get anything else or because someone had offered him money for them.'

'Exactly! Now, if he was merely going to steal and photograph anything of value he could find, he would realize that the B2 papers were, for his purpose, valueless. Would he risk his life getting away with something that he knew to have no market value? No; someone wanted the B2 stuff and Borovansky is being paid to get it. The worst of it is that nothing can be done to stop him until he gets into Austria. Berlin wants an excuse for another anti-Soviet drive and we don't want to provide it. We must hope that he does not deliver the goods before he leaves Germany.'

'Why in Heaven's name wasn't he stopped before he could leave Soviet territory?'

'They didn't know anything was wrong. Borovansky was acting as liaison between Moscow and our people in Riga. If the man who took the photographs hadn't grown suspicious and made up his mind to tell the police about it, we should probably still be in the dark. Borovansky was a fool, too. He might have remained unsuspected for several extra days if he'd had the sense to report at Riga before he made for Germany.'

'Still, it's no affair of ours.'

'No, I suppose not.'

But he still looked thoughtful. Suddenly he rose abruptly, walked to a cupboard in a corner of the room, took a bulky file from it and started turning the pages absently.

'A report came in from the Basel agent this afternoon,' said Tamara. 'He says that the British agent has moved. The Englishman used to work from an office in the Badenstrasse. It was called the Swiss Central Import Company. Now he's gone to the Koenig Gustavus Platz and is working from the apartment of a dentist named Bouchard. It's a very good idea. You can't keep a check on everyone who visits a dentist.'

Zaleshoff, immersed in the file, grunted.

'Oh, and the Geneva agents reported this morning that it's not Skoda, but Nordenfelt who did the bribing over that new Italian order for howitzers; and they're going to ship them from Hamburg to Genoa,' Tamara went on. 'He also reports that one of the South American League delegates is visiting a woman calling herself Madame Fleury. He says that she is actually a Hungarian named Putti and that she worked for Bulgaria in nineteen-sixteen. He doesn't say who she's working for now, and anyway I don't see how he expects us to keep track of all these South American peccadilloes.'

Her brother went on reading.

'There's one rather interesting thing in his report. He says that the British, the Germans and the Italians met at a small hotel across the lake to decide what the Germans and Italians are going to reply to the Note the British are sending them next week. He hears that the Italians objected to one question in the Note – something to do, he thinks, with Italian intentions in the Sudan – and that the English agreed to leave it out if the Italians would accept loans from London and guarantee to use them to subsidize Italian heavy industries. That means that London wants the lira forced down a point or two.' She paused, then: 'I don't believe you are listening, Andreas Prokovitch.'

'Yes, yes, Tamara, I am listening. Go on, please.' But he was clearly finding the file of absorbing interest.

'The Geneva agent also reports,' said Tamara, 'that the Pan-Eurasian Petroleum Company of London has failed to obtain a revision of their oil concession by the Roumanian Government. Pan-Eurasian Petroleum is, he reminds us, an English company under the control of Joseph Balterghen of Gracechurch Street, London, who also holds thirty-five per cent of the ordinary shares of Cator and Bliss Limited, the English munition firm, and is a director of the Imperial Armour Plating Trust. I have turned up Balterghen's record. He is an Armenian by birth and was naturalized English in nineteen-fourteen. From nineteen hundred to nineteen hundred and nine he sold arms for the Nordenfelt company, but he had his fingers in the oil business as early as nineteen hundred and seven. In nineteen-seventeen he endeavoured to negotiate a concession for the Baku fields with Kerensky. It is believed that he had actually reached some arrangement with the Provisional Government immediately before Kerensky's fall. In nineteen-eighteen he arrived in Odessa and again tried to negotiate for the Baku fields, this time with General Almazoff, a White Army commander in the sector. He worked through an agent named Talbot. He—'

But Zaleshoff had leapt across the room and was shaking her by the arm.

'What name did you say, Tamara?'

'Talbot.'

'And Odessa in nineteen-eighteen? Balterghen was there?'

'Yes.'

'Then look, Tamara, at this!'

He thrust the file into her arms and dashed into the outer office. A second or two later the girl heard the hook of the telephone rattling furiously.

She sat down, lit a cigarette slowly, then, nursing the file in her lap, began to read from the strips of typewriting pasted to thick yellow paper.

DOSSIER S8439 Copy 31 Zürich.

Name. Stefan Saridza.

Place of birth. Adrianople (believed).

Date of birth. 1869 (about).

Parents. Not known.

Political sympathies. Not known.

Remarks. No useful photograph obtainable. This man has been known since 1904. See below.

Following details transferred in 1917/18 from Ochrana archives (Kiev). Court martial of General Stessel 1904. Subject: Stessel's failure to hold fortress of Port Arthur against forces of Japanese General Nogi. Stessel pleaded betrayal of fortress. Examination of suspects negative. Stessel accused Bulgarian named Saridza (or Sarescu). Failed to secure Saridza for examination. Reported in Athens January 1905.

Trial of Heinrich Grosse, Winchester Assizes, England, 1910, for espionage. Man named Larsen described as Grosse's employer at trial. Believed Saridza. (Identification claimed by D.24.)

Trial of Captain Bertrand Stewart (British) in Berlin 1911 for espionage. Stewart victim of *agent provocateur* named Arsène Marie Verrue, alias Frederic Rue (see Dossier R77356) stated to have been employed at instance of German contra-espionage bureau by R. H. Larsen, alias Muller, alias Pieters, alias Schmidt, alias Talbot. Believed Saridza.

Following details supplied by Commissariat for Interior,

Odessa. December 1918. Reported (K. 19) that agent named Talbot (see above) attempted negotiations with General Almazoff for petroleum concession at Baku. Believed acting for English oil interest.

Commissariat for Foreign Affairs. March 1925. Reported (V. 37 Barcelona) that agent named Luis Gomez engaged in anti-Soviet propaganda particularly with reference to Soviet petroleum imports in Spain. Believed acting for English oil interests.

Note. Above agent identified as Saridza 1929. See remarks below.

February 1930. Case heard before Judge Mahoina in New York City. Cator and Bliss (New York) Inc. (defendant) versus Joshua L. Curtice (plaintiff). Curtice alleged non-payment of $100,000 expenses in connection with work done at second disarmament conference Geneva. Nature of work: Alleged contra-disarmament propaganda. Curtice employed by London directors of Cator and Bliss Limited. Hearing of case in New York arranged by plaintiff. Judgement on case given in accordance with agreement reached between litigants. Curtice claimed Swiss citizenship. Identified as Saridza by B. 71.

Remarks. Saridza is understood (Report ZB356/28) to possess large organization, principally in Europe and Near East. Activities now mainly political propaganda on behalf of industrial and banking groups. Excellent organizer. Unscrupulous. Speaks English (slight accent), French (bad accent), German, Russian and Slovene.

Appearance. Height, average. Thin build. Grey hair, nearly bald, sallow complexion. Small grey clipped moustache stained with nicotine. Has been known to carry fire-arms. *Important Note*. On every occasion on which Saridza has been identified it has been through the fact that his left arm is incapable of full articulation at the elbow. This disability produces an unmistakable awkwardness in the use of the arm.

Standing Instructions (May 1926). Any agent securing information, even from an unreliable source, of Saridza's activities, to report immediately.

Tamara closed the file and crushed out her cigarette. Through the open door she could hear her brother speaking rapidly.

'. . . the Pan-Eurasian Petroleum Company, there is not a doubt of it, Petroff. The affair becomes a little clearer, my friend, does it not? You have heard of Balterghen's failure in Roumania? . . . yes, yes, that is so . . . but I will leave you to notify Moscow . . . no . . . yes . . . I shall go straight away to Linz . . . yes . . . I shall take Tamara. I will recall J12 from Berne to take charge here. Please be good enough to warn Vienna . . .'

There was a long pause. Tamara could feel her heart beating.

'Ortega?' went on Zaleshoff. 'Yes, I remember his face. Who could forget it? He has a skin like elephant hide and eyes like a snake. *Au 'voir.*'

There was a clatter as he hung up. When he came bustling back into his office, Tamara was looking at the file again.

'You have read it? You heard me speaking to Petroff?' He was looking excited.

'Yes. But why do we go to Linz?'

'You have read the dossier. It was I who identified Saridza in New York. I know his face well.'

'But our people in Vienna . . . ?'

'They do not know him as I do. It is lucky for us. Saridza is an important enemy. It will be a great *coup* for us. Now, please, Tamara, get me Berne on the telephone.'

Waiting in the dark little outer office for the call, she heard him rummaging furiously in his desk. He was humming *Tchoubtchik* softly to himself. Once he stopped and swore, and she called to ask him if he wanted anything; but it was only ammunition for his revolver and he had found it. Then:

'Andreas! We are going back to Moscow next month?'

'Yes, Tamara, next month.'

'For three months?'

'Perhaps.'

She was silent for a moment. With her finger she drew a long straight line in the dust on the shelf beside her. When she spoke again, her voice had dropped slightly.

'Andreas, shall we always do this work?'

'I hope so. We are good at it.'

She heard him slam and lock a drawer in the desk. The telephone pressed to her ear, she stared at the clumsy, old-fashioned typewriter on the table as she went on.

'I suppose Borovansky will be dead by the time we reach Linz?'

'Ortega has instructions not to kill, but to get the photographs at all costs; but you must not let your imagination dwell on it. Borovansky would be no great loss. There is a story of a man and a woman at Essen that is unpleasant to hear.'

She pressed the shift key on the typewriter thoughtfully.

'Do you remember his eyes, Andreas? One would not think that anyone with such soft brown eyes could be treacherous.'

'A man's eyes, a man's nose, his forehead, his ears – none of those things, Tamara, has anything to do with the mind behind them. Small men have large heads and great men small ones. There were never two people in the world who understood each other's minds by looking at each other's faces.' There was a pause and she heard him open a cupboard.

'We are a long time getting through to Berne, Tamara. There is a train in twenty minutes.'

'You must take a thick scarf, Andreas. It will be cold.'

Zaleshoff came through the door behind her. He wore a heavy grey ulster; round his neck was a wool muffler. He leant forward and kissed her lightly on the cheek.

'Have you got your pipe, Andreas?'

'No.'

The telephone crackled suddenly.

'The Berne agent,' said Tamara.

3

Room 25

For most of the three and a half hours it took to get from the frontier to Linz, Herr Sachs talked incessantly.

'One should learn,' he told Kenton, 'to judge one's fellow men.' He wagged a dirty finger. 'Take yourself, Herr Kenton. The moment I saw you on this train I said to myself that here was a man on whom a man could rely – a man with whom one could leave one's hard-earned savings in absolute safety.'

He paused dramatically.

It occurred to Kenton that Sachs must have judged him to be a perfect fool if he imagined that the Jewish refugee story was still believed.

'But why,' Sachs went on, 'why should an honest man not receive payment for his honesty?' The brown eyes were round with wonder. 'I am satisfied to pay. It is good.'

He started picking his teeth.

Kenton fidgeted. He would, he told himself, have earned his six hundred marks. At the moment, he was not quite sure whether Herr Sachs was delivering subtle threats or seeking by flattery to restore his courier's self-esteem. If it were the latter, he was failing. The one thing that was puzzling Kenton was why the man should be prepared to pay six hundred marks to a perfect stranger to carry the envelope to an hotel in Linz.

His curiosity on the point almost overrode his distaste for the role of hired mercenary to which he had committed himself. Sachs was very obviously afraid of something or someone – his spate of talk was like a nervous twitch – but of what or of whom? One thing, and one thing only, was clear. All this talk of securities, Jewish suspects and Nazi spies was sheer nonsense. Kenton had, in his time, interviewed some of the most agile liars in Europe. Herr Sachs was wretchedly unconvincing by comparison. But it was one thing to interpret a story correctly when you knew a little more than you should; it was quite another matter when you knew nothing at all about the story-teller or his probable motives. The whole business was very puzzling.

'The psychology,' Herr Sachs was saying, 'is a strange work. I know many good psychologies.'

He nodded his head twice and wiped his nose.

'When I was in the foundries at Essen, there was a man who had such a psychology. Strange, you understand; bizarre. There are men who are small and humble and make one think they are always afraid. Hoff was like that – small and afraid. You have been in a foundry, *mein Herr*? No? It is a great thing to see. Thousands of kilogrammes of molten steel held in a great ladle swung from a gantry that moves slowly towards the moulds. Then the control operates and the steel gushes out like blood from a pig. It is certainly to be seen.'

He closed his eyes reminiscently, then opened them suddenly, a look of horror on his face.

'But I am boring you, *mein Herr*. I am sorry, I regret it deeply.' He dissolved into contrition.

'No, no!' protested Kenton politely.

'You are too kind.' He patted Kenton on the knee. 'I see you are a man after my own heart. We value the psychology. It is a great thing.'

Kenton said he thought so, too.

'The case of Hoff is very strange,' pursued Herr Sachs, 'and also of great interest. Hoff it was who controlled the ladle. He was a good workman, for he obeyed perfectly the signs from those below, and kept good watch so that the casting was not spoiled. The foreman was named Bauer and he hated Hoff. There were those who said it was because of Hoff's woman, and perhaps that was so, for she was good to look at and liked men; and Hoff, as I have said, was small and humble. Bauer always tried to make Hoff a fool.

He would shout at him and speak against him to the manager, but he would never dismiss Hoff – only make his life in the foundry a bad thing. Other men would have gone away or grumbled; but Hoff only smiled in his nervous way and said that Bauer was really a good fellow. Some said that Hoff was a coward, but he only smiled and said that it did not matter. You, Herr Kenton, would perhaps have said that Hoff was a coward?'

'Such cases,' said Kenton tactfully, 'are always difficult.'

Herr Sachs looked cunning.

'That is so. For myself, I have given much thought to the case of Hoff. But I will tell you the story,' he went on. 'The affair was as I have said for many months. Then one day Bauer became angry and beat Hoff on the face with a steel rod. It was over a small matter; but it was the first time that Bauer had struck Hoff. Some of the men wished to wait for Bauer and beat him, but Hoff still smiled his nervous smile and wiped the blood from his face, saying that it did not matter. The next day we were pouring some heavy castings and Hoff was controlling a ladle with over ten thousand kilos of metal. Bauer was by the moulds, waiting for the ladle to move overhead. The gantry moved slowly across and the men made ready below. Suddenly it stopped and they saw that the ladle was over Bauer's head. It started to tilt. They shouted to Bauer, but that was too late. The next instant the metal poured. The men ran. Bauer only did not run. He cried out and fell to the floor screaming. Later that day, he died in hospital. Hoff said that the control gear was not good, and there were many who had hated Bauer to swear it was an accident. But the control gear was good.' He beamed. 'So, Herr Kenton, Hoff was not a coward, you see.'

'Then what was he?' Kenton could not help asking the question.

'Hoff,' said Sachs with a chuckle, 'was clever, very clever. To wait, to smile, to be afraid, to be humble to those who pry, and then to strike – that is to be clever.' He became suddenly serious. The brown eyes narrowed, his lips tightened and drew back slightly, showing his teeth. 'It was good, that moment, when Bauer looked up and saw death coming to meet him – from the hand of the poor fool Hoff.

In that last second before the metal got him, Bauer knew; one could see that he knew.' Herr Sachs began to laugh. 'It was a good revenge and Hoff was very clever. Do you not think so, Herr Kenton?'

'Yes, very.'

'To wait, to smile, and then – to strike,' said Sachs; 'that is a good psychology.'

He smiled complacently. Then, with a sudden movement, he wiped the mist off a patch of window and peered through. 'There are lights on the Danube,' he said; 'soon we shall be at Linz.'

'But, Herr Sachs,' said Kenton thoughtfully, 'you haven't told me what happened to Hoff's woman. That, I think, would be even more interesting to learn.'

For a moment he thought that the other had not heard him. Then Sachs raised his head. His eyes as they met Kenton's held a strange light.

'Hoff's woman, ah, yes,' he said slowly. 'Soon afterwards she, too, died.' The words came slower. 'There was an accident with some acid. Her face was hurt – it was merciful that she died – merciful. But sad for Hoff, for he was there at the time, and there was much prying and probing and lying.'

Kenton saw that his eyes had wandered to the corridor.

'A curious affair,' he murmured.

But Herr Sachs seemed to have lost interest in the matter and did not answer. Having licked the fingers of both hands, he started smoothing long wisps of straight black hair over a bald patch on the top of his head. Then he put on his hat, buttoned up the collar of his overcoat so that it concealed his mouth and nose, hauled his battered case from the rack and announced that he was ready.

'The Hotel Josef,' he said, 'is near to the river, beyond the *Weinzinger* in the old town. You will find it. But please to delay half an hour before you come. I have business to attend to before that.'

Kenton nodded.

'Good. I trust you, Herr Kenton, as I would my own mother. You will be there and I will give you the money I have promised. I, too, am to be trusted. You shall see. Please,' he added, 'to see if the corridor is empty.'

On Kenton's assuring him that the coast was clear, he scuttled down the corridor to the exit. When, some three minutes later, the train drew into Linz, Herr Sachs was out and away before it had come to a standstill. Kenton, from the compartment, watched him picking his way round some piles of packing-cases until the shadows hid him. Then he saw another figure move into the light for a moment and disappear after Sachs. Kenton paused for a moment as he prepared to leave and then shrugged. Nazi spy or no, the man with the small eyes and unwholesome face had to leave the station with the rest of the passengers. The fact that he was following Sachs meant nothing. He picked up his suitcase and left the train.

Few things are more dispiriting than the railway station of a strange town in the early hours of the morning. As Kenton walked along the platform, he vowed that, whether he could afford it or not, he would spend the night in a comfortable bed. The sky was starry and it was horribly cold. Somewhere behind him a man was coughing ceaselessly and the sound depressed him.

He found an open café near the station, went inside and ordered coffee.

It is said that at two o'clock in the morning man's vitality is at its lowest ebb; that it is during those dark hours that suicides reach the nadir of desolation, where thought and action meet and triggers are pulled. It may be so. For Kenton, the minutes that passed while his coffee grew cold enough to drink were among the most dismal he had ever spent. Here was he, nearly thirty years of age, a comparatively responsible member of a dignified profession, throwing his money away like an undergraduate, and having to accept dubious commissions from unknown men with murderous 'psychologies' and fire-arms in their pockets. He elaborated the theme. Supposing he had been caught at the frontier? Well, that would have served him right. It had got to stop. He would discharge his end of the bargain he had made, collect his money, go straight back to Berlin and get down to some real work. Meanwhile, there was the envelope. He took it from his pocket and examined it.

It was made of cheap grey paper and was stuck down firmly. There was no writing on it and the usual dark paper lining of

Continental envelopes fulfilled its purpose by preventing him from seeing anything by holding the envelope against the light. He felt the contents carefully. He was unfamiliar with the shape and feel of engraved script, but it occurred to him that the bundle of paper inside was too stiff and resilient for the purpose.

He put the envelope back in his pocket, drank his coffee and smoked a cigarette. Then, having left his suitcase with the café proprietor, he set out for the Hotel Josef.

The first part of the journey took him through wide streets plentifully scarred with examples of that brand of baroque architecture of which Austrians are so strangely proud. Then, as, after crossing a narrow steel bridge over the river, he made his way towards the landing-stages – the 'port' of Linz – the streets became narrow and squalid. A solitary policeman of whom he inquired the way looked suspicious and directed him down a series of dark and deserted alleyways. He came at last to a short street of old houses. About half-way down it, a dimly lit box sign announced that rooms with two beds were to be had at the Hotel Josef for five *schillings*. He was twenty minutes late; but he had arrived.

The entrance to the Hotel Josef was not imposing. Two worn stone steps led up to a narrow door. The top half of this was of frosted glass from which the words 'Hotel Josef', in black paint, had begun to peel. A glimmer of light showed through the glass. Kenton pushed the door open and walked in.

He found himself in a narrow passage. On the left was a small counter set in a shallow alcove and labelled 'AUSKUNFT.' On the right a letter and key rack hung on the wall. The fact that most of the keys were in their places seemed to indicate that the Hotel Josef was not doing a roaring trade.

There was no one behind the counter and he stood for a moment or two looking for some means of attracting attention. Then he heard the sound of somebody snoring close at hand. It seemed to be coming from along the passage and he moved forward, a little uncertainly, to investigate.

Two or three steps brought him to a room leading into the passage. The door was half open and he looked in. A candle, burnt down and guttering in a pool of wax, cast a flickering light on a man wearing an apron and carpet slippers, stretched full length on a red plush sofa. This, Kenton assumed, was the night porter.

The man grunted and stirred in his sleep as Kenton rapped on the door. The second knock woke him and, rubbing his eyes, he raised himself to a sitting posture on the sofa.

'*Herrn Sachs?*' asked Kenton.

The man rose unsteadily to his feet and moved towards Kenton. Reaching the door, he leaned heavily against the wall and, throwing back his head, regarded the journalist through half-closed eyes. He smelt strongly of stale wine and Kenton saw that he was drunk.

'*Was ists?*' he demanded thickly.

'*Herrn Sachs, bitte.*'

The man digested this information for a moment, then looked up again inquiringly.

'*Herr Sachs?*'

'*Jawohl,*' said Kenton impatiently.

The night porter breathed heavily for a moment or two, moistened his lips and looked at Kenton a little more intelligently.

'*Wen darf ich melden?*'

'*Herr Kenton.*'

'*Herr Kenton! Ach ja! Man erwartet Sie. Wollen Sie bitte hinaufgehen?*'

The porter prepared to return to his sofa. Kenton, it seemed, was expected to guess the room number.

'*Auf Zimmer nummer . . . ?*' he said encouragingly.

The man sat on the edge of the sofa and blinked at Kenton irritably.

'*Zimmer fünfundzwanzig, dritter Stock,*' he said and, with a heavy sigh, lay back on the sofa. As Kenton started to climb the stairs to the third floor, he heard the snoring begin again.

Once out of range of the passage light, the stairs were in pitch darkness and, having failed to find any switches, Kenton had to keep striking matches to light his way.

The house had obviously never been intended to serve as an hotel. The proprietor's efforts to create the greatest possible number of rooms, by means of extensive partitioning, had turned the place into a maze of small corridors in which doors were set at unexpected angles and culs-de-sac abounded. When he reached the third floor it took him several minutes and many matches to find Room No. 25.

He knocked and the door swung ajar with a slight creak.

Except for a shaft of light from a source he could not see, the place was in darkness. It appeared to be a small sitting-room. He listened, but could hear no sound of movements. He called Sachs' name softly; but there was no response, and he repeated the name in a louder tone. Then he pushed the door open and stepped inside.

The light was coming through a communicating-door from a single naked lamp in the bedroom. From where he stood, he could see that the bedclothes were turned back ready for the occupant. But of Herr Sachs there was no sign.

He stepped back into the corridor and waited for two or three minutes. Then he lit a cigarette, but after a few puffs crushed it out. The Hotel Josef was getting on his nerves. He went back into the sitting-room and stood facing the light.

He called once again without result and went to the bedroom door.

The next instant he stood stockstill. Into the small area of floor that had come into view beyond the bed protruded a man's foot.

His spine crawled. With an effort he remained motionless. Then he edged forward, slightly increasing his field of vision. A second later he stepped into the bedroom.

The man was half lying, half kneeling in a pool of blood that was still creeping slowly along the cracks in the pinewood boards. The knees were drawn up. The hands were clasped tightly on the handle of the knife that had been driven hard into the right side just below the rib cage. He had been in his shirt sleeves when he had fallen. On the floor beside him his jacket lay with the lining ripped out.

Kenton glanced quickly round the room.

On the floor the other side of the bed were the remains of the composition suitcase, ransacked and slashed all over with a knife. Then his eyes returned to the body.

He took one step forward. The slight movement was enough. With scarcely a sound it rolled over on to its back.

The brown eyes were no longer luminous. This time Herr Sachs had waited and smiled too long. This time he had been too late to strike.

4

Hotel Josef

There are persons who can, like undertakers, adopt a matter-of-fact attitude towards dead bodies; who can touch and move them, close the eyes. Kenton was not one of those. He had been in Spain during the worst months of the civil war and had seen many, too many corpses. But in a battle area, among buildings wrecked by gun fire and streets strewn with the pitiful debris of war, dead men (and women) were a part of the scene – shapeless patches of dark colour against the vaster destruction about them.

In the silence of Room 25 in the Hotel Josef, however, death was no longer incidental. Here it was grotesque. Kenton found that he wanted to be sick and forced himself to look away.

He knew that, useless though it might appear, he ought to find out if Sachs were still alive, and if he were, to go for a doctor. As he stood trying to overcome his nausea, he could hear the watch ticking on his wrist. It seemed that he had been there for ages. Then, carefully avoiding the blood, he went down on his knees beside the body.

He had read of such things, but could not remember the exact procedure. He had an idea that a 'faint fluttering of the heart' was the thing to look for; but the mechanics of detecting it was another matter. It was, he knew, useless for him to attempt to feel the pulse. He had always found it extremely difficult to locate even his own. Perhaps he should undo Sachs' grimy shirt and rest his hand over the heart. He gritted his teeth and started on the waistcoat. Then he noticed that his fingers were slipping on the buttons and realized that he had got blood on his fingers. He stood up quickly. The perspiration was running from his forehead. He stumbled over Sachs' torn suitcase to the wash-basin, poured some water and rinsed his hands. Then he looked once again at the body. Suddenly he felt himself losing control. He must give the alarm, call the police, anything. This was no affair of his. He must get out as quickly as possible. He walked rapidly through the sitting-room into the darkness of the corridor.

With Sachs' remains out of sight, however, he felt his self-possession returning. Outside the door, he stopped and began to think.

What exactly was he going to do? The night porter was asleep and drunk. It was no use attempting to explain things to him. The nearest policeman was probably streets away. The thing to do was to telephone to the police from the bureau downstairs.

He was about to carry out this intention when another aspect of the situation occurred to him. How was he to account for his own presence on the scene? The Austrian police would certainly demand an explanation. They would ask certain questions.

What was his profession?

Journalist.

Ah, yes, and of what journal?

No particular paper – a free-lance.

Indeed! And where had he come from?

Nuremberg.

And for what purpose?

To borrow money in Vienna.

Then he was short of money?

Yes.

And why had he not gone on to Vienna?

He had met the deceased in the train and the deceased had requested him to execute a commission.

So? And what was the commission?

To carry an envelope containing documents of value to the Hotel Josef.

But the deceased was himself going to the Hotel Josef: why should he wish documents of value taken where he himself was going?

He did not know.

Did Herr Kenton expect payment for this service?

Yes. Six hundred marks.

Kenton imagined the incredulity with which that statement would be received.

And how did Herr Kenton know that the deceased possessed that sum?

Herr Sachs had shown him in the train.

Ah, then he had had an opportunity to inspect the wallet of the deceased?

Yes, but—

And Herr Kenton was going to Vienna to borrow money?

Yes.

And so he decided to save himself the trouble?

The deceased had pressed him to accept the commission.

Herr Kenton then followed the deceased to the Hotel Josef?

Yes, but—

And there Herr Kenton stabbed the deceased?

Nonsense.

Then, horrified at his deed and thinking to put the police off the scent, he telephones for their aid. Is it not so?

Absurd!

The night porter deposes that Herr Kenton asked for Herr Sachs soon after that gentleman arrived; he adds that Herr Kenton was nervous and impatient.

He always appeared nervous, and as for his impatience, that was explained by the stupidity of the hall porter. Besides, Herr Sachs had left word that he was expecting him.

Indeed? The night porter has no recollection of it.

The night porter was drunk.

Perhaps; but not too drunk to identify Herr Kenton.

He went back into the sitting-room. It was, he decided, out of the question to allow himself to be identified with the affair. Even if he succeeded finally in convincing the police that he had nothing to do with the stabbing, there would be endless delays. He would have to remain in Linz perhaps for weeks. The only thing was to go while the going was good. But first there was some thinking to be done. There must be no mistakes.

He hesitated, then walked into the bedroom and took a small

shaving-mirror off a nail in the wall. Turning it glass downwards, he went over to the body, and bending down, held the mirror against Sachs' mouth for a minute or two. There was no trace of moisture on the glass when he looked.

Satisfied that there was nothing a doctor could do for the man, he replaced the mirror and returned once more to the sitting-room. There, he shut the door leading into the corridor, seated himself in a chair facing the bedroom door and lit a cigarette.

One thing, he decided, was evident. Whoever had murdered Sachs had wanted the envelope that was now in his, Kenton's, pocket. The slashed and ransacked suitcase, the ripped jacket and Sachs' own concern for its safety pointed to that conclusion. Point two; the murderer had not got it. Kenton found that a disturbing thought, for it meant that the murderer might still be in the immediate neighbourhood. Dismissing a strong desire to look under the bed, he drew his chair into the light from the bedroom.

The first thing to be looked into was the envelope. He took it from his pocket and ripped it open hastily.

At first he thought that the contents consisted of nothing but blank paper. Then he saw that, placed carefully between the folds, were a series of glossy half-plate photographs.

He took them out one by one and flattened them. There were fifteen prints in all. Two were of large-scale sectional maps, heavily marked with crosses and numbers; the remaining thirteen were miniature reproductions of closely typewritten sheets of foolscap proportions.

He examined them closely. The language was Russian and he glanced through the photographs until he came to what was evidently the title page. His knowledge of Russian was sketchy, but he knew enough to decipher the heading.

He read:

COMMISSARIAT FOR WAR

Standing orders (B2, 1925) for operations contra Bessarabia. To be observed only in the event of attack by Roumania or Roumanian allies on Ukraine along front Lutsk–Kamenets.

There followed twelve and a half pages of telegraphic but highly complicated instructions concerning bridge-heads, stores, communications, water supply, railway rolling stock and engines, fuel, roads and all the other essential details of organization attendant upon a modern army on the move.

Kenton glanced through it all hurriedly. Then he stuffed the photographs into his pocket. He was, he felt, getting into deep waters. Whoever wanted Herr Sachs' 'securities' had not hesitated to commit one murder; in view of the nature of those securities, it would not be unlikely that the man or men were ready to commit another. As far as he was concerned, the affair had assumed a different complexion. From his point of view there was now only one proper place for the photographs – the British Consulate. Meanwhile, however, both he and the photographs were in the Hotel Josef with a murdered man. All things considered, it would be as well to reconnoitre the position.

He went to the window.

By drawing aside the curtains and pressing his face against the pane, he found that he could see the length of the street in front of the hotel. The moon was on the wane, but he could see enough. Standing in the partial shadow of a doorway a few yards up on the other side of the road were two motionless figures. A little farther down, drawn up facing his way, was a big saloon car. Kenton did not attempt to deceive himself. The way out of the hotel was closed and he was in a nasty corner.

He let the curtain fall and stood there for a moment. The men outside might owe their allegiance to one of two parties: the owners of the documents, the photographs of which were now in his pocket, or those who wanted the photographs. On which side had Sachs been? Assuming that he had known what his envelope actually contained, probably the latter. The real owners would have destroyed the photographs. But as he, Kenton, had the photographs, he was an object of interest to both parties. Did Sachs' friends know that he had them? Sachs had said that he had had business to attend to before going to the Hotel Josef. He might have told them then. At all events, one of the parties was now waiting outside in force. The other was – where?

Kenton had never regarded himself as a particularly courageous man. Such scenes of physical violence as he had encountered in the course of his work had upset both his digestion and his mental processes. Now, however, he had no time to consider his digestion; while as for his mental processes, he told himself that if he were to escape from his present predicament unscathed, he had to think fast.

He went into the bedroom, put on his gloves and with his handkerchief wiped everything he could remember touching. He had no desire to leave his fingerprints for the police. Then he buttoned his coat and, after a last look round, prepared to go.

As he moved away from the bed, he felt something soft beneath his foot. Looking down, he saw that it was Sachs' wallet. He picked it up. He was about to look through it when, through the bedroom door, he heard the faint creak of a floorboard in the corridor. Slipping the wallet into his overcoat pocket, he tiptoed into the dark sitting-room and stood by the door.

There was silence for a moment, then he heard a slight movement outside and the door handle began to turn slowly.

His heart thumping painfully, he saw the door creak open and pressed himself against the wall behind it. Then a man stepped into the room and closed the door carefully behind him. Kenton was close enough to hear the other's breathing. The man's back was towards him, but as he moved away into the light from the bedroom door, the journalist saw that he was short and thick-set and wore a woollen muffler wound twice round his neck.

From his place in the shadows Kenton watched the man with the muffler walk into the bedroom, glance, without evident surprise, at Sachs' body and look slowly round the room. Then he moved out of sight and Kenton heard sounds that suggested that the room was being searched. Now was the time to go.

He edged carefully towards the door handle, reached it without making a noise and began to turn it. The lock made no sound, but he remembered the creaking as the door had opened before, and as he eased the catch clear, he lifted the door a fraction to take the weight off the hinges. He reached the corridor without a sound, and having closed the door as carefully as he had opened it, he moved, treading close to the wall to avoid loose boards, to the head of the stairs.

There he paused. Who was the man in the muffler and which party did he represent? The whole affair was getting most complicated. He decided that, for the moment at any rate, there were more important things to think about. How, for example, was he to get out of the Hotel Josef?

He strove frantically to remember something of the geography of the place as he had seen it by the light of matches on his way up. There must be some exit at the rear of the building. He remembered vaguely having felt the draught from a window as he had climbed, but could not recollect on which floor. He felt for his matches and found that he had now only two left – one for each landing. He would have to do the best he could and trust to luck.

He felt his way down to the next landing and struck the first match. The stalk broke in his fingers. He struck the last match. It lit safely and, shielding it carefully, he looked round. There were two corridors ending in blank walls and one that made a right-angle turn. The window was, therefore, on the landing below. He tried to preserve the light long enough to serve on the next landing, but it burnt too quickly.

He had now to depend upon touch to find the window. Keeping the fingers of one hand brushing lightly against the wall and the other arm stretched out in front of him he moved carefully down the corridor. The thought crossed his mind that he probably looked like an old lithograph of Florence Nightingale and he experienced a desire to giggle. This desire he diagnosed as nerves and suppressed firmly.

After about six paces he felt the corridor turn half left. The next moment he was pulled up by a bedroom door. He was in a cul-de-sac. He retraced his steps, but he must have followed the wall too far, for he failed to regain the head of the stairs. Another few paces brought him up against a blank wall. He had begun to grow desperate and was trying to make up his mind what he should do next when he felt a slight but very cold breeze on his face. He was near the window. He felt the wall, took a few cautious steps in the direction of the draught and collided with another wall. He felt his way along it to a corner, rounded the corner and saw the window in an alcove facing him.

The moon was now hidden, but its reflection showed him that he was no longer facing the street. He leant out. About ten feet below, he could discern the dim shape of a small outbuilding. He climbed out on to the ledge. Then it occurred to him that the roof below might be of glass. For a minute or two he crouched there, trying to make up his mind what to do. Deciding, finally, that he could not stay perched on the ledge all night, he made up his mind to risk a glass roof, and lowered himself carefully until he was hanging in mid-air. Then he shut his eyes and let go.

He had underestimated the distance to the roof and the impact took his breath away. In addition, the roof, though not of glass, sloped a little, and he had to clutch at the tiles to prevent himself rolling to the ground. The noise he made sounded to him appalling, and for several minutes he clung there waiting for the alarm to be raised. But nothing happened and he clambered from the roof to the ground without trouble.

He found himself in a small and very dark courtyard. His eyes, however, were by now accustomed to the blackness, and he made for a pool of shadows which looked as though it might mark a way out. His right hand had touched a concrete wall and he was feeling his way along it when he heard a slight sound somewhere ahead of him.

With a sinking heart he stood still and listened. There was complete silence. He was still a trifle breathless and, as he strove to breathe noiselessly, the blood thumped in his head. He was beginning to think that the noise had been made by a rat, when it came again. This time it was more distinct – the scatch of shoe leather on a gritty surface.

Suddenly there came a soft whisper from the darkness ahead.

'Is that you, Andreas?'

The voice was a woman's and she spoke in Russian.

He held his breath. Then a little gasp of terror came from the darkness. The next instant a blinding light shone full in his face for a second and went out again.

He ducked sideways and ran forward blindly. A concrete wall brought him to a sharp halt and bruised his hand. He stood where he was and stared helplessly into the darkness; but he could see or hear nothing. He began to work his way round the curve in the wall.

He had moved about four yards when his fingers felt the latch of a wooden door. He turned the latch slowly. It left the socket with a faint *click*. He drew a deep breath. Then, in a single movement, he opened the door, slid through it and shut it again. For a moment he hung on to the latch the other side. Then he saw that he was in a back street and waited no longer. He ran.

5

Hotel Werner

He was soon lost in a network of streets and slowed down to a sharp walk. Once or twice he looked back to see if he was followed, but saw no one. His idea was to make for the river, and when he had found that to get back to the station.

He had no intention of remaining in Linz longer than he could help; but it was out of the question to knock up the Consul and hand over the photographs at that hour of the morning. He would spend what remained of the night in an hotel and see the Consul just before he left for Berlin. The first thing was to collect his suitcase from the café.

The sky was beginning to lighten when he reached the river and the stones were white with frost. He was feeling very tired, but it was purely physical fatigue. Questions were jostling each other in his brain.

What was the special significance of the photographs in his pocket? For whom had Sachs been working? Who had killed him? Who were the sinister-looking gentry outside the Hotel Josef? Who was the thick-set man with the muffler? And who was the woman who had mistaken him for someone else in the courtyard?

He could, he thought, answer the first of those questions.

The trade in military secrets was, he knew well enough, a very busy one. With the nations arming as fast as they could, the professional spies were prospering. He himself knew of two cases of military attachés paying fabulous prices for what, to him, had seemed trifling pieces of information – in one case the maximum angle of elevation of a new field gun; in the other case confirmation of a slight inaccuracy in a previous report on the thickness of the armour plating on a new tank. He supposed that the Russian plans for military organization in the event of war with Roumania would be welcomed at Bucharest.

He had an uncomfortable feeling, however, that this answer was not the right one. The question of Bessarabia's incorporation in Roumanian territory had, he knew, been a bone of contention between Bucharest and Moscow in the past. Early in 1918, when Roumania had been driven back into a small corner of her territory by Germany and her allies, when Bucharest was occupied by the Central Powers and the Roumanian Government had moved to Jassi, the Roumanians had established themselves in Bessarabia. As Roumania's ally, nominally at all events, Russia had not objected. In any case, the Russian Government had at that time been too preoccupied with the White armies in the south-west, and other problems, to deal with the situation. But later in 1918 trouble had arisen between the Russian and Roumanian soldiery in Bessarabia, and the Soviet Government had demanded that Roumania should evacuate the territory. The latter had pointed out with some reason that, as a state of extreme famine existed in what was left of Roumania, the return of an unpaid and unfed army would probably precipitate complete anarchy. Russia had been preparing for war with Roumania, and things had looked hopeless, when Roumania had finally succeeded in persuading a suspicious Russia of the purity of her intentions. Reluctantly the Russians had agreed to a treaty by the terms of which Roumania promised to evacuate Bessarabia within a specified time. She had never fulfilled that promise, and Russia, again preoccupied with more immediate troubles, had allowed Roumanian dominion over Bessarabia to go unchallenged until the *fait accompli* was generally recognized abroad and it was too late for anything but protests. Under the circumstances it was hardly likely that Roumania would have failed to allow for the fact that, in the event of a general European conflict, Russia might attempt to assert her undoubted legal rights by annexing Bessarabia. Besides, the orders were dated 1925. If Roumania had been able to do without the information they contained for so long, they couldn't be so very valuable. Very odd.

As for Herr Sachs, he was as much of a mystery as ever. Kenton now knew for certain what he had suspected all along; namely, that the man had not been what he claimed. The fact that he had been carrying military secrets of a somewhat unsensational nature instead of dangerous drugs or stolen banknotes merely confused.

The credit for the murder might, he decided, be awarded to the 'Nazi spy'. The man had looked quite capable of it. It was also possible that, having failed to find the photographs, the murderer had summoned his friends to await the arrival or departure of an accomplice with the photographs. In that case the man with the muffler might have been an ally of Sachs.

That explanation, however, would not do. The man with the muffler had behaved as though he already knew of Sachs' murder.

Then there was the woman. Judging by her voice, she was young, and since she had spoken in Russian, probably interested in the destination of the photographs. She had addressed him as 'Andreas'. Who was Andreas? The murderer, the man with the muffler, or someone else?

He gave it up; but, rather to his surprise, he found himself speculating as to the girl's appearance. Her voice had possessed an oddly attractive quality. The chances of his ever meeting her face to face were, he thought, remote. A dark courtyard, a single whispered sentence, the momentary glare of a torch and – that was all. How curious it was! Until the end of his life probably, at odd moments separated perhaps by intervals of years, he would remember and wonder what the owner of the voice had looked like. His mental picture of her would change with time. If his life were unhappy, he would imagine her to have been very beautiful, and would regret that he had not stayed in the courtyard. When he was very old he would tell other old men of a curious experience he once had in Linz when he had been young; and declare that he had been a romantic young fool at the time, and that the girl had probably been as unattractive as a glass of sour wine.

He was contemplating, with some distaste, the sentimental trend of these reflections, when his thoughts were interrupted by the squeal of brakes.

He had crossed the river and was within a few minutes of the station. He looked round quickly, but he could see no sign of a car, and concluded that the noise of brakes had come from a side street which he had just passed. He walked on a little way and looked round again.

The road was fairly broad and well lighted, but deserted. Suddenly there was the whine of a car being driven hard in reverse gear and a big saloon swung out of the turning backwards and pulled up with a jerk. A second later it shot forward in the direction from which he had come. With an unpleasant start he recognized it. It was the car that he had last seen waiting outside the Hotel Josef.

He watched it disappear round a corner with relief. Evidently they had not spotted him. Then he mentally kicked himself. How could they 'spot' him? They did not, could not know of his existence. Or if they did, if Sachs had told them, they couldn't know what he looked like. He walked on, cursing himself for a nervous fool. When, turning the next corner, he glanced back and thought he saw a figure dissolve quickly into the shadows by the wall, he decided that the sooner he got some sleep the better.

He was still considering the dangers of an over-wrought imagination when he arrived at the Café Schwan.

Having reclaimed his suitcase and learnt that the Hotel Werner, two streets away, was both good and cheap, he decided that after the excitements of the past hour or so, a cup of hot chocolate would be a good introduction to sleep.

While it was being prepared, he bought some matches, and was feeling in his pocket for his cigarettes when his fingers met the wallet he had picked up in Sachs' room.

He fingered it a trifle unhappily. He should have left it for the police to find. He had not meant to take it and had slipped it into his pocket without thinking. However, now he *had* got it, he might as well learn what there was to be learnt from it. He took it out of his pocket.

It was of imitation leather with the initial 'B' in one corner and had obviously cost very little. Inside, however, were over eight hundred marks in notes, four hundred and fifty of which belonged by right to him. The only other thing in the wallet was a small green note-book. All but two pages of it were blank. The two pages contained addresses; but the writing was so bad that Kenton postponed the task of deciphering them. He tore them out and stuffed them into his overcoat pocket.

There remained the money. After a good deal of quibbling with himself, he decided that he had a legitimate claim against the estate of Herr Sachs. Accordingly, he transferred four hundred and fifty marks to his own wallet.

He finished his chocolate and thought for a moment. Then he asked the man behind the counter for envelopes and stamps.

In the first he placed the balance of the money and addressed it to Herr Sachs at the Hotel Josef. The police would take charge of it. In the second he put one hundred marks with a note of thanks to the Havas man. In the third he put the photographs.

The first two he stamped. The third he marked with his own name and handed it over, accompanied by five marks and a circumstantial story, to the man behind the counter for safe keeping.

He had cleared his conscience on the subject of Herr Sachs' money. The Havas man's loan had been repaid. He had relieved himself of the compromising presence of the photographs. He had five hundred-odd marks in his pocket. Moreover, he was feeling sleepy. Later on that day, he would return to Berlin. With something approaching a light heart, he posted his letters and made his way to the Hotel Werner.

The sky was greying by the time he got to his room.

He flung his suitcase on the bed, drew the curtains and sank into a chair. His eyes were aching and, leaning over to the bedside lamp, he switched the light off. He sat still for a minute, then started to take off his tie. But even as he fumbled with the knot he felt sleep pressing on his eyelids. His fingers relaxed and his head fell slowly forward as he slid into an uncomfortable doze. It must have been about twenty minutes later that he was disturbed by a knock at the door.

He rose wearily to his feet. The knock was repeated. He walked to the door.

'What is it?'

'Service, *mein Herr,*' said a voice. 'The gentleman may be cold. I have brought extra blankets.'

Kenton unlocked the door, and turning away, started once more to remove his tie.

The door opened. There was a quick movement behind him. The next instant he felt a teriffic blow on the back of the neck. For a split second an agonizing pain shot through his head and he felt himself falling forward. Then he lost consciousness.

6

Ortega

Zaleshoff and Tamara arrived in Linz at ten o'clock in the evening and drove from the station, in a taxi, to an address on the other side of the town.

Kölnerstrasse 11 was a grocer's shop in a quiet residential quarter. Leaving his sister to pay off the taxi, Zaleshoff rang a bell at a side door. After several minutes' waiting, the door opened an inch and a woman's voice demanded hoarsely who it was who rang.

'Rashenko?' said Zaleshoff.

The woman opened the door. Motioning Tamara to follow him, Zaleshoff went in. Just inside the door was a flight of bare wooden stairs and, with the woman puffing and blowing ahead of them, the two went up slowly.

On the second landing the woman opened a door leading off it and, grunting that Rashenko was on the top floor and that she couldn't be bothered to go any farther, went inside and left them. Three more flights brought them to a landing over which the ceiling sloped steeply. There was only one door. Zaleshoff stepped forward to knock, paused, then turned to his sister.

'You have never met Rashenko?'

Tamara shook her head.

'You must not be surprised at him. He was taken by some Czarist officers and badly treated. As a result he is, amongst other things, dumb.'

The girl nodded and he rapped loudly on the door.

The man who opened it was tall, white-haired and stooping. He was incredibly thin and his clothes hung about him in long folds, as though there were no body beneath them. His eyes were set deep in his head, so that it was impossible to see the colour of them, but they gleamed like two pin-points of light from the dark hollows. His thin lips stretched tightly in a smile of welcome when he saw Zaleshoff, and he stood aside to let them in.

The room was so full of furniture that it was almost impossible to move. An unmade bed in one corner and a small stove in another contributed considerably to the general air of confusion. A wood fire burnt in the stove and the place was insufferably hot.

Rashenko waved them to chairs, then sat down himself and looked at them expectantly.

Zaleshoff took off his coat, folded it carefully over the back of his chair and sat down. Then he leaned forward and laid his hand gently on the other's arm.

'How are you, my friend?'

The dumb man picked up a newspaper from the floor, produced a pencil from his pocket and wrote in the margin. Then he displayed it.

'Better?' said Zaleshoff. 'Good. This is my sister Tamara.'

Rashenko wrote again and held the paper up.

'He says,' said Zaleshoff, turning with a smile to Tamara, 'that you are very beautiful. Rashenko was always considered an expert in these matters. You should be flattered.'

The girl smiled. She found it extraordinarily difficult to say anything to the dumb man. He nodded vehemently and smiled back at her.

'Have you heard from Vienna?' asked Zaleshoff.

Rashenko nodded.

'Have they told you that I am taking charge of this business here?'

The other nodded again and wrote on the paper: *'Ortega will come here when he has interviewed Borovansky.'*

Zaleshoff nodded approval and surveyed the dumb man sympathetically.

'Go to bed when you are tired,' he advised. 'Tamara and I will wait.'

Rashenko shook his head wearily, rose to his feet, and going to a cupboard, produced two glasses which he filled with wine from a stone jar and handed to them.

'You are not drinking with us?' said Tamara.

Rashenko shook his head gravely.

'He is not allowed by the doctors to drink wine,' explained Zaleshoff; 'he is too ill.'

The dumb man nodded and, smiling reassuringly at the girl, made a gesture of distaste towards the wine.

'Rashenko,' remarked Zaleshoff, 'is a very obstinate fellow. In Moscow they wished to send him to a sanatorium in the Crimea to recover his health; but he prefers to serve his country here.'

The dumb man smiled again – very pathetically, Tamara thought.

'Did you ever hear of a man called Saridza?' said Zaleshoff.

Rashenko shook his head.

'He was with Almazoff's army.'

The dumb man raised his head quickly and looked from brother to sister. Then he opened his mouth and seemed to be struggling to speak. At last a guttural noise came from his throat. Then he snatched at the fallen newspaper and started scribbling furiously.

Zaleshoff stood up and looked over his shoulder; then, firmly but gently, he pushed him back into the chair. Tears were streaming down the sick man's face and he fought feebly to shake off Zaleshoff's hands. Suddenly he was still and the lids drooped over his burning eyes.

Zaleshoff turned to the girl.

'It was Almazoff's men who tortured him,' he said. 'It was over eighteen years ago, but they did their work well,' he added quietly.

Rashenko's eyes opened and he smiled apologetically at them. Tamara looked away. The heat of the room was making her head ache.

A telephone bell shrilled suddenly.

Rashenko rose painfully to his feet and, going to the cupboard in the wall, lifted the instrument from a hook inside and put it to his ear. Then he pressed a small Morse key and signalled three sharp buzzes into the transmitter. For a moment he listened; then he signalled again, replaced the telephone and turned to Zaleshoff.

'Vienna?'

Rashenko nodded, reached for his pencil, wrote a message and passed it to Zaleshoff.

The latter turned to Tamara.

'Vienna says that Ortega telephoned twenty minutes ago from Passau. He and Borovansky arrive at two-thirty.'

For the girl the next hundred and fifty minutes were an unbearably slow procession of as many hours. There were two clocks in the room, and for a time their different rates of ticking fascinated her with the seemingly endless rhythmic variations they evolved. Soon, however, she found that the changes of rhythm were part of a pattern that repeated itself every three-quarters of a minute. She glanced at the two men. Her brother was frowning fiercely into the fire and twiddling a key between his fingers. Rashenko's eyes were closed and he looked asleep. Murmuring that she was going to smoke a cigarette, she put on her coat and went out to the landing.

After the heat of the sick man's room, the cold air was immediately refreshing. Through the sloping skylight, just above her head, she could see the sky. It was a bright, clear night, and the stars, dimmed by the rising moon, seemed infinitely derisive. Gusts of wind buffeted the house with increasing force. She found the sound curiously soothing and stayed there until the sharp rattle of a bell far below told her that the man they were waiting for had at last arrived.

The moment the Spaniard came into the room it was obvious that something was wrong. He was out of breath from running, and the grey, puffy cheeks were flecked grotesquely with two patches of colour. His dull pebble-like eyes, blinking in the light, darted suspiciously round the room, like those of a cornered animal. One corner of his mouth twitched slightly. Zaleshoff, who had let him in, followed him into the room and shut the door.

'Well,' he said in German, 'you have what you were sent for?'

Ortega shook his head and strove to regain his breath.

'No,' he said at last, 'they were not there.'

Zaleshoff looked at him steadily for a moment; then, stepping forward, he gripped the sleeve of the man's coat and jerked him towards him.

'No lies, my friend,' he said grimly. Then he let go of the coat and held up his hand. Tamara saw that it was smeared with blood.

'What happened?' he added dangerously.

The Spaniard was recovering his breath. He assumed a jaunty air. His dry, bloodless mouth twisted a little.

'I kill him perhaps, eh?' He snickered and his eyes wandered towards the girl, seeking approbation. 'He saw me on the train and tried to escape me at the station; but I was too quick for him perhaps. He took a taxi and drove about to escape me, but though he was cunning, I was more cunning, and I follow him to the Hotel Josef.'

Zaleshoff turned quickly to Rashenko.

'The Hotel Josef, where is that?'

The dumb man wrote quickly. Zaleshoff looked at the paper and nodded. Then he turned again to Ortega.

'Go on.'

'I follow him to his room.'

'How did you know which room?'

Ortega shrugged disdainfully.

'It is a poor hovel, not such as I am perhaps used to in my native country, where I am rich. I wait outside the door and hear the porter give him the number. He named himself Sachs. It was room twenty-five on the third floor. Then he ask to telephone and I do not hear that. But also I hear him tell to expect a Herr Kenton who would call.'

'Kenton? That is an English name.'

'Perhaps. On the train with him from Ratisbon there is an American or perhaps he may have been English. Perhaps this American has the photographs. I do not know. I could not wait.'

Zaleshoff made a gesture of impatience.

'Quick, what did you do?'

'I go to his room by the back way so that no one sees me and I knock at his door. He says to come in, Herr Kenton, and although my name is not Kenton, but Ortega, a great family name in Spain, I go in. When he sees me he cried out and go for the gun he had. But I reach him first and get him. It hurt him,' added the Spaniard reminiscently.

The veins stood out on Zaleshoff's forehead.

'You were ordered not to kill,' he said quietly.

Ortega shrugged.

'It was a small thing – nothing.'

'You fool!' shouted Zaleshoff suddenly. 'You were ordered not to kill. You kill. You were ordered to get the photographs from Borovansky. You do not get them. There is only one place for you, my friend.' His voice dropped suddenly. 'You know where that is, Ortega, do you not? Lisbon, my friend, Lisbon.'

'There were no photographs, no photographs at all.'

'Or perhaps,' went on Zaleshoff viciously, 'you would prefer the Austrian police to the Portuguese. The telephone, please, Rashenko.'

'Mother of God,' screamed the Spaniard, 'I tell you that there were no photographs.'

Zaleshoff sneered.

'So you say. But, you see, I do not believe you. There was no doubt a wealthier bidder for your services. How much, Ortega? How much did they offer you to turn traitor?'

'*Madre de Dios, juro que es mentira!*' Sweat was pouring from his face.

'Where did you look?'

'His coat, his luggage, everything.'

'The lining of his coat?'

'I tear it to pieces; also his luggage. There is nothing.'

'He had hidden it in the room.'

'He had no time.'

'Did you look?'

'It was necessary that I go perhaps.'

'And this Herr Kenton; did he arrive?'

'I do not know. I go.'

'What did this American on the train look like?'

'Tall, thin, a soft hat, young perhaps.'

Zaleshoff turned to the others.

'It is necessary that we search that room immediately. You, Tamara, and I will go. You have a pistol, Rashenko?'

Rashenko nodded.

'Good. Ortega the traitor will remain here with you. If he tries to go, shoot him.'

The Spaniard burst into excited speech.

'*No hara Vd. esto! Debo ir. El hijo de zorra tenia una pistola – a que dudar? Lo maté porque era necessario. No tengo fotografías, lo juro. Dejeme escapar, seré perseguido por la policia – tenga piedad!*' His voice rose hysterically.

Zaleshoff, struggling with his overcoat, took no notice of him.

'He says,' said Tamara in Russian, 'that he must go.'

'Tell him,' said her brother in the same language, 'that he is a fool, and that it is safer for him to remain. Safer, because the police will not look here for him, also because if he tries to leave, Rashenko will shoot.'

When, a few minutes later, they hurried away, Rashenko was sitting in his chair, a large revolver in his hand. Ortega had taken a rosary from his pocket and was kneeling by the fire, the beads clicking through his fingers and words bubbling from his lips. As the Russian listened a smile spread over his drawn face, for he knew a little Spanish. Señor Ortega's orisons would have made even a Bilbao docker blush.

Andreas Prokovitch Zaleshoff was, as many could have testified, a deceptive character. For one thing, he gave the impression of being almost childishly naïve; for another, he possessed a subtle sense of the value of histrionics. Violent displays of emotion, if well timed, distract the shrewdest observer and hamper his judgement. Zaleshoff's timing was invariably perfect. He rarely said what he really thought without making it sound like a clumsy attempt to dissemble. Passionate conviction was with him a sign of indifference to the point at issue. For Tamara, who understood him better than he supposed, he was a constant source of entertainment.

As she kept watch in the darkness behind the Hotel Josef she was, however, worried. His anger with Ortega had been very nearly genuine. That could mean only one thing: that he was badly puzzled. He did not, she knew perfectly well, expect to find the photographs in the murdered man's room. She also knew that he was taking an unnecessary risk to confirm the obvious.

She was turning these matters over in her mind when she was startled by the noise of Kenton's arrival on the roof of the outhouse. Wondering why her brother had not returned the way he had gone (by the tradesmen's door), she moved away from the wall to meet him.

Tamara was not used to automatics. But for that fact, the career of a little-known but promising journalist might have been cut short by death in, as the newspapers say, mysterious circumstances. As the light from her torch showed for a split second that the man before her was not her brother, her forefinger jerked involuntarily at the trigger of the gun Zaleshoff had slipped into her hand before he had gone inside. If the safety catch had been disengaged, not even Kenton's leap for the wall would have saved him.

Zaleshoff joined her some five minutes later with the expected news that the photographs were missing. Hurriedly she told him of her encounter. He listened thoughtfully, then asked for a precise description of the man. The description she gave would not have flattered Kenton, but he would have been struck by the accuracy of it.

'He might easily,' she concluded, 'have been an American or possibly English.'

'Did you see his tie?'

'No, his coat collar was turned up. But the hat looked American or English.'

Zaleshoff was silent for a moment or two. Finally, he led the way into the street again.

'Go back to the Kölnerstrasse and wait there until I telephone you,' he said.

He watched her out of sight, then turned and made his way by a circuitous route to the street in front of the hotel. As he drew nearer, he slowed down and kept in the shadows. When he was about twenty yards from the saloon car which stood near the entrance he stopped.

So far as he could see there were four men in the car besides the two gazing up at the hotel windows from farther up the street, and for a quarter of an hour they sat motionless. He began to get stiff with cold. Suddenly a door of the car swung open and two men got out, walked slowly towards the hotel and went inside. It was too dark to see their faces, but as they disappeared through the frosted glass door, the leading man raised his left hand with an awkward gesture to the inside breast pocket of his coat. His arm seemed slightly stiff at the elbow. If Tamara had been there, she would have recognized the look of stony indifference that spread over her brother's face. Andreas Prokovitch was feeling pleased with himself.

The two had been gone about three minutes when the door of the hotel was flung open and they came hurrying out again. Zaleshoff heard a sharp order in German to the driver of the car as they climbed in. He caught only two words – '*der Engländer*' – then the door slammed and the car roared away.

Zaleshoff went in search of a telephone booth. Five minutes later he was speaking to Tamara, to whom he gave certain instructions. An hour later he stepped out of another telephone booth near the station and asked a man hosing the roadway how to get to the Hotel Werner.

But as he turned the corner of the street in which it lay, he saw by the cold grey light of the early morning that he was too late. Two men were carrying between them what looked at first like a large limp sack from the entrance of the Hotel Werner to the waiting car. *Der Engländer* had been found.

7

'Colonel Robinson'

When consciousness began to return to Kenton's brain it brought with it several varieties of pain. The most immediate was the horrible ache in his head. Then he became in turn aware of cramp in his legs, a hard surface battering his left thigh, and a sharp edge crushing the back of his left hand. He opened his eyes.

The first thing he saw was a trouser leg made of coarse material in an unpleasant shade of fawn. Following this down, he saw that its owner's foot was pinning his hand to a fibre mat. Then he realized that he was lying on the floor of a car moving fast over rough ground. Instinctively he made to lever himself into a sitting position. There was an agonizing throb in his head and he let out a gasp of pain. The sound evidently reached the man on the seat above him, for the foot shifted to his fingers and a hand pushed him down again. Striving to keep his head from contact with the vibrating floor, he lay still and closed his eyes. For a time he slipped into semi-consciousness, and there was only the steady whine of the car climbing fast in lower gear to remind him where he was. Then the car slowed down and he felt his body dragging on the mat as the driver turned a sharp corner. The vibration ceased suddenly, the wheels rolled smoothly over concrete for a few yards and stopped.

The door at his feet opened and two men clambered over his legs to get out. There was a muttered conversation too low for him to hear and the sound of receding footsteps. He opened his eyes again and, raising his head slightly, looked out through the open door of the car. The back of a man wearing chauffeur's uniform partly obscured the opening, but what he could see through the gap was sufficiently astonishing. He was looking at a ridge of snow-capped hills, their summits radiant with the halation of the rising sun behind them.

Kenton was one of those persons, of whom there are many, who find the contemplation of scenery very boring. For him, half an hour in a pavement café at, say, the lower end of the Cannebière was to be preferred to all the peaks in the Dolomites, with a dozen Aegean islands thrown in. He would have exchanged a valuable Corot for a not-so-valuable Toulouse-Lautrec and considered himself the gainer. He preferred Satie to Delius, George Gissing to Richard Jeffries, and the feel of pavements beneath his feet to that of the springiest turf ever trod by Georgian poet. But for a moment now he contemplated and was not bored; for a moment he forgot his aching head; then, as he eased his cramped legs and his head swam when he tensed the muscles in his neck to raise himself, he began to think again and to remember. He had had a room in the Hotel Werner. It had been getting light when he had arrived there. If the sun were only just rising, he must be somewhere in the hills very near Linz. What on earth had happened?

His mind was still searching feverishly among a jumble of impressions when someone shouted in the distance and the chauffeur turned round and tapped him smartly on the leg with the barrel of a revolver.

'*Aussteigen.*'

Kenton slid forward until his feet touched the ground, hauled himself gingerly to his feet and looked round.

He was standing on a concrete runway leading to a garage surrounded by bushes of mountain ash and tall fir trees. Through them he could see the top of a white house, with two small spired turrets, set in a niche in the hillside. Behind him, the hill sloped away to the foot of a deep and narrow valley and rose again to the early snow altitude. The entire landscape was carpeted with firs. The only indications of contour were given by the roads – thin streaks of white laid here and there at odd angles across the dense green-black masses.

He shivered. The air was clean and exhilarating, but very cold; and he had no overcoat. The chauffeur prodded his arm with the gun.

'Los! Vorwärts!'

Not yet feeling well enough to translate his resentment into words, Kenton obeyed the man's gesture and started along a path sloping up to the house through the firs. The path ended at a flagged courtyard in front of the house. Waiting for them at the door was the owner of the fawn trousers.

He was a tall, lean, middle-aged man with a hard, stupid, rather handsome face. A small fair toothbrush moustache bridged a very short upper lip. He wore a belted raincoat with shoulder straps and carried what looked like a short thick stick in one hand. He dismissed the chauffeur with a nod and gripped Kenton's arm tightly. To the journalist's surprise, the man addressed him in English.

'Feeling a bit dicky, are you, old man?' He grinned. 'Neat little tap I gave you, wasn't it? Well, well; better pull yourself together a bit; the chief wants to see you. Come on.'

'Look here—' began Kenton angrily.

'Shut up and come on.' His fingers moved slightly on the muscles in Kenton's upper arm. Suddenly he tightened his grip. The journalist cried out with pain. It was as though a red-hot poker had been jabbed into his arm.

The other laughed.

'Good trick that, isn't it, eh? Better get a move on, old man, or I'll do it again.'

He jerked Kenton forward through the door.

There are houses which can give the impression of wealth and luxury without the aid of soft carpets and splendid furniture. This was one of them. With the exception of two or three fine rugs, there was no covering on the waxed pine floor of the spacious entrance hall. On the far side a broad staircase curved up to a small gallery. In the recess below the balustrade a narrow table stood against the wall. On it stood a pair of exquisite Cinquecento candlesticks. On the wall to the right was a good copy of Tintoretto's *Miracolo dello Schiavo*. A fir-cone fire roared in a massive grate.

The Englishman led Kenton across the hall to a small door below the gallery, opened it and pushed him in.

The first thing he noticed was a very pleasant smell of freshly made coffee. Then the door closed behind him and he heard from the other end of the room the clink of a cup being placed in a saucer. He looked round. Sitting behind a large desk with the sunlight now streaming through the tall windows glinting on his grey hair, was a man eating breakfast from a tray.

The man looked up. There was a pause. Then he spoke.

'Good morning, Mr Kenton. I think you could probably do with a cup of coffee.'

He was an impressive-looking man in the late fifties, with a smart grey cavalry moustache and a monocle. At first sight, he looked like a cross between a *Punch* drawing of a retired general and a French conception of what the continent of Europe so oddly terms 'the English sporting'. That he spoke with a pronounced Russian accent, and that the skin of his face was stretched like creased yellow parchment over a bone structure which was certainly not Nordic, indicated, however, that he was not English. That below the grey moustache there was a loose and curiously cruel mouth, and that the monocle did nothing to hide a pair of pale, calculating and very dangerous eyes, suggested that he was probably not 'sporting' either. Kenton experienced an immediate and powerful sense of dislike. He came to the point.

'I should like to know by what right—' he began angrily.

The other held up his hand imploringly.

'Mr Kenton, Mr Kenton, please! I have not been to sleep all night. I must ask you to spare me your outraged feelings. We are all feeling outraged this morning, aren't we, Mailler?' He addressed the last words over Kenton's shoulder.

'My God, yes,' said Kenton's escort.

'All the same,' continued the man at the desk, 'I understand your indignation. What right have I, a perfect stranger, to tell my men to club you and to carry you off in so high-handed and uncomfortable a manner – you, an English journalist, if the Press card in your pocket does not lie? What right, I say?' He thumped the desk with his fist.

'Exactly,' said Kenton, a little bewildered by this vigorous presentation of his case.

The grey-haired man sipped at his coffee.

'The answer is,' he said, 'none! No right at all except my own wishes.'

'And those are?'

The man raised his eyebrows.

'Surely,' he said, 'you are in no doubt about that?'

'I'm afraid I am,' said Kenton with rising irritation. 'I can only conclude that you have mistaken me for someone else. I don't know who you are or what your game is; but you have placed yourself in a very awkward position. The British Consul in Linz will not, I should think, be disposed to intercede with the police on your behalf and, unless I am immediately released and taken back to Linz, nor shall I. Now, if you please, I wish to go.'

The man at the desk smiled broadly, disclosing a row of long, uneven yellow teeth.

'Excellent, Mr Kenton, excellent. I can see that Mailler is appreciating your performance, too. You and he would, I feel sure, grow to like each other very much. You must get him to tell you about some of his experiences. Captain Mailler was in the Black-and-Tans, and was also, at one time, the only professional strike-breaker in America with an English public school education. At the moment, of course, he is hoping that you will attempt to leave this room. I hope you won't, because then we shall have to postpone the rest of our talk for an hour or two. Eh, Mailler?'

'I vote we give the beggar hell now, chief,' said the Captain.

'That's typical of Mailler,' said the grey-haired man to Kenton. 'He has very little tact. Though, to be sure, with his experience, he can usually get what he wants without it.'

Kenton studied an ink-well on the desk. He had an uncomfortable feeling that no mistake had been made and that he could guess only too well what was wanted. He looked up. The man behind the desk was lighting a cigarette; he was doing it rather awkwardly, as though his arm were very stiff at the elbow.

He blew a long, thin jet of smoke into the air, watched it dissipate, then turned to Kenton again.

'Still puzzled, Mr Kenton?'

'Very.'

'Well, well. Sit down, Mr Kenton. You, too, Captain. I am always in favour of doing business in comfort.' He favoured Kenton with another of his yellow smiles.

Kenton sat down.

'Business?' he said.

The skin creased suddenly round the other's eyes.

'Yes, Mr Kenton, business. Let us come to the point.'

'Yes, let us.'

'Why did you kill Borovansky?'

'Who?'

'Borovansky.'

'I don't know what you're talking about.'

'You may have known him as Sachs.'

'Never heard of him.'

Captain Mailler gave a short laugh. The man behind the desk sighed wearily.

'It may be,' he said with an air of great patience, 'that you doubt my motives. You may think that I inquire after the fate of Borovansky out of some petty desire for revenge. That is not so. Borovansky, personally, was not of the slightest interest to me. He was, however, carrying certain property of mine. I wish you to restore that property to me. You have probably examined it. You will know, then, that the photographs are of no monetary value to you. You will also realize that anyone being so fool-hardy as to interfere in such affairs places himself in a very delicate position. Borovansky's pocket-book with all his money in it was gone when we found him. It is, I find, in your pocket. You see, Mr Kenton, it was hardly tactful of you to mention the police, even in fun. Austria is, I believe, one of the countries which has abolished capital punishment, but a life sentence is hardly worth risking. Now, please, what have you done with the photographs?'

'You're talking nonsense. I did not kill Sachs.'

'Ah, then you did know him?'

Kenton stirred in his chair. It might be due to the crack on the head he had received, but he did not seem to be doing very well out of the interview. He changed his tactics.

'You can hardly expect me to treat you with a great deal of confidence. Quite apart from the fact that your professional thug here has assaulted me and that you are holding me prisoner, I have not the least idea who you are.'

'I shouldn't get cheeky if I were you, old man,' advised the Captain.

Kenton ignored him.

'Now, now,' said the grey-haired man reprovingly. 'Let us keep calm. You have asked me for my name, Mr Kenton. I fail to see that it can be of the slightest help to you to know it. It is, however, Robinson – Colonel Robinson.'

'English?'

Colonel Robinson smiled with his cigarette between his teeth.

'No, Mr Kenton. Why should I bother to deceive you? My accent is not, as you perfectly well know, quite perfect.'

'You are very fluent.'

'It is good of you to say so.' He leaned forward. 'Now, supposing we dispense with these courtesies and come to the point, my friend? Where are the photographs? And before you answer me please remember that you will save yourself a lot of unpleasantness if you discard the various clumsy evasions that you are turning over in your mind. I know the photographs are not on your person. Where are they and how can they be got at?'

Kenton hesitated. His first impulse was to give the man the information he wanted and get out of the place. He glanced at the two men. The ex-Black-and-Tan Captain was lounging in his chair, absently biting his nails. Across his knees lay the short, shiny black stick. 'Colonel Robinson' was leaning forward in his chair, a cigarette smouldering between his lips. In their eyes, watching him intently, there was a hint of amused expectation. Then, rather to his surprise, he became conscious of a new and unfamiliar sensation. For the first time in his adult life someone was trying to coerce him with threats into making a decision, and his mind was reacting with cold, angry, obstinate refusal. He drew a deep breath. Slightly above the solar plexus there was a curiously hollow feeling, his heart was beating faster, and the blood was tingling away from his face. He realized that for the first time in years he was within a few seconds of a complete and violent loss of temper. He pulled himself together and felt the blood rushing back to his cheeks. But there was an edge to his voice when at last he answered.

'I am afraid I have no intention of telling you any such thing. Certain property was entrusted to my care. The man who entrusted it to me is now dead. He was no friend of mine. To be accurate, I met him on the train coming to Linz. But he paid me well for safeguarding his property and I accepted the responsibility. That he was subsequently stabbed to death does not seem to me to affect that responsibility in the slightest.'

'Then how, may I inquire, do you intend to relieve yourself of the responsibility?'

'The photographs,' Kenton replied cautiously, 'would seem to be the property of the Russian Government. If you can show me credentials authorizing you to act on their behalf, I shall be pleased to hand over the photographs when I am released.'

There was dead silence in the room for a moment or two. Then the Captain rose slowly to his feet.

'Now,' he began, 'you're going to get—'

The man at the desk waved him into silence and turned to Kenton.

'I don't think you understand the position, Mr Kenton.'

'No?'

'No. Borovansky, or, if you prefer it, Sachs, was working for me. It was to me that he was delivering the photographs.'

'Then why did he hand them over to me?'

'He was afraid that he would be attacked and the photographs stolen from him before I could provide him with protection.'

'And yet he was murdered.'

'Shortly after you arrived, Mr Kenton,' said the Colonel pointedly. 'When he arrived at the Hotel Josef, Borovansky telephoned to say that you were carrying the photographs. My men were on the spot in time to see you go in. They did not see you leave.'

'Sachs was already dead when I arrived. I left by the back entrance.'

'With the photographs?'

'Certainly.'

'Don't you think you are being rather foolish, Mr Kenton?'

'Why?'

Colonel Robinson's yellow skin tightened suddenly.

'Because, whatever your prim notions of responsibility may be, I want those photographs and intend to have them. Furthermore,' he added slowly, 'I am prepared to take any steps that may be necessary to overcome your scruples.'

'Such as?'

The Colonel's face relaxed. Rising to his feet with a smile, he walked round the desk and laid his hand in a friendly gesture on Kenton's shoulder.

'Come now, Mr Kenton, don't let us spoil this delightful morning with talk of unpleasant things. Be sensible, Mr Kenton. The welfare of the Russian Government is, I feel sure, of no interest to you. Borovansky, poor fellow, is dead. Hand over the photographs, forget the whole affair and we might even discuss the question of a substantial honorarium in recognition of your own trouble and discomfort. What do you say?'

Kenton nearly smiled. Two bribes in twelve hours! Not bad going!

'What do you suggest?'

The Colonel became almost eager.

'Tell us where the photographs are, and the moment they are in my possession you will be released with a thousand marks in your pocket.'

So his price had gone up! What a trusting fool the man must think him!

'And the alternative?'

The Colonel reached for the cigarette-box and offered it to Kenton, who shook his head. The Colonel lit up, extinguished the match carefully and sank into his chair.

'Do you ever read Machiavelli, Mr Kenton?'

'I have done.'

'"*Fa bene la fortuna questo, che ella elegge un uomo di tanto spirito e di tanta virtu che egli conosca quelle occasioni che ella gli porge."* You probably know the passage. Machiavelli is always so beautifully to the point, don't you think?'

Kenton nodded. The man clearly loved the sound of his own voice.

'You see,' continued the Colonel with relish, 'fortune has placed you in rather an unfortunate position. For instance, my intuition tells me that you did not kill Borovansky. That fact, however, will not prevent my handing you over to the police with the evidence of my men who saw you enter the hotel, and that of the wallet in your pocket.'

'But then,' objected Kenton evenly, 'you would not get your photographs and I should almost certainly go free.'

The other affected to consider this.

'It is a possibility.' He shrugged. 'I will not labour the point. The leniency of the police has always irritated me. I merely wished to suggest one of the possibilities of your present situation. There are others. For example; what paper do you work for?'

'I am a free-lance.'

'Indeed? Dear me, that makes it very easy. Do you know, Mr Kenton, that I could, through my principals in London, make it impossible for you to carry on your profession?'

'How?'

'By having your name black-listed by the proprietors of every important group of newspapers in England.'

Kenton smiled.

'I'm afraid I can't take that very seriously, Colonel. You see, quite apart from the fact that many editors make a point of circumventing that sort of order from a proprietor, I use at least six pseudonyms in my work, none of which is anything like Kenton. Under the circumstances, your principals might find you a little tiresome.'

The moment he had finished speaking, he knew that his flippancy had been a mistake. The man behind the desk was silent; not a muscle of his face seemed to have moved; but in some subtle fashion the mask had changed from one of watchful geniality to one of malignant fury. When at last he spoke his accent had become very pronounced.

'I can see,' he said slowly, 'that you are going to be foolish. That is a pity. I had hoped for a reasonable attitude on your part, that this matter could be settled across this desk and that extreme measures would not be necessary. I see I have wasted my time.'

Out of the corner of his eye Kenton saw Captain Mailler's hand drop to the shiny black stick.

'I'm extremely sorry,' he said, with not quite as much suavity as he had intended.

'You will be very much sorrier before long, Mr Kenton,' was the reply. He fingered his lower lip and gazed at Kenton thoughtfully. 'The art of persuasion,' he went on, 'has always interested me. The days of the rack, the wheel and the thumbscrew are past. We can afford to smile a little at the narrow limits of mediæval thought on the subject. To-day we look towards new horizons. The early nineteen-twenties brought with them a renaissance of the art which has not yet reached its absolute fulfilment. That renaissance is no decadent sham. The men who have brought it about have not needed new media, new tools with which to express themselves. With the sublime simplicity and humility of all true artists they have used the materials that were available. Castor oil, for instance, that homely stuff, has been used with amazing success as a persuasive agent. You see, when administered by the pint it produces a painful effect very much like that resulting from eating green apples, but many times magnified. To Fascist Italy must go the credit of the discovery, as also must that of the *bastonatura in stile*, a process that consists of treating the lower part of the face with rubber truncheons, such as the one Captain Mailler is holding, until the jaw is shattered. Pins and tooth-picks under the fingernails are, of course, a little jejune; but from the other side of the Atlantic, the authorities have given us, beautiful in its simplicity, the dentists' burr drill to grind the teeth of reluctant mouths. Rubber hose, blinding arc lights, lighted cigarettes and well-placed kicks all have their advocates. For myself, I have no special likes and dislikes, but you will, I think, see what is in my mind. Do you, Mr Kenton?'

The journalist was silent.

Colonel Robinson smiled slightly.

'I think you do. But I will make myself quite clear. I am going to place you in a room by yourself for twelve hours. If at the end of that time you have not decided to be frank with me, then I shall hand you over to Captain Mailler and his assistants for interrogation.' He nodded to the Captain. 'All right, Mailler, put him in the top room.'

'Get up,' said Mailler.

Kenton got up. His face was white with fatigue, his swollen eyelids were twitching with the pain in his head; but his mouth had set in an obstinate line.

'Your name might actually be Colonel Robinson,' he said. 'I doubt it. But whatever your name is, you are, in my opinion, a nit-wit. At one stage in this conversation I was not unwilling to wash my hands of the entire business and hand over the photographs to you. You made the mistake of supposing that I could be successfully intimidated. It is a mistake that quite a number of persons of your kidney are making in Europe to-day. The Nazi concentration camps and the Italian penal islands are full of men who have refused to compromise with violence. To compare my present attitude with their amazing courage is absurd, but I find now that I have an inkling of their point of view. I used to wonder how they could suffer so much for the sake of such transitory things as political principles. I realize now that there's more in it than that. It's not just a struggle between Fascism and Communism, or between any other "-isms". It's between the free human spirit and the stupid, fumbling, brutish forces of the primeval swamp – and that, Colonel, means you and your kind.'

Mailler's fist with the truncheon in it dashed into his face. He reeled backwards, caught his foot in the chair and went down. For a moment he lay still; then he crawled slowly to his feet.

Blood was trickling from the corner of his mouth. His face was deadly white, but he was smiling slightly.

'You, too, Captain,' he said.

Mailler knocked him down again and this time Kenton had to haul himself up by the chair. Mailler went to the door and called two men in. Next, he went over to Kenton, pulled the chair from under his hand and gave him a shove that sent the journalist sprawling. Then he gave the two men a sharp order in bad German and Kenton was dragged to his feet and taken out. At the foot of the stairs he fell down again and was carried to a room at the top of the house, where he was dumped on the floor. The shutters were pulled to and fastened with a padlock and chain. Then the door slammed and a key was turned in the lock.

For a time Kenton remained where he had been dropped. At last he raised his head painfully and looked round.

The sun was sending long, slanting bars of light through the shutters. By its reflection, Kenton could see that there was no furniture in the room. For a moment he contemplated the pattern of sunlight on the floor thoughtfully. Then, resting his head in the crook of his arm, he lay back and closed his eyes.

A minute or two later he was asleep and on his lips was the slight, contented smile of the man who remembers work well done.

8

The Truncheon

When Kenton awoke the sun had gone. The room was in almost complete darkness and for some seconds he did not realize where he was. Then he remembered and got stiffly to his feet. His face felt badly bruised, and when he put his hand to his mouth he found that his lower lip was swollen. His head, however, though extremely sensitive to the touch, was no longer aching. He struck a match and went to the window. By crouching down he could see a black sky through the slats. He had taken off his watch in the Hotel Werner, but it was evidently quite late. Colonel Robinson's ultimatum must expire very soon.

Sleep is not always an unmixed blessing. It brings relief to the nerves and strength to the body; but it also brings cold sanity to shatter the flimsy emotional structures of the night before. Kenton's reactions to the methods employed by Colonel Robinson and his *aide* to secure the Sachs photographs had been emotional. Now, nearly twelve hours of sleep had left him wondering why on earth he had made such a lot of fuss. If they wanted the wretched photographs, let them have them. All that absurd fit of heroics had produced was a swollen lip and a bruised face. A nice mess he had landed himself in! The best thing he could do was to hand over the photographs as soon as possible and get back to Berlin.

He sat on the floor with his back to the wall below the shutters and considered his plight.

First and foremost, he badly needed a drink; water for preference, but anything else would do. He did not feel very hungry; but that was probably because he was so thirsty. His last meal had been off Sachs' garlic sausage in the train. That seemed a long time ago.

Sachs was now lying dead in the Hotel Josef. No, the police would have taken him away by now. He found it a little difficult to get the events of the past twenty-four hours into perspective. What curious business had he become involved in? Who had Sachs, or, rather, Borovansky, been? The fact that his other name was Russian fitted in with his odd accent. It would appear, too, that he was working against the Russian Government; that was always assuming that the 'Colonel' had been speaking the truth – a questionable assumption. Then there was that question of the Colonel's 'principals in London'. Who were they, and what 'business' was the man transacting for them? Kenton felt that if he knew the answer to the first part of that question, the second part would be answered automatically. Principals in London who were in a position to influence newspaper proprietors sounded suspiciously like Big Business.

It was difficult, Kenton had found, to spend any length of time in the arena of foreign politics without perceiving that political ideologies had very little to do with the ebb and flow of international relations. It was the power of Business, not the deliberations of statesmen, that shaped the destinies of nations. The Foreign Ministers of the great powers might make the actual declarations of their Governments' policies; but it was the Big Business men, the bankers and their dependents, the arms manufacturers, the oil companies, the big industrialists, who determined what those policies should be. Big Business asked the questions that it wanted to ask when and how it suited it. Big Business also provided the answers. Rome might declare herself sympathetic to a Hapsburg restoration; France might oppose it. A few months later the situation might be completely reversed. For those few members of the public who had long memories and were not sick to death of the whole incomprehensible farce there would always be many ingenious explanations of the *volte face* – many explanations, but not the correct one. For that one might have to inquire into banking transactions in London, Paris and New York with the eye of a chartered accountant, the brain of an economist, the tongue of a prosecuting attorney and the patience of Job. One would have, perhaps, to note an increase in the Hungarian bank rate, an 'ear-marking' of gold in Amsterdam, and a restriction of credit facilities in the Middle-West of America. One would have to grope through the fog of technical mumbo-jumbo with which international business surrounds its operations and examine them in all their essential and ghastly simplicity. Then one would perhaps die of old age. The Big Business man was only one player in the game of international politics, but he was the player who made all the rules.

Kenton found a cigarette in his pocket and lit up. It looked as if Big Business was, in this case, interested in either Bessarabia or Roumania. He drew at his cigarette and the end glowed in the darkness. He watched it thoughtfully. Somewhere and recently, he had heard something about Roumania that had interested him. Ah yes! It had been that business about Concession Reform. A newspaper that had printed an article against it had been beaten up. Well, there didn't seem to be much to be got out of that; though, of course, you never could tell. That was the trouble. One end of the game was played in the rarefied atmosphere of board-rooms and weekend shooting parties; the other was played, with persons like Sachs as counters, in trains, in cheap hotels, in suburbs of big cities, in murky places away from the bright highways dedicated to the rosy-cheeked goddess of *tourisme*. Someone spoke in an office in Birmingham or Pittsburgh, or maybe on board a yacht off Cannes, and a few weeks later a Mills bomb burst in a printing works in Bucharest. Between those two events, unknown both to the man who had spoken and to the man who had pulled the pin from the bomb, was a misty hinterland in which the 'Colonel Robinsons' of the earth moved silently about their business. Yes, he would certainly give up the photographs. His role had always before been that of spectator; let it remain so.

He crushed his cigarette out on the floor and rose to his feet. As he did so, he heard the sound of approaching footsteps, a pause, then the rattle of a key in the lock.

His heart beating a little faster, he stood by the window and waited. The door opened, the beam of a torch cut across the room, swung round and shone straight into his eyes.

'Well, old man,' said the voice of Captain Mailler, 'are you going to be sensible or do I have to knock hell out of you first?'

For about five seconds Kenton did not speak. In those five seconds all his resolutions, all his sane reflections on the desirability of giving in gracefully and keeping out of trouble, were swept away by just two things – Captain Mailler's voice and Captain Mailler's words. In those five seconds the entire structure of resentment, anger, obstinacy and defiance that reason had so completely demolished was re-erected. And this time it was supported by a body no longer tired, a brain no longer distracted by the after-effects of concussion.

'You can do exactly what you like,' he said at last; 'but if you think you can bully me into doing anything, you've made a mistake.'

'Don't be silly, old man,' said the Captain evenly. 'You don't know what you're talking about. A nigger out in the States once felt that way about things, and those fellows are really hard eggs. But by the time I'd finished with the beggar he would have jumped over the moon or razored his own father and mother if I'd told him to.'

'I'm an orphan.'

The Captain clucked reprovingly.

'Shouldn't get cheeky if I were you, old man. Doesn't pay. The chief didn't care for you much and he's given me a free hand. To tell you the truth, old man, I don't much care for you, either. As a matter of fact, I shouldn't be so sorry if you did try to keep your mouth shut for a bit. I could do with a bit of fun.'

Kenton did not answer.

The torch wavered slightly.

'*Vorwärts!*' said the Captain.

Two men appeared from the blackness of the passage outside and seized Kenton's arms. He shook them off, received a kick on the ankle, the pain of which took his breath away, and was hauled out of the room and downstairs to the hall.

Mailler vanished into the Colonel's room. A minute later he reappeared and signalled to the men holding Kenton.

'The chief wants to see you, old man,' he said. 'If I were you I'd watch my step. He's not feeling very pleased with you.'

'I'm not feeling very pleased with him,' retorted Kenton.

For a second he thought the Captain was going to strike him. Then Mailler grinned unpleasantly.

'You and me'll be having a little chat soon, old man,' he said.

He nodded to Kenton's escort and they went in.

The Colonel was standing in front of the fire; and in a suit of tweeds and by the subdued amber light of the desk lamp he looked a picture of landed respectability. He stared at Kenton for a minute or two in silence. Then:

'Are you ready to be sensible yet?' he asked coldly.

'If by that,' replied Kenton promptly, 'you mean am I prepared to hand over to you what is obviously somebody else's property, the answer is no.'

The Colonel's arm shot out; he caught hold of Kenton's jacket and jerked him forward.

'Listen, my friend,' he said quietly, 'I am in no mood to indulge in drawing-room pleasantries. I need those photographs and I am not going to be stopped by any blockhead of a reporter from getting what I want. When you left the Hotel Josef you went to the Café Schwan. You had the photographs then. When you arrived at the Hotel Werner you had not got them. My men report that you went to nowhere else but the Café Schwan. What did you do with the photographs?' He struck the journalist across the face with the back of his hand. 'What did you do with them?' he repeated savagely.

Kenton's hand went to his face. Then he looked at his fingers. The Colonel wore a ring and it had opened up his cheek. He decided on revenge.

'I – I don't remember,' he stammered weakly.

The Colonel shook him violently and struck him again.

'Perhaps that'll help you.'

Kenton cringed.

'Yes, yes,' he babbled, 'I will tell you.'

He saw the Colonel glance triumphantly at Mailler.

'Come on then.'

'I put them in an envelope and gave it to the *patron* of the café to be called for.'

The Colonel drew a deep breath and turned to Mailler.

'Quickly now. Take the car and one man with you and get to the Café Schwan immediately.'

He turned to Kenton's escort.

'Take him away and lock him up.'

'But you promised to release me if I told,' Kenton burst out angrily.

The Colonel smiled.

'I'm afraid we shall have to change our plans, Mr Kenton. Perhaps in a week or two we might go into the matter again. Now, Mailler.'

The Captain started for the door.

'Just a minute,' said Kenton loudly.

Mailler stopped.

'I am sorry,' went on Kenton smoothly, 'to dash your hopes so soon, but in the excitement, in my terror of the Colonel, I quite forgot to add one little piece of information to my statement.' He grinned at the Colonel.

'Well, let's have it,' snapped Mailler.

'It's such a trifling thing,' said Kenton deprecatingly.

He saw the Colonel's lips tighten.

'Come on,' shouted Mailler.

'Well,' he said slowly, 'it's just that when I gave the photographs to the *patron* of the Café Schwan for safe keeping, I said that on no account was he to give the envelope up to anyone but me in person, and you know what a reputation for discretion these café proprietors have. I hinted that it was an affair of the heart. The *patron* would, I am afraid, regard Captain Mailler as the villain of the piece, the wicked fairy, if he tried to get that envelope.' He smiled reproachfully at Mailler.

For fully a minute there was not a sound in the room except the ticking of a clock. At last, the Colonel cleared his throat.

'It seems, Mr Kenton, that we shall have to insist upon your co-operation.'

'You won't get it.'

'I think so.'

'My God, yes,' said the Captain; 'you leave the little swine to me.'

The Colonel caressed his lower lip.

'Yes,' he said thoughtfully, 'I shall leave him to you. Only don't take too long about it, Mailler. Bastaki is expecting me in Prague to-morrow. And don't forget that this man's face must not be damaged and that he must be able to walk.' He turned to Kenton. 'In view of your claim, Mr Kenton, that your possession of the photographs is purely accidental, I find your attitude completely incomprehensible.'

'You would,' retorted Kenton rudely. 'But for your enlightenment I may as well explain again that your treatment of me leaves me no alternative. Anything I can do to cause you and your charming principals inconvenience and discomfort gives me the liveliest satisfaction.'

Colonel Robinson warmed his hands at the fire, smiled slightly and shook his head sorrowfully.

'Believe me, Mr Kenton,' he said slowly, 'my treatment of you until now will seem like a mother's caress compared with what you will experience in the next few hours.' He nodded to Mailler. 'All right, take him away and get on with it. Mr Kenton,' he added, 'they are taking you downstairs to the cellars. You will be separated from this room by several metres of stonework and earth, but I think I shall be able to hear you react to Captain Mailler's persuasive methods.'

'I'll make the beggar squeal all right,' said the Captain. '*Los! Hinunter in den Kellern!*'

Kenton was marched across the hall to a door under the stairs which when opened revealed a flight of narrow stone steps. Mailler went ahead, switching on lights. The two men, after a brief consultation in German, held him by his wrists and drew him after them.

At the bottom of the stairs was a long stone-flagged corridor the sides of which were pierced with archways which led, Kenton saw as he was marched past them, into a series of well-stocked wine cellars. Mailler turned through the last archway, pressed a switch and a naked lamp bulb glowed yellowly on a dusty collection of broken and mouldering furniture, rusting ironwork and old curtains. The four walls were lined with empty wine bins.

Mailler extracted a chair with sound legs from the rubbish and dumped it in the middle of the floor.

'Tie him up,' he ordered in German.

The two men pushed Kenton into the chair, produced a hank of thick cord and proceeded in impassive silence to lash his legs to the frame. They seemed, thought Kenton, to be rather bored by the whole business. He glanced at Mailler.

The Captain seemed to be far from bored. He had taken the rubber truncheon from his pocket and was weighing it in his hand and flicking it viciously against the side of the arch. It made almost no sound. Kenton looked at Mailler's face. An unpleasant change had come over it. The jaw had dropped slightly, his cheeks were sunken, he was breathing rather quickly and kept darting little sidelong glances at Kenton with eyes that had become curiously glazed. Already rather frightened, Kenton began to feel an almost hysterical terror stealing over him.

The two men tested their knots carefully and stood up. One of them grunted at Mailler, who turned and stared dully at Kenton. Then he walked over and stood in front of him. There was a slight white froth in the corners of his mouth.

Suddenly he lifted the truncheon high into the air and went up on his toes. Kenton clenched his teeth. The truncheon came down with lightning speed and stopped an inch from his cheek.

Kenton broke out into a cold sweat. The two Germans laughed. Mailler's lips smiled and he tapped the side of Kenton's head playfully with the truncheon. It was cold and had a certain hard greasiness about it. The next moment Mailler's smile changed to a glare of animal ferocity and he brought the truncheon round in a vicious arc. Again it stopped just short of Kenton's face. Again Mailler smiled.

'Enjoying yourself, Kenton?'

Kenton said nothing.

Still smiling, Mailler flicked him lightly across the face with the truncheon.

For a moment Kenton thought that his jaw had been shattered by the blow. The pain was agonizing.

Mailler stood back.

'Going to be sensible, old man,' he said, 'or do I have to make a real start on you?'

Kenton did not answer. His silence seemed to madden the Captain, for he suddenly stepped forward and lashed furiously at Kenton's knees and legs.

At last the rain of blows ceased. Almost fainting with the pain, the journalist felt that his will-power was going. If Mailler repeated his attack, principles or no principles, he would agree to anything.

'Had enough yet?'

Kenton looked at the man for a moment. He opened his mouth to speak, but the words would not come from his throat. It was as if a great weight were pressing on his lungs, stifling him. He wanted to shriek, to scream that he was ready to give in, that they could have their photographs. But his conscious brain had lost control of his body. He gasped out a single syllable:

'No.'

He saw Mailler raise the truncheon again, saw the man's face contorted with vindictive fury. He shut his eyes and his body stiffened to receive the blow.

But no blow came. An uncanny quiet seemed to have fallen. Slowly he opened his eyes.

Mailler was still standing in front of him; but the truncheon had fallen to the floor and his hands were raised high above his head. Beyond him the two Germans stood in similar postures. Kenton turned his head. Standing in the entrance to the cellar stood a stocky little man with a dark pugnacious face. Wound twice round his neck was a thick woollen muffler. In his hand was a large blue revolver with the hammer cocked.

'The first one that moves,' said Zaleshoff in German, 'I will kill.'

9

Zaleshoff Fires Twice

Zaleshoff stepped forward a pace or two and his eyes met Kenton's for a second.

'Mr Kenton?' He spoke English with an American accent.

Kenton nodded.

Zaleshoff looked at Mailler.

'Who is this man?'

'Captain Mailler.'

'Are there any more upstairs?'

'There's a man who calls himself Colonel Robinson; I haven't seen any more.'

'Has he a stiff arm?'

'Yes.'

Zaleshoff jerked the barrel of the revolver towards one of the rather bewildered Germans.

'Lass ihn los!'

Under the Russian's watchful eye, the man produced a large clasp-knife and hacked at the cords which bound Kenton. The journalist eased his muscles and tried to get up, but the battering Mailler had given his legs made this process painful.

'Can you stand?' asked Zaleshoff anxiously.

'I'll be all right in a minute.'

'O.K. Be as quick as you can.'

'My God, you'll get hell for this,' the Captain burst out suddenly.

Zaleshoff bent down, picked up the rubber truncheon and, keeping his eyes on the three men in front of him, held it out to Kenton.

'Here you are. Do you want to try it on him?'

'Very much; but at the moment I should prefer to get away from here.'

'Good. Take that rope he's cut off you, tie their hands behind them, put them against the wall and tie them to the bins. Then gag them. I'll keep watch.'

Kenton did as he was told; but when he came to the gagging process he was at a loss.

'Tear pieces off those old curtains,' directed Zaleshoff, pointing to the corner of the cellar, 'screw them up, stuff them in their mouths, then tie them in with the mouth open.'

Kenton followed instructions. Mailler swore and then refused to open his mouth, but Zaleshoff tapped his jaw with the truncheon and the Captain gave no more trouble.

'Now,' said Zaleshoff, 'if you're ready, we'll go.'

Kenton followed him down the corridor, past the foot of the steps, to the hall. At the end of the corridor there was a door, but Zaleshoff ignored this and led the way down a narrow boarded passage to the right. After a yard or two he halted, and turning to Kenton, whispered to him that they must go quietly now. A few more steps and they were in the open air.

As Kenton had seen through the shutters earlier on, the sky was black with cloud. There was no wind, but his teeth started to chatter with the cold. Then he felt something warm and soft being pushed into his hand and found that his companion was giving him his muffler. Murmuring his thanks, he put it on and felt better. The other's hand pressed his arm, enjoining silence, and drew him forward along a loose stone path. It went downhill for about twenty yards, then sloped sharply upwards. A black mass loomed suddenly and Kenton realized that they had reached the fir trees.

They turned left and pushed their way as silently as possible through a fringe of bushes. Suddenly Zaleshoff gripped Kenton's arm tightly. They stood still. For a moment there was no sound but the faint rustling of the bushes. Then, out of the darkness, came the sound of a man whistling a German love song softly and with a curious sweetness.

A second or two later the glare of a powerful electric lamp lit up the leafy screen ahead, the whistling ceased and there was the clatter of an empty petrol tin being dumped on concrete.

Zaleshoff cupped his hands and put them to Kenton's ear.

'We must pass the garage to get to the road,' he whispered. 'The way through the forest would take too long.'

'The chauffeur's got a gun,' returned Kenton.

The other was silent for a moment, then, whispering to Kenton to stay where he was, he crept forward to the edge of the garage clearing. Kenton saw his head and shoulders faintly silhouetted against the light, then he disappeared to the left. Kenton leaned against a tree and waited.

The stranger's very timely intervention in the cellar and the obvious urgency of putting as much country as possible between himself and Colonel Robinson and staff, had given him no time to consider the question of his companion's identity. The vicinity of the Colonel's house was hardly the ideal place for an exchange of life histories. Left to himself, however, he began to ponder the question. He had no doubt that this was Andreas, the man who had entered and searched Sachs' room at the Hotel Josef, and for whom he had been mistaken in the courtyard. There was no mistaking that stocky figure with the large muffler. That meant that the Russian might be Sachs' murderer. Not a very comforting possibility! The American accent was a little baffling; but then, quite a lot of English-speaking Continentals had American accents. However, the man seemed to know his name and to be on his side – whatever that might be – and had so far exhibited no homicidal tendencies. He turned his attention to the more pressing question of how to keep his hands and feet from going numb with cold.

Zaleshoff was away about three minutes. When he returned, he drew Kenton back the way they had come until they were out of possible earshot of the chauffeur.

'He's doing something to the car,' Zaleshoff reported; 'but we must get past without his seeing. We can't stay here. If Saridza goes to see how those men in the cellar are progressing, we shall be caught.'

'Saridza?'

'Colonel Robinson. His name's Saridza.'

Kenton decided that that question also could wait.

'All right. What's your plan?'

'I have a car, but it is about two kilometres down the road. We must get there before they can get after us. It will be easy for them to find us on the road.'

'Where do we start?'

'The drive to the garage is cut through a rise in the ground. It is narrowest at the top of the rise; but there the sides of the cutting are too high. We must cross nearer and choose a moment when the chauffeur is looking the other way.'

'All right.'

They returned to the edge of the bushes and began to work their way carefully to the left. Part of the way was easy going, but there were places where the bushes were close together and they had to worm their way below the branches to avoid the rustling leaves. At last the garage light showed through the bushes to the right and Zaleshoff halted.

'We are near the edge of the cutting,' he whispered; 'there's a drop of about two metres to the drive.'

They went forward. Suddenly Kenton saw a patch of brightly lit concrete six feet below him. He leaned forward to get a better view. About fifteen yards away stood the black saloon car. The bonnet was up and the chauffeur was working on the engine.

Zaleshoff gripped an overhanging branch and began to lower himself down to the edge of the concrete. Kenton followed, and they were soon crouching in the shelter of a bush at a point from which they could see both the chauffeur and the bank on the opposite side of the drive.

For several minutes they stayed there, watching the chauffeur working. The man seemed to be doing something to the lighting circuit, for every now and then he would go round to the instrument board inside the car and switch the headlights on and off. Kenton had begun to despair when the chauffeur felt in his pocket for something, peered at the assortment of tools on the running-board, then went into the garage.

'Now,' whispered Zaleshoff.

He rose and walked calmly across the drive towards the bushes on the other side. Kenton stood up to follow him, but his bruised legs had become stiff with crouching. He stumbled and his foot scraped loudly across the concrete. He recovered himself, but the damage was done. There was a quick patter of feet from the garage, a shout, and the next instant that thudding *crack* which signifies that the hearer is in the direct line of fire of a large-calibre revolver.

Two more shots crashed out as he scrambled across to the shelter of the bushes. Then there was a flash and report from the shadows ahead and a cry of pain from the direction of the garage. Kenton crashed blindly into the undergrowth and hit his head sharply against a branch. Then a hand grabbed his coat and hauled him up a steep gravel slope.

'Quick, run,' hissed Zaleshoff.

Kenton staggered to his feet and blundered through the trees after his companion. The ground sloped downwards, but was fairly smooth as far as a long gully. On the opposite side of the gully was a wire fence. As they scrambled through it, they heard the piercing scream of a Bosch motor horn sounding the alarm behind them. They began pushing their way through the tangled undergrowth of ferns beyond the fence.

'That gives us about five minutes to reach the car,' gasped Zaleshoff.

'Did you shoot the chauffeur?'

'In the arm; but it would not have helped to kill him. Those shots would have wakened the dead. It won't take long to release the three in the cellar.'

Two minutes later they slid down a steep bank on to the road and set off at a run in the direction of Zaleshoff's car lower down the valley.

The experiences of the past twenty-four hours and the weakness resulting from lack of food had left Kenton in no condition for running long distances. By the time they had gone half a kilometre, Kenton was ready to drop. His legs felt as if he were trying to run with loose sand up to his waist. His chest was aching from lack of breath. There was an unpleasant light sensation in his head. Zaleshoff urged him on ruthlessly, but at last he slowed down to a walk. As he did so there was a faint sound of a car engine higher up the hill and the beams of two headlights swung round into space and disappeared.

'They're after us,' panted Zaleshoff. 'No use going any farther. They mustn't know about the car. If they find that, we're cornered. Our only chance is to let them know that we're still about here and wait for an opportunity to get to the car.'

Kenton, struggling to recover his breath, nodded.

'Come on,' said Zaleshoff, 'up here. Hurry.'

They were at the foot of a long straight slope in the road. To the left the ground dropped away almost vertically to another section of the road which lay beyond a hairpin bend three hundred feet lower down the side of the valley. To the right the ground rose steeply to the summit of the hill and was densely covered with fir trees. It was to the right that Zaleshoff went. Soon they were about twenty yards up among a maze of large, straight tree trunks.

'When they come, stand behind a tree and do as I tell you.'

Kenton, who had reached a stage of exhaustion where he was incapable of anything but dazed obedience, mumbled agreement, propped himself against a tree and stared into the pitch blackness of the forest.

'Here they come.'

Kenton turned his head and saw a pin-point of light moving in the distance. Then it grew suddenly, became elongated and glowed through the trees.

'They're turning the spotlight on the car up the hillside as they go. Keep behind the tree.'

The light came closer, sending long shadows twisting over the floor of the forest. As it reached them, Kenton saw Zaleshoff rest his revolver on a small shoot on the side of the tree behind which he was standing and take careful aim. A second later the gun crashed once and the light went out. There was a shout from below.

Zaleshoff gave vent to a Russian crow of self-congratulation.

'Bull's eye at twenty paces!' he added. 'Now we make for the road higher up the hill.'

They started to move across the face of the slope and had gone about fifteen yards when there was the sound of a twig snapping below. They stopped. Suddenly a torch flashed momentarily in the darkness.

'Down,' hissed Zaleshoff.

The next moment there was the sharp crack of a small automatic and the quick whine of a ricochet as the bullet hit a stone higher up the slope.

Zaleshoff let out a howl of agony and Kenton heard Mailler's voice raised in triumph.

'Are you hit?' asked Kenton stupidly.

'No, but they must think so. Get on.'

They were going downhill now and the darkness ahead was broken as the moon, showing faintly behind a patch of thin cloud, threw the trees on the edge of the forest into dim silhouette. Behind there were stabs of light every now and then as their pursuers tried to locate them.

'Stop,' whispered Zaleshoff.

They were near the road. Fifty yards or more downhill was the rear light of the black saloon.

'Now,' he went on, 'cross the road as quietly as you can, get down the hillside so that you can't be seen from the edge of the road and wait for me.'

'What are you going to do?'

'See if there's anyone left in Saridza's car.'

'Why?'

'Explanations later. You get across the road and be quiet about it.'

'All right.'

Kenton tiptoed slowly across the road and started to pick his way down the steep slope beyond. For a few yards the way was littered with large stones and he had to take great care to avoid dislodging them. Then the trees started again and he was able to zigzag down from trunk to trunk. He was soon in pitch darkness once more and sat down to wait for his companion.

For ten minutes he waited, speculating miserably on his chances of avoiding pneumonia. Then there was a slight noise from above, and Zaleshoff called his name. He answered and the Russian scrambled down to him.

'We are out of luck,' he reported; 'Saridza's standing by with a rifle. I had hopes that they might have left the car unguarded. I would have put a bullet in the gasoline, but it was too dangerous.'

'What are we to do?'

'We shall have to get straight down here on to the lower bend in the road. It will be tough going and I dare not use a torch. They would see it. Still, there's nothing else we can do.'

The descent was, for Kenton, the worst sort of nightmare. The face of the hill was covered with deep hollows, so that he kept missing his footing and slithered down wildly, to be brought up with sickening force by the trees. The steep slope of the ground made it necessary to go on all fours in places and one trouser leg was ripped in the process by a dead branch. His face and hands were badly grazed and he wrenched a wrist. The absolute darkness induced a feeling of panic-stricken helplessness. By the time he reached the road at the bottom, he was in a state of collapse.

Zaleshoff, whose clothes had also suffered from the climb down, took Kenton's arm and hurried him along the road.

It seemed to Kenton that they kept going for hours. At last Zaleshoff slackened his pace and Kenton saw, through half-closed eyes, the shape of a large touring car with the hood up and no lights. By the driver's door stood a girl.

She started forward to meet them.

'What is it, Andreas?' said a familiar voice.

Kenton began to laugh hysterically.

'Andreas,' he panted, 'there's no need to introduce me. We've met before.'

He withdrew his arm from Zaleshoff's, took a step forward and stood still. His knees seemed to give way and there was a rushing noise in his head. Then, for the first time in his life, he fainted.

10

Zaleshoff Talks

Kenton became conscious of a pleasant burning sensation in the pit of his stomach and a taste of something like a mixture of turpentine and olive oil in his mouth.

A man's voice said something in Russian that he did not understand and a glass clinked against his teeth. The next moment he sat up choking and coughing, and opened his eyes.

He was lying on a red plush sofa in what, at first sight, looked like a second-hand furniture shop. Bending over him was an elderly man with white cadaverous cheeks and sunken eyes that gleamed. He held a bottle with a pale-green label and a small glass half filled with a colourless liquid. Kenton realized the reason for the warm glow inside him and the curious taste in his mouth. He had been drinking vodka.

Seated at a table, watching him gravely, was the man he knew as Andreas.

'You are feeling better?' said Zaleshoff.

Kenton nodded a little uncertainly and raised his hand to wipe the remains of the vodka from his chin. The hand was stained with iodine. The man with the vodka offered him the bottle. Kenton shook his head, looking inquiringly towards Zaleshoff and opened his mouth to speak. The Russian forestalled him.

'You are in a house in the Kölnerstrasse in Linz,' he said. 'My sister and I brought you here. Thinking you might be hungry, she has gone out to buy some food.'

'That is very good of her,' said Kenton. 'I seem to be causing you a lot of trouble.'

'Yes,' said Zaleshoff blandly, 'quite a lot of trouble; but not in the way you think, Mr Kenton. Our host here, Rashenko, is very pleased to be of service to you. Please do not trouble to thank him,' he added as the journalist turned; 'he does not understand English, and he is, poor fellow, dumb.'

Kenton murmured his thanks in German and Rashenko smiled and nodded encouragingly. The journalist was feeling rather bewildered. He turned again to Zaleshoff.

'I'm sorry to be a nuisance,' he said; 'but do you mind answering a few questions? For instance, do you mind telling me who you are and why I am here? I should also like to know how you knew my name, why you rescued me from that house and, if I'm not being indiscreet, whether you were responsible for the death of a man called Sachs or Borovansky. I think I know why you searched his room, but should welcome fuller information on that subject. I am curious, too, about the man calling himself Colonel Robinson. Why do you call him Saridza? There are other things that are puzzling me, but I'm sure you will see the general idea. Incidentally, what time is it?'

'Just after midnight,' said Zaleshoff. He pursed his lips. 'As for the rest of your questions, Mr Kenton, I suggest we wait until after we have refreshed ourselves with food before we start on the explanations. Tamara should be back by now. She and Rashenko shall cook for us. You and I will drink vodka.' He thumped the table like an auctioneer. 'What do you say?'

Kenton smiled.

'I like you, Andreas,' he said; 'you know perfectly well that I have got something that you want; you hear with well-concealed surprise that I saw you search Sachs' room and yet you propose that we eat and drink before we talk! Why, I haven't even thanked you for rescuing me!'

Zaleshoff shook his head gravely.

'You mistake my motives, Mr Kenton. Try to stand up.'

Kenton obeyed. His head swam and a wave of nausea swept over him. He sat down again quickly.

'You see, Mr Kenton, it would be a waste of time to start talking just at the moment. Rashenko used to be a doctor. He reports that you are in a state of extreme nervous and physical exhaustion. You are suffering from severe shock, the after-effects of concussion and lack of food. The wild elation you are experiencing at the moment is produced by the vodka. You had better have some more.'

Rashenko was now busying himself at the stove. Zaleshoff reached for the bottle, poured out two large tots and handed one to Kenton.

'Vodka,' he said, 'should not touch the palate. It should be poured straight down the throat. I will show you. *Pros't!*'

He raised the glass to his lips, jerked his head back and swallowed once. Then he set down the empty glass.

Kenton followed suit and felt the liquid burn in his stomach.

'All the same,' he resumed obstinately, 'I should like to know who you—'

A knock at the door interrupted him. Zaleshoff turned in his chair and Kenton saw that the blue revolver was in the Russian's hand. Rashenko glanced at him inquiringly and received a nod. The door was opened and Tamara came into the room carrying a bulky string bag.

'Mr Kenton,' said Zaleshoff, flourishing the revolver in a grand gesture, 'this is my sister Tamara. Tamara, this is Mr Kenton.'

The girl nodded gravely to Kenton.

'Please, Andreas,' she said, 'do not wave that pistol about so. It is dangerous.'

Her brother took no notice and turned to Kenton.

'What do you think of her, my friend?'

'She is remarkably beautiful,' said Kenton; 'as beautiful as her voice.'

Zaleshoff slapped his knee delightedly.

'You see, Tamara, what vodka will do even to a cold-blooded Englishman. "Remarkably beautiful; as beautiful as her voice." You heard him, Tamara?' He translated for the benefit of Rashenko, who smiled and nodded at them.

'You will embarrass him,' said the girl calmly, and emptied the string bag on to a chair. 'Be careful, Mr Kenton,' she added over her shoulder. 'My brother is endeavouring to lull you into a sense of false security in the hope that you will take him into your confidence.'

Zaleshoff bounded to his feet, overturning a chair, and swore. Then he pointed a denunciatory finger at his sister.

'Look,' he roared at Kenton, 'hampered and thwarted at every turn by my own mother's daughter! I soothe you, I give you vodka to drink, we become friendly, we are *en rapport*, then – piff – Tamara breaks the spell with her foolishness.'

He sank back into the chair and buried his head in his hands.

'Very amusing,' said Kenton evenly. 'Do you think I might have a glass of water?'

Zaleshoff raised his head slowly and stared sullenly at Kenton. Suddenly he brought the flat of his hand down on the table with a crash and started to roar with laughter.

'There, Tamara,' he gasped at last, 'we do not deceive him, you see. He is unmoved. He sees through our little tricks to gain his confidence. We see why the English are such great diplomats.'

'Do we?' said Tamara, taking off her coat.

'But of course!' He turned, beaming, to Kenton. 'My apologies, Mr Kenton. One should have realized that such foolish histrionics were an insult to your intelligence. We have your forgiveness?'

'Naturally,' said Kenton uncomfortably. Really, he thought, the man was rather childish.

The Russian sighed with relief.

'That is good to know,' he said fervently; 'if only we knew,' he went on dreamily, 'if only we knew a little more of Mr Kenton's thoughts.' He leaned forward suddenly. 'Why, for instance, is Mr Kenton prepared to go to such lengths to preserve the property of the Soviet Government?'

The suddenness of the attack took the journalist completely by surprise. He was silent for a moment. There was no sound in the room except the ticking of the clocks and a faint hiss from the stove. The atmosphere had changed in some indefinable way. Even Rashenko sensed it and paused in his work. The girl, standing with her back to the door, was staring at the table. Zaleshoff, no longer benignly theatrical, was watching him intently with blue eyes that had become extraordinarily shrewd and calculating.

All this he saw in the fraction of a second. Then he smiled easily.

'I thought we had postponed business until after we had eaten. Still, if you wish . . .'

Instantly Zaleshoff was all apologies.

Yes, yes, of course, Mr Kenton was right. Meanwhile, the glass of water or perhaps some more vodka. No? Rashenko would hurry.

There followed a quick patter of Russian and nods from Rashenko. Zaleshoff began to give the girl a wildly exaggerated and over-dramatic account of their escape from the house on the hill. It seemed to Kenton that his presence had been entirely forgotten.

The meal came at last.

It consisted of *bortsch* with sour cream and little pasties filled with chopped vegetables and, except for a sudden pæan of congratulation directed by Zaleshoff at Rashenko, it was eaten in silence. Kenton was thoughtful and extremely puzzled; but he was also extremely hungry and ate steadily. The moment they were finished Rashenko began to clear the dishes from the table.

'A cigarette, Mr Kenton?'

'Thanks.'

He lit it and inhaled deeply. He was beginning to feel better.

Zaleshoff turned to the girl.

'Where did you put that paper, Tamara?'

She went to the cupboard and returned with a sheet of grey paper covered with small writing. Her brother took it, pressed Kenton into a seat on the sofa and sat on a chair facing him. The girl sat behind the table with a pencil in her hand and a note-book in front of her.

'A court of inquiry?' said Kenton.

He saw a look of faint amusement flicker across the girl's face.

'Not at all,' said Zaleshoff, a little too emphatically. He held up the grey paper. 'Do you know what this is, Mr Kenton?'

The journalist shook his head.

Zaleshoff held it out for him to take.

Kenton looked at the paper. It was headed 'Dossier K.4596' and began: 'Desmond d'Esterre Kenton, journalist, born Carlisle 1906.' It went on to describe, in German, his parents and their histories, his appearance, his character, his career, his political leanings and his work for various papers, with an accuracy and insight that he found very disconcerting. He read it through twice and handed it back.

'Very good,' he said; 'but you're wrong in saying that I spent most of nineteen thirty-four in Hungary. I was in Rome for most of that year.'

Zaleshoff frowned and made a noise of disgust.

'Tamara, please make a note of that and report it.' He turned to Kenton. 'It is so difficult,' he went on plaintively, 'to get people to take proper steps to check up on their information. One is constantly made to look a fool.'

Kenton did not feel that he was expected to comment on this statement.

'I showed it to you, however,' the other continued, 'more to make my position clear than to impress you. It is unimportant.' He threw it on the table. 'Tamara, you may tear it up.'

Kenton noticed, however, that the girl put the paper carefully in the back of the note-book.

'And now to business,' her brother went on affably. 'Supposing you tell us, Mr Kenton, exactly how you came to be in the Hotel Josef the other night.'

Kenton examined his cigarette.

'I shall be glad to do so,' he murmured; 'but I think you have overlooked a very necessary preliminary.'

'Yes?'

Kenton raised his head and his eyes met those of the Russian.

'I want to know first to whom I am talking,' he said.

There was a slight pause, punctuated by a clatter of plates from the other end of the room.

Zaleshoff frowned fiercely.

'I do not see,' he said at last, 'what my name has to do with this business. It will convey nothing to you. However' – he shrugged – 'it is Andreas Prokovitch Zaleshoff.'

'Zaleshoff?'

The Russian scowled his confirmation. Kenton leaned back on the sofa thoughtfully. Then he snapped his fingers.

'Got it!'

Zaleshoff raised his eyebrows.

'I remember now,' Kenton went on. 'Weren't you deported from the United States for Communist agitation in nineteen twenty-two? Pittsburg, I fancy, though it may have been Detroit. Which was it?'

He waited, expecting an outburst of theatrical indignation. Then, to his intense surprise, he saw a deep blush creeping over the Russian's face.

'Chicago,' muttered Zaleshoff almost sheepishly.

The girl began to laugh.

It was, thought Kenton, a very pleasant sound, but her brother rounded on her angrily and pounded the table with his fist.

'Stop, Tamara, stop at once!' He turned to Kenton. 'You are right,' he said with a comical attempt at jauntiness. He shrugged his shoulders deprecatingly. 'I was very young at the time. A boyish escapade, nothing more. But it was nineteen twenty-five, my friend, and in Chicago.' He laughed rather unconvincingly. 'It was good to remember the name, but your facts were quite wrong.'

'That,' said Kenton, 'is hardly to be wondered at. When you were being deported from Chicago I was a rather pimply adolescent. Until you spoke just now I had never heard your name before in my life.'

Zaleshoff leaned back in his chair and breathed noisily through his nose. It was the girl who spoke first.

'Do you mean, Mr Kenton,' she said, her voice broken with suppressed laughter, 'that you had no idea of our having been in America and that you made up that story about my brother?'

Kenton nodded.

'Yes, I made it up. You both speak English with an American accent and you speak it as fluently as I do. You must have spent a number of years in America. I had every reason to believe that your brother was employed by the Soviet Government. I wanted to annoy him into showing his hand. The deportation business had the right circumstantial feeling about it.'

'Well, I'll be—' began Andreas Prokovitch Zaleshoff, but the girl interrupted him.

'Our father was killed secretly by the Ochrana in nineteen hundred and ten. Our mother escaped from Baku with us to America, through Mexico, where I was born. But she never took out the proper papers and when Andreas got into trouble with the police for his propaganda they found out about us and we were deported. Our mother was dead; we spoke Russian better than English, so we claimed Soviet citizenship. It is quite simple.'

'If, Tamara, you have quite finished these domestic revelations,' snarled her brother, 'I wish to talk to Mr Kenton, myself.' He turned to the journalist. 'Now, Mr Kenton, we seem to have answered your question. You know who I am. Supposing you answer mine? How did you come to be at the Hotel Josef?'

Kenton considered for a moment. Then:

'Very well, there seems to be no harm in that.'

Zaleshoff listened intently while Kenton described his meeting with Sachs, his reasons for accepting Sachs' offer and his visit to the Hotel Josef. When he came to his interview with 'Colonel Robinson', however, the Russian began to interrupt with questions. What exactly had been said? Had the subject of oil been mentioned? How far did Mailler seem to be in his master's confidence? When Kenton mentioned the Colonel's principals in London, Zaleshoff's eyes gleamed and he rapped out an excited comment in Russian to his sister. The Colonel's intention of going to Prague was noted carefully.

'And then,' Kenton concluded at last, 'you appeared on the scene; how, I cannot imagine.'

'That is easily explained. I saw Saridza's men carry you out of the Hotel Werner. Later, I searched your room. I found a small piece of paper torn from a note-book in one of your overcoat pockets. It had two addresses on it, both obviously written by a Russian. One was the Hotel Josef, the other was the Villa Peschik. That was the name of the house in which I found you.'

'But how did you know of my existence?' A thought struck him. 'I suppose that pasty-faced specimen that Sachs told me was a Nazi spy wasn't one of your little friends?'

Zaleshoff looked mystified.

'Who murdered Sachs?' persisted Kenton.

The two Russians exchanged a quick look of understanding. Then Zaleshoff shrugged.

'Who can say?'

'All right,' said Kenton irritably, 'let it go. Is there any further information I can give you?' he added ironically.

His head had begun to ache.

'Well, Mr Kenton,' purred Zaleshoff, 'there are just two things more.'

'What are they?'

'I heard the end of your conversation with Saridza from outside the window before you were taken to the cellar. Why, Mr Kenton, did you not surrender the photographs and save yourself that rather painful interlude with Captain Mailler?'

Kenton laughed shortly.

'Zaleshoff,' he said, 'my father was Irish, my mother was French. Rather to my surprise, I find that I have inherited from them two curious qualities – obstinacy and the faculty of resentment.'

The Russian glanced at his sister.

'Does that make sense to you, Tamara? I have told you what they were doing to him.'

The girl nodded. Her brother turned again to Kenton.

'The only other thing I want to know,' he said, 'is where I can find those photographs.'

Kenton thought swiftly. Zaleshoff had obviously not heard enough of his interview with the Colonel to know about the café.

'You really don't know?'

Zaleshoff shook his head slowly. Kenton sensed a revival of the slight hostility in the other's attitude that had coloured the earlier part of their conversation.

'Then, Monsieur Zaleshoff,' he said, 'I'm going to bargain with you.'

'Indeed?'

'Yes. During the past twenty-four hours quite a lot of unpleasant things have happened to me. I demand compensation.'

The Russian's lips tightened and his jaw thrust forward aggressively.

'How much?' he said quietly.

Kenton registered horror.

'Dear me, not money! That makes the third time I have been offered bribes in connection with this bunch of rather uninteresting photographs. I didn't think it of you, monsieur,' he added reproachfully.

Zaleshoff's face darkened.

'Come to the point, please.'

'Certainly. I am a reporter. Just before I met the late lamented Borovansky, I was wondering where I was going to get a news story that wouldn't be hogged by all the news-agency men and foreign correspondents in Middle Europe five minutes after it had broken. Well, now I think I'm on the track of it. I want to know more of friend Saridza's principals in London. I want to know who they are and what they are, and why they're so interested in Bessarabia and Roumania. I want to know what oil has got to do with it and exactly where you came in. I want the dope, the low-down, the works, or whatever you used to call it in Chicago, in exchange for the photographs. How does the idea appeal to you?'

Zaleshoff looked grim.

'I'm afraid, Mr Kenton, that you are doomed to disappointment. I am, indeed, a little surprised that a man of your experience should make such a suggestion. I can assure you that I, at least, have no sensational revelations to make.' He smiled slightly. 'Perhaps Tamara can think of something?'

'Don't you want your photographs?'

'Yes, Mr Kenton, I do; but I am not empowered to make statements to the Press. In any case, the affair is purely commercial. It has no political significance.'

'I am inclined to doubt that.'

'No paper would publish anything so unimportant.'

'I'll tell you about that when I've heard the facts.'

There was a long pause, then the girl spoke.

'I think, Andreas,' she said, 'that we shall have to compromise with Mr Kenton.'

The Russian glanced at the journalist for a moment or two. Then he shrugged.

'Very well. I suppose it makes no difference.'

'No difference?' Kenton found the statement a little odd.

But Zaleshoff did not explain.

'One can only regret,' he was saying viciously, 'that one did not leave Mr Kenton to the excellent Captain Mailler for just a little longer.'

Rashenko brought them tea in glasses. Zaleshoff crushed a slice of lemon into his glass and stirred the contents moodily.

At last he looked up.

'You must understand, Mr Kenton,' he said with an air of brisk candour, 'that my connection with this affair is purely accidental. I am a private Soviet citizen with business interests in Switzerland – the importation of machinery, to be precise.'

He paused.

'However,' he went on, sipping at his tea, 'the Soviet citizen is, in common with other nationals abroad, always ready, should the occasion arise, to place his country's interests before his private business affairs. When, therefore, I was requested, for various reasons that would not interest you, to assist in a rather unusual matter of Government business, I had no alternative but to agree. That, Mr Kenton,' he concluded a trifle defiantly, 'explains my position in this affair.'

Kenton, secretly amused at this naïve evasion, nodded solemnly and lit a cigarette.

'And Borovansky's murder?' he said.

Zaleshoff waved the question aside.

'An insignificant incident. We will talk about it later.' He leaned forward earnestly. 'You are a journalist, Mr Kenton; you know more than the ordinary man; I do not need to do more than hint and you will understand. When I tell you that a certain prominent exile from Russia seeks once again to taste power, much will be clear to you. In nineteen-seventeen and -eighteen this man rendered great services to Russia; but there was in him the taint of personal ambition. He craved power. Russia has no room to-day for those who place the service of their vanities above the service of the people. He was expelled.'

'Are you talking about Trotsky?'

Zaleshoff nodded portentously.

'It would have been better, perhaps, to have shot him,' he said regretfully, 'for he has not ceased to plot against the State. Round him he has gathered a brood of fanatics drunk with the desire for power. They are dangerous. France expelled them. Norway and Sweden expelled them. Of the other countries of the world, only Mexico would receive them. They have worked for the downfall of the Soviets for years; many great servants of the people have been corrupted by their subtle poison. Those unhappy men have had to pay the price. When a limb is poisoned it must be amputated, lest it infect the health of the whole body.'

'The nineteen-thirty-six trials?' queried Kenton.

Zaleshoff assented rather impatiently to this intrusion of the specific.

'The nineteen-thirty-six trials brought the danger to the notice of the people; but it still remains. The aim of these vermin is to discredit the Soviet Union in the eyes of her neighbours. They pursue that aim with relentless determination. They will go to any lengths. You, Mr Kenton, have experienced some of their methods. Borovansky was a Soviet citizen, a man of the people. By chance, these impudent forgeries, which you yourself have examined, fell into his hands. He informed Moscow and was ordered to lay aside his work and bring them here to Linz for examination. Like the true patriot he was, he set out immediately. But they were swiftly on his track. He handed them to you, an Englishman whom he saw he could trust, for safe keeping. Then the fiends murdered him and turned their attention to you. The results you know only too well. What our enemies reckoned without was the loyalty of the Soviet citizen to the people of whom he is but an insignificant unit. I was called upon. I answered the call and was able to save you from the torture. I take up Borovansky's work where he left off. Now you know all. In Borovansky's name, Mr Kenton, I request you to return to me the photographs entrusted to you.'

He flung out an appealing arm. He was glowing with sincerity. The girl stared at her note-book.

Kenton surveyed them both for a moment, then leaned back and put his hands in his pockets.

'You wish me to understand,' he said slowly, 'that the photographs are forgeries, that Borovansky was a Russian patriot, and that Colonel Robinson and Captain Mailler are in the employ of the Trotskyites?'

Zaleshoff nodded.

'Those are the facts.'

Kenton stood up.

'Well,' he said bitterly. 'I've known myself behave like a fool. I have even been told I was a fool. But I never before realized that I must look the biggest nit-wit in Europe.'

'What do you mean?'

'I mean that I have never before heard so much unmitigated nonsense from the mouth of one man in the space of five minutes. I congratulate you. It was a magnificent achievement. But it is late and I am tired. I feel sure you will excuse me if I return to my hotel and get some sleep.'

He started towards the door.

'Just a minute, Mr Kenton.'

He turned. Zaleshoff was standing behind the table. In his hand was the blue revolver.

The journalist shrugged.

'I am getting a little bored with all this melodrama,' he said acidly. 'What is it?'

'The photographs, Mr Kenton.'

'I have already made you an offer.'

Zaleshoff's jaw shot forward angrily.

'What you ask is absurd. You are interfering in a matter that does not in the least concern you. Be sensible, Mr Kenton.'

'Colonel Robinson was anxious, too, that I should be sensible.'

'I am not interested in Colonel Robinson's anxieties.'

'Nor I in yours. I am going to be sensible from my own point of view. I am interesting myself professionally in this affair.'

For a moment the two men glared at each other in angry silence.

'I think,' said Tamara, 'that it would be better and more comfortable if we all sat down again.'

'You keep out of this.'

The girl flushed slightly.

'I will not keep out of it, Andreas. You have bungled this affair badly and you know it. If you would not persist in treating this man as if he were a cretin like Ortega and—'

'Be silent,' roared her brother.

'Very well, Andreas. I will be silent. But I say first that you had better talk things over again before you go too far.'

'Don't be silly, Tamara. What is the use of further talk?'

'It depends what sort of talk it is. I think, Andreas, that you will have to accept Mr Kenton's terms.'

For a moment Kenton expected an outburst of rage from the Russian; but it did not come. Suddenly, he dropped the revolver into his pocket, sat down and began pouring himself out some fresh tea. Kenton glanced at the girl uncertainly. She motioned him back to the sofa. Zaleshoff looked up from his tea with a sneer.

'So,' he said sardonically, 'you are feeling sure of yourself, eh? Andreas Prokovitch is forced to give way to the demands of the gutter Press.'

'A question of *quid pro quo*, surely?'

'*Quid pro quo!*' repeated Zaleshoff with deep contempt. 'There is a great deal too much *quid* and not enough *quo* about this business.'

'He will stop talking nonsense in a minute,' said the girl calmly.

'Quiet!' snarled her brother. 'This interfering busybody of a reporter pays you a stupid compliment and you lose your senses completely.' He turned to Kenton suddenly. 'Why, my interfering friend, do you suppose I wish you to give me those photographs?'

'Because the original documents are not forgeries,' said Kenton promptly.

'Very clever of you. The photographs were taken illegally by a man in a Government department in Moscow.'

'Borovansky?'

'Yes. The man who told you his name was Sachs.'

'And where does Colonel Robinson come in?'

'Saridza was the man who bribed Borovansky to take the photographs.'

'Then he was speaking the truth when he said that Sachs was on his way to deliver them?'

'Yes.'

'Who was the man in the train of whom Sachs was afraid?'

'I know of no man in the train,' said Zaleshoff shortly. 'It was probably Borovansky's guilty imagination.'

Kenton decided to shelve the point for the moment.

'Who is Saridza?'

Zaleshoff's face darkened.

'I think that on the whole you would do well to forget that name,' he said slowly. 'So far as I know, only one newspaper in Europe ever printed it. Saridza was calling himself something else at the time; but the newspaper, in probing some sort of financial scandal that he was connected with, used the real name. I don't know how it had become known. The newspaper may have had Saridza's dossier on their files. Anyway, the day after the article appeared, the man who wrote it was shot dead with his wife on the steps of their home.' He looked thoughtfully at the glass in his hand and it seemed to Kenton that the Russian was talking to himself. 'They say that persons like Al Capone and John Dillinger are products of America's corrupt administration and clumsy law-making. Saridza and his kind must be the products of the world business system. The principal difference between Al Capone and Stefan Saridza is that while Capone worked for himself, Saridza works for other people. When Capone ordered his hoodlums to machine-gun a couple of men on the side-walk from an armour-plated coupé, it was to maintain or increase his own income. When Saridza ordered that Captain to beat you with a *Totschläger* until you gave him some photographs, it was to increase the income of what he called his principals in

London – gentlemen who would, in all probability, hesitate before they swatted a fly. You see, your business man desires the end, but dislikes the means. He is a kind-hearted man. He likes an easy conscience. He likes to think that the people he exploits are pleased and happy to be exploited. He likes to sit in his office and deal honestly with other business men. That is why Saridza is necessary. For at some point or other in the amazingly complicated business structure of the world, there is always dirty work to be done. It may be simple bribery, it may be the manipulation of public opinion by means of incidents, rumours or scandals, it may even be an affair of assassination – but whatever it is, Saridza and his kind are there to do it, with large fees in their pockets and the most evasive instructions imaginable . . .

'Saridza started his career in Bulgaria in the early nineteen hundreds. His business then was intimidating shopkeepers – the "protection racket," as it is called now in America. But he has progressed. To-day, his speciality is moulding public opinion, and he is a person of curious importance. He has been decorated by most European Governments. Those same Governments also have his dossier on their files of dangerous foreign agents. He calls himself a propagandist. A better description would be "political saboteur".'

Kenton fidgeted.

'But what would he want with those photographs?'

Zaleshoff wagged an expressive finger.

'Ah! There you have it. What indeed? As soon as I had positively identified Saridza with this affair, we set ourselves to examine the problem.'

'We?'

'Tamara and me,' said Zaleshoff blandly.

Kenton shrugged.

'All right.'

'We concluded,' Zaleshoff went on, 'that the key to the situation was in Roumania.'

'That wasn't difficult.'

'No. But that simple fact alone did not get us any place. We had to look farther.'

'Just you and your sister still?'

'Certainly. We had one clue only. It was that Saridza had some years previously been in touch with the Pan-Eurasian Petroleum Company and that he had also been employed apart from that by the present chairman of the Pan-Eurasian Company, Mr Balterghen.'

'Balterghen? He's a big man in the City of London, isn't he?'

'Very big. More important, it is his company that has been behind the agitation for oil-concession reform in Roumania.'

'Wait a minute. There was some business about a newspaper being beaten up for printing an article about that, wasn't there?'

'There was. We have learned this morning that the orders to wreck the newspaper offices originated with the agent of the Pan-Eurasian Company in Bucharest. The idea was, apparently, to kill the issue in which the article appeared, but the paper was already distributed before the thing happened. It wasn't a very good article, but it upset the Concession Reform proposals and resulted in an official inquiry. That was over three months ago.'

'You mean that Saridza's principals in London are the Pan-Eurasian Petroleum Company?'

'It seems likely.'

'Hm! It seems rather circumstantial to me. Still, even if it's true, I still don't see where Sachs and his bundle of photographs come in.'

'Neither did we. But a little investigation gave us a further hint.' Zaleshoff lit a cigarette and gazed raptly at the ceiling. 'Have you studied Roumanian politics recently, Mr Kenton?'

'Consistently.'

But the question had evidently been rhetorical, for Zaleshoff removed his eyes from the ceiling and went on as if the journalist had not spoken.

'Until nineteen thirty-six,' he said, 'Roumania could be summed up politically in one word – Titulescu. Titulescu's foreign policy was based on friendship with Soviet Russia. The Little Entente was the first link in the chain round Germany. The last link was the Franco-Soviet pact. But there is reaction in the air of Roumania as there is in every other European country. With Fascism in Italy, National-Socialism in Germany, the Croix de Feu in France, Rexism in Belgium, and Nationalism in Spain, it was hardly likely that Roumania would escape the contagion. Even in England the symptoms are apparent in the rising power of bureaucracy. Roumania's little Hitler is Cornelius Codreanu, and he has a Goering in the person of General Zizi Cantacuzino. Codreanu was a lawyer until he formed a party called the League of the Archangel Michael. The name was afterwards changed to the Iron Guard. Later on he called it the All-for-the-Fatherland League. The name, however, is unimportant. The party's policy is a familiar one – anti-Semitism, a corporate state, an alliance with Germany, and the "saving of Roumania from the Jewish and Communist menace". The party wears green shirts and occupies its time almost exclusively with the collection of funds and political assassination and terrorism. When Tatarescu forced Titulescu's resignation and Titulescu fled from Roumania, a contingent of Codreanu's men followed him. Titulescu's attack of poisoning in St Moritz was believed by many to have been their work. It is not unlikely. The point was that in place of Titulescu, Antonescu became foreign minister, and Roumania and Poland formed an alliance aiming at strict neutrality towards *both* Germany and Russia. In one way it was a good move. It killed any German idea of an attack on Russia by way of the Ukraine. But, unless something serious happens, personal power and the German alliance are as far away from Codreanu as ever. Now do you see where Saridza stands, Mr Kenton?'

'You mean that Saridza has been employed to provide that "something serious"?'

'Exactly. You are familiar with the old Bessarabian quarrel between Russia and Roumania. The Iron Guard is out to drive Roumania into the bosom of Germany, by inflaming public opinion against Russia. The Soviets, they will declare, are planning to attack and seize Bessarabia. They will create a scare; then, suddenly, dramatically, they will produce the evidence – those photographs – as proof of Russia's intentions. It is merely a question of skilful timing. Mass hysteria will do the rest.'

'Would it? I wonder.'

Zaleshoff snorted irritably.

'My dear Mr Kenton, if you were to search long enough in the British War Office, you would probably find a complete plan of attack by England against France. It is part of the business of war offices to evolve such things. Nobody in England dreams of attacking France. The two countries are allies. But supposing you published that plan of attack in France, and swore that England was greedy for French Morocco – what sort of effect do you suppose it would have on public opinion there? A disposition to distrust England's motives in the future would be the least of the damage done. Yet England and France are as friendly now as two nations can be in this world. Imagine, then, the damage to the relations between two countries in the position of Russia and Roumania. Wars have been fought over less.'

'I see your point. But where does Pan-Eurasian Petroleum come in?'

'On the ground floor. The price of Saridza's assistance in gaining power is the immediate use of that power to revise the oil concessions in Pan-Eurasian's favour. It's an old game. The big oil interests played it in Mexico for years. That's why there used to be so many revolutions.'

Kenton was thoughtful for a moment.

'What makes you so sure,' he said at last, 'that what you have told me will not prevent me from giving up the photographs? For all you know, I might be a die-hard Tory with a nice holding of Pan-Eurasian shares.'

Zaleshoff smiled grimly.

'Please give me credit for a little sense. If you had held any shares of any value at all, you would not have needed money in Nuremberg so badly as you told me. You might have lied, but I should have detected that. In any case, your dossier credits you with a sort of modest radicalism, very common among English journalists.'

Kenton yawned.

'Well, you needn't worry. I'll let you have the photographs. You were right, of course, about there being nothing in it from my point of view. Something that nearly happened isn't news. You've given me an idea, though. I might go to Bucharest and do some stuff on Codreanu. By the way, for my own satisfaction, you might just tell me if it *was* you who killed Sachs.'

Again he noticed that curious exchange of glances.

'No, Mr Kenton, it wasn't.'

The journalist shrugged his shoulders.

'That's that then. You won't mind, will you, if I draw my own conclusions?'

'Not at all.'

'Right. Well, I'll be getting back to my hotel.' He stood up.

'You're not forgetting the photographs, Mr Kenton?' It was the girl who spoke.

'Of course not. They're with the *patron* at the Café Schwan. I arranged with him that he was to hand them over to nobody except me in person. He's open all night, and it's near the Hotel Werner. We'll go now if you like.'

'Is the envelope deposited in your name?' said Zaleshoff sharply.

'Of course.'

Zaleshoff looked inquiringly at the girl.

She shook her head.

'We cannot risk it,' she said.

Zaleshoff nodded and turned again to Kenton.

'I regret,' he said, 'that you will have to spend what remains of the night here. In the morning we will consider what to do.'

Kenton looked grimly from one to the other.

'I don't quite understand.'

'It will be more comfortable—' began Zaleshoff in a conciliatory tone; but the girl interrupted him.

'He had better know the truth,' she said. 'Mr Kenton, it is quite impossible for you to return to your hotel. It is equally impossible for you to claim that packet at the Café Schwan. It would even be dangerous to be seen in the streets.'

'Why?'

'Because,' said Tamara, 'there is not a newspaper in Austria to-night that does not carry your name and description and a large reproduction of a fingerprint found on the wash-basin in room twenty-five at the Hotel Josef. Every policeman in Austria is on the look-out for you. There is a price on your head of one thousand *schillings*. You are wanted for the murder of Herman Sachs.'

At a quarter past two that morning the proprietor of the Café Schwan telephoned the police with news that, ten minutes earlier, three masked men had driven up in a black closed car, menaced the occupants with revolvers and ransacked his premises. One of the two clients present at the time, a railway official from the station, had attempted to resist the bandits and had been shot in the foot. No money had been taken, but a small packet, left by a young American, had been taken from the poste restante box. The packet, he understood, had contained compromising letters from a lady. The man who had shot the railway official was tall and thin. The other two had been of medium height. The arm of one of them, the left arm, he thought, had appeared to be rather stiff at the elbow – but he could not be sure. They had declared that it was an affair of honour. No, he could not describe the men, owing to the masks. He had not remarked their clothes. No, he had not noticed the make or number of the car – who would, under the circumstances? No, he could not remember the name of the American – if he were to remember the name of every traveller who left things to be called for, he would have no head left for the conduct of his business. The name might have been Krause.

The police promised to investigate the affair.

II

Kenton Thinks

The more fanciful among recent interpreters of history have frequently drawn attention to the grotesque intrusion of the trivial on the larger affairs of mankind. They have elaborated the idea. What, they ask, might have been the course of history had, say, Napoleon fought the battle of Marengo with his judgement impaired by a cold in the head?

Such whimsical speculations are symptomatic of an a-religious age. Yet, in the complex anatomy of cause and effect, in that crazy *pastiche* which some dismiss as 'the blind workings of Fate,' there is often to be observed a certain artistry.

In 1885 there lived in Salzburg a young married couple named Hoesch. Karl, the husband, was employed in the office of one Buscher, a maker of glass beads. Early in 1886 Herr Buscher died. In his will, among other bequests to his employees, he left his clerk Hoesch two books 'for the nourishment and improvement of his mind and that of his good wife'. One of the books was a *Life of Charlemagne*, published in Berlin in 1850; the other was a German translation of the Iliad. With a generosity as characteristic as it was pointless (for Frau Hoesch was unable to read) Karl shared his good fortune with his wife by giving her one of the books. This, the *Life of Charlemagne*, was carefully packed away with the lady's Sunday dress and some keepsakes from her mother. The Iliad Karl read assiduously, both to himself and to Frau Hoesch. When, in 1887, it was known that their first child would soon be born, the pair decided immediately that if it were a girl her name should be Helene; while that if, as Karl secretly hoped, it were a boy, then he should be called Achilles. In the August of that year, Achilles Karl Hoesch was baptized.

It might be expected that as he grew up the young Hoesch would have become ashamed of his first Christian name. But he did not. That may have been because his mother invariably called him by his second name. After two or three years' nightly readings of the Iliad, Frau Hoesch had taken an almost active dislike to Homer. Once, she had suggested turning to the *Life of Charlemagne*; but her husband had refused, pointing out that he had given the book to her, and could not take back his gift. She had accepted this punctilious verdict without question; but her dislike of the Iliad had intensified. It was then that she had begun to call the boy Karl.

To the world outside his family, however, the young Karl was always Achilles; and, as he was a lusty and pugnacious lad, the name was regarded with envy instead of scorn by his contemporaries. It was perhaps the self-confidence engendered by the distinction that caused him, on leaving school, to reject his father's plan for a career in the glass bead factory and enter the service of the State Railways.

Of the career of Achilles Hoesch little need be said. In a dim way he prospered. After twenty-six years' service in various capacities he was made a sub-inspector of goods traffic at Linz; and it was about two years after this appointment that he formed the habit of dropping into the Café Schwan when he was on night shift, to drink a *Kaffee ausgeheitzter* and eat a piece of *Kuchen*.

He had been thus occupied when Colonel Robinson and his assistants had appeared on that November night with pistols in their hands and threats on their lips. Quivering with a rage worthy of his namesake, Achilles, on being invited to put up his hands, had grabbed a chair and hurled it at Captain Mailler's head.

The Captain ducked, fired at Achilles' legs and hit him in the foot. At the hospital it was found that the bullet had passed through the fleshy part of the heel.

Almost every town of any size has its nightly quota of violence. Only the character of it changes from country to country and district to district. In the East End of London the knuckleduster, the razor, and the broken bottle are the common weapons. In the Paris suburbs knives and pistols share the work. In Central Europe, north of a line Basle-Trieste, the revolver comes into its own. Newspapers rarely report these drab incidents. Unless the case possesses that mysterious quality called 'news value,' little is heard of it. The wounding in the heel of an unknown Linz railway official would have possessed no news value. Nor would the wounding in some unspecified part of the body of Achilles Hoesch. But the wounding in the heel of a man named Achilles *did* possess news value – it was a good joke.

Half an hour after Achilles was carried into the hospital, an agency message was being ticked out by tape machines in the offices of every Vienna morning paper. All but one extreme left wing sheet promptly squeezed it in on the front page of the late editions. It was headed 'ACHILLES' HEEL.'

Shortly after half-past seven that morning, Zaleshoff rose stiffly from a chair beside the stove in Rashenko's room in Kölnerstrasse 11, felt his way in the semi-darkness to the washstand and sluiced his face and hands with cold water. This done, he peered at his sister curled up in an armchair.

'Tamara,' he whispered softly.

'Yes?'

'I'm going out to get some air.'

'All right.'

He listened for a moment to the faint snores coming from the sofa and to Rashenko's heavy breathing from the bed.

'Don't wake them,' he added.

The door squeaked slightly and he was gone.

The girl gazed for a moment at the dull glow of the dying fire, then shut her eyes again. It seemed to her that she had scarcely done so before her brother was by her side, shaking her arm and whispering to her to get up and put on her coat. In his hand was a newspaper.

When, two hours later, Kenton awoke, Zaleshoff and Tamara had gone. A shaft of pale sunlight filtering through the gap between the curtains was shining in his eyes. He sat up on the sofa and something fell to the floor beside him. It was a piece of paper folded in three. He opened it.

Dear Mr Kenton (he read),

On the table in the middle of the room there is to-day's newspaper. There are two news items on the front page that will interest you. The one which concerns yourself should not, I think, be taken too seriously. Since when have the police not expected to make an arrest within the next few hours? The other item will, when you find it, explain itself and our absence. The race is to the swift. Do not attempt to communicate with anyone. I suggest that you remain here with Rashenko until I am able to arrange for you to be moved out of Austria. As you so forcibly intimated last night, I am not without responsibility for your unpleasant predicament. My sister, whose maternal instincts are clearly aroused, sends her best wishes.

The note was unsigned. Zaleshoff was nothing if not careful.

Kenton read of the 'latest developments' in the Linz murder with detached interest.

His first reaction to the news that he was wanted for murder had been to laugh. Then the evening papers had been produced and laughter had been replaced by a feeling of amused indignation. He would go to the police immediately, curse them for their stupidity, exact apologies, lodge complaints right and left. Finally he had lost his temper and accused Zaleshoff of murdering Sachs. There had been a stormy scene.

The girl had calmed them both down.

As she had pointed out, the suspicions of the police were not, after all, unreasonable. It must look as though Kenton had been the last person to see Sachs alive. There was money missing. There was the damning testimony of the Hotel Werner. She had ended by suggesting that rest was needed by all concerned and that decisions were best taken in the morning.

Well, the morning had come and Zaleshoff and his sister had decamped. He looked a little doubtfully for the news item to which the note referred. Finally, the facetious little paragraph recording the wounding in the heel of Achilles Hoesch caught his eye and he understood. So Saridza had got his photographs after all! That was that. Meanwhile . . .

He moved the curtains aside and gazed out of the window, down at the pavement far below. There were a few children playing, an old woman, one or two hurrying men. He experienced a sudden desire to get out of Rashenko's cramped, stuffy room and walk in the open air. There was, after all, no reason why he shouldn't do so. He had done nothing criminal. It was absurd that they should suspect him. Absurd that . . . but, he thought suddenly, they didn't *suspect* him. This was Austria, not England. Until he should prove his innocence, he was not merely suspect – he was guilty!

He let the curtain fall and stood up. The bottom half of his body ached badly. This, he discovered, was due partly to the stiffness of his joints and partly to a colourful display of bruises. His arms and back had, however, suffered less. A small mirror on the wall showed that, except for an unsavoury growth of beard, his face had returned to its normal proportions. His clothes had fared badly. In addition to the huge rent in his trouser leg, there were minor tears on the sleeves and back of the jacket. His linen was all that could be expected after the stresses of seventy-two hours' continuous and unusually hard wear. A bath was badly needed. He stripped and, going to the washstand, did what he could with the small hand-basin and a jug of cold water.

Rather to his surprise, he found that being wanted for murder produced in him an effect almost identical to that of a dentist's waiting-room – a sense of discomfort in the intestinal region, a certain constriction in the chest. He supposed that the same glands discharged the same secretions into the blood stream in both cases. Nature could be absurdly parsimonious. That, perhaps, explained why real murderers so often behaved with such hopeless lack of discretion when confronted by the police. Too much assurance could be more dangerous in those circumstances than blind panic. He must do nothing hastily.

He dried himself somewhat inadequately on a small hand-towel and put on his shirt and trousers again. When Rashenko awoke he would borrow a razor from the Russian and shave himself. He found some cigarettes, lit one and sat down to think.

The immediate question was whether or not he should accept the suggestion in Zaleshoff's note.

The decision might be easier to make if he really had murdered Sachs, for then he would have to think only of saving his skin. As it was, there was the complicating necessity of having to prove his own innocence. A real murderer would not bother about that. With the evidence available, the last thing he would want would be a trial. For that matter, the last thing he, Kenton, wanted was a trial; but he had not yet come to the point of admitting it as a possibility. He had not killed Sachs; therefore they would not, could not, try him for doing so. The whole thing was fantastic. The Consul would put things right.

Then another thought began to germinate. Supposing they *did* convict him of murder. Supposing his efforts to prove his innocence failed and that the Consul could do nothing. It was all very fine to say that Right triumphed in the end, that Justice sought out the guilty and punished them. In actual practice, Right and Justice were far from infallible. Stupid, honest and blind, they blundered in pursuit of their quarry. The innocent sometimes crossed their paths. Right and Justice pounced. The innocent were sometimes convicted; and with conviction Justice was satisfied. The case was closed as far as the police were concerned. Not much use then to hope for the triumph of Right.

His heart beat a little faster. He snatched a newspaper from the table and began to read more carefully the account of police activity in connection with the crime. Fingerprints! He had thought he had wiped everything he had touched. He must have forgotten the basin where he had washed his hands of Sachs' blood. There was the evidence of the night porter. The description was fairly good, though the name was spelled Kent*en*. The man could not have been as drunk as he had looked. There was money missing. Sachs had paid in advance for his room and the porter had seen the wallet. There was no mention of the money he had posted to the hotel, but the police were no doubt keeping the handwriting on the envelope as a conclusive titbit for the trial. What a fool he had been to send it! The Hotel Werner had contributed handsomely to the evidence. The murderer, stated the manager, had arrived in the early hours of the morning looking very dishevelled, as if he had been struggling with someone. When his flight had been discovered later that day, the room had been in great confusion. This, Kenton concluded, was not unlikely in view of the fact that both Saridza and Zaleshoff had searched his things. It was a watertight circumstantial case. His only defence could be the rather feeble assertion that Sachs had been already dead when he, Kenton, had arrived. The story of the photographs would do more harm than good. Even if it were not regarded as a piece of impudent bluff, it could only serve to provide the prosecution with an additional motive for the crime. One thing was clear. It would be far too dangerous to give himself up. His one chance lay in finding the real murderer and bringing him to book. The only other alternative was to get back to England, either with Zaleshoff's help or on his own, and stay there. You could not, he seemed to remember, be extradited from your own country.

He paced the room distractedly. If only Zaleshoff had not slipped away. He would have forced the Russian to tell the truth about the murder. Either the 'Nazi spy' or Zaleshoff himself had stabbed Sachs; of that he was convinced. He should have wrung the truth out of the man the previous night. If only he had thought more and talked less. Still, if you weren't used to being suddenly and unjustly accused of murder, you were, he supposed, liable to let your sense of outraged innocence obscure the realities of the situation. He had, he remembered bitterly, gone to sleep complacently coining the ironical phrases with which to scourge the blunderers responsible for the mistake.

The prospect of lurking in Rashenko's room for days on end was something he could not face. Apart from the risk of discovery, there was the all-important fact that his chances of clearing himself of the charge against him would decrease with every day that passed. Zaleshoff, acting, no doubt, on the information he had given him the previous night, was on his way to Prague. The pasty-faced thug of the Nuremberg-Linz train might be, and doubtless was, hundreds of miles away. Zaleshoff, of course, did not care a tinker's curse what happened. As long as his Government's aims were achieved, the fate of an obscure English journalist was a matter of minor importance. Kenton raged at the man's perfidy. As for the girl; she, at least, might have had a little more consideration for him. He smiled dryly. Consideration! What a prim, respectable word to use in connection with so grotesque a business! He was, he decided, losing his sense of proportion. Recriminations were a waste of time. The point was: what was he to do now?

Should he make for England? The idea was not altogether unattractive. There, at least, he would be sure of physical safety. On the other hand, his freedom of movement would be severely hampered. If he ventured to set foot outside England, he could and probably would be immediately arrested. In England itself he might be under surveillance. It was, he decided, the sort of thing about which you ought to consult a solicitor. In any case, the prospect of clearing himself of the charge while in England would be remote. Perhaps he would have to rely ultimately on the real murderer making a death-bed confession. Meanwhile, life in England would, to say the least of it, be anything but a bed of roses. A man wanted for a particularly sordid murder would not be a very welcome member of society. It all came back to one thing – find the murderer and bring him to justice.

He examined this proposition gloomily. It seemed hopeless. Even if he could find Zaleshoff, he would still have to persuade the Russian to help him. Wring the truth out of him! Yes, but how? He remembered the blank looks, the cold denials that had met his previous inquiries about Sachs' murder. He sighed. If only he'd played his cards a little better. Zaleshoff and his sister had been too clever for him. Before they had told him about the police they had found out what he had done with the photographs. All that haggling over the price of his surrender of the photographs had been mere play-acting to divert his attention from the real issue. How relieved they must have been that he had not insisted on the name of Sachs' murderer! He remembered significant little incidents: the girl hastily pushing a crumpled newspaper out of sight, those curious glances whenever

Sachs' murder was mentioned. Yes, he had been very competently 'handled'. He found himself feeling almost pleased that they had after all failed to get the photographs. They . . .

He started.

Zaleshoff badly wanted those photographs. He, Kenton, had surrendered them for a news story that he couldn't use. They had been his only bargaining weapon. Supposing, by some means or other, he could regain possession of that weapon. Then . . .

He relaxed again disgustedly.

It was crazy, hopeless. How could he possibly get hold of the photographs? Saridza was probably already in Prague. Zaleshoff was by now speeding after him. What chance had he, Kenton, of forestalling the Russian? Moodily he crushed his cigarette out and rested his head in his hands.

A psychiatrist would have observed the journalist's behaviour during the succeeding two minutes with gloomy professional interest. After a minute and a half the expression of utter dejection on the face changed suddenly and curiously. The lower jaw drooped, the eyes opened wide, the forehead creased thoughtfully. Then the forehead returned to normal and the mouth spread slightly in the beginnings of a grin. He stood up quickly, snapped his fingers once, said 'Ha!' and whistled softly. For he had remembered something – something all-important – the fact that Colonel Robinson was going to Prague *to meet someone named Bastaki.*

In his hurry to tell Zaleshoff his story and answer the Russian's stream of questions, he had forgotten all about the name. He had not, indeed, paid particular attention to it. His thoughts at the time had been concentrated largely on Captain Mailler's rubber truncheon. Afterwards, the business of getting away and of coping with Zaleshoff's mental acrobatics had driven that apparently insignificant piece of detail from his mind. In any case, he had not regarded Saridza's destination as being of importance. He had thought the photographs safe enough at the Café Schwan.

Now, however, things were different. Saridza's destination had become important; and the measure of its importance to him was determined by the single fact that he, Kenton, possessed a piece of information that Zaleshoff did not possess. That information might make it possible for him to regain possession of the photographs before the Russian could do so, in spite of the latter's start. Prague was a large place. With nothing at all on which to work, Zaleshoff's task was a formidable one. The name 'Bastaki', it was true, might prove worthless as a lead; but it was just possible that it might be invaluable. At all events, he told himself, he had nothing to lose. If he failed to find Saridza or if, having found Saridza, he failed to get the photographs, he could still try to get to England through Poland. In any case, Czechoslovakia was the best country to make for. The Swiss frontier could be reached only travelling right across the longest route in Austria, while, as he dare not use his passport, Germany and Italy were too risky. In either of the latter countries he would have to register his actual passport with the local police wherever he stopped. A mere filling up of hotel identity forms with a name and passport number only would not be enough. To get into Hungary would merely land him farther away from England and accomplish nothing. Prague it should be.

The feeling of having a definite object in view cheered him enormously. In his heart he knew that his chances of doing anything useful in Prague with his clue were fantastically slender; but he also knew that, short of remaining cooped up in Rashenko's room, there was no other course open to him. He concentrated with relish on the more immediate problem – that of getting from Austria to Czechoslovakia without being arrested or inviting capture by showing his passport.

The first necessity was clothes. His hat and overcoat were at the Hotel Werner or had been removed to the police station. His trousers were useless if he wanted to get anywhere without attracting attention. The next essential was money. He counted the contents of his wallet. He had four hundred and sixty-five *Reichmark* and a little loose change. If he spent the sixty-five on clothes, that should leave enough to last a week or two. He would soon know whether or not he was wasting time in Prague. If necessary, he would be able to get to Danzig and buy a passage on a Hull-bound boat.

He walked over to the bed.

Rashenko was lying on his back, his eyes closed. His breathing was inaudible and Kenton judged that the Russian was awake. 'Rashenko,' he said.

The eyes opened.

'You know,' said Kenton in German, 'that Zaleshoff and his sister have gone?'

Rashenko nodded. Then he clambered slowly out of bed and wrapped an old dressing-gown round his shoulders. The journalist watched him go to a table and scribble rapidly on a piece of paper. At last he held up the paper for Kenton's inspection.

'*You have made up your mind to go,*' he read, '*but I beg that you remain here. It is safer. Andreas Prokovitch will not fail you.*'

'How did you know that I was going?'

Rashenko scribbled again:

'*I have been watching your face. I saw you make up your mind. It is not safe to go. You will be caught.*'

His eyes met Kenton's and he nodded vehemently.

'If you will help me, I shall not be caught.'

Rashenko shook his head.

'Do you mean,' said Kenton, 'that you won't help me or that I shall be caught?'

Rashenko smiled wanly and wrote:

'*It is our wish to help you; but if you leave this house we can do nothing.*'

'I must take my chance.'

'*Where do you go?*'

'To England. Then I am safe from arrest.'

'*You will be caught at the German frontier, if not before.*'

'I shall go via Czechoslovakia.'

For a second suspicion gleamed in the Russian's sunken eyes, then he shrugged his shoulders slightly and, turning to the stove, began to make coffee and heat some rolls that he took from the cupboard.

Over the coffee and rolls, Kenton stated his wants – a razor, some Austrian money in exchange for his German notes and some clothes. Rashenko nodded gloomily, took one of Kenton's hundred-mark notes and showed him where the razor was. Then he disappeared through the door leading to the stairs and the street.

Wondering whether the Russian intended doing his shopping in a dressing-gown and nightshirt, Kenton started on his beard. He had decided to leave himself a moustache. When, however, he came to the point of shaping it he was in a difficulty. He had never before attempted to wear a moustache and was uncertain of the technique. A tooth-brush effect would look too English. He decided finally to let the stubble finish at the corners of his mouth. The result, he was interested to note, made him look extremely bad-tempered.

He was examining the work critically when Rashenko reappeared with a large bundle of clothes.

Kenton took it eagerly. On the top was a little pile of Austrian money. The clothes consisted of a grey soft hat with a round, flat, continental brim, a pair of thick brown trousers and a voluminous dark-grey overcoat. They were obviously not new.

'Where did you get them?' he asked.

Rashenko smiled, but made no attempt to answer.

Kenton put on the hat and looked at himself in the mirror. There was something curiously familiar about the way the crown was pinched in that he could not identify. He had seen the hat before somewhere. He shrugged. There must be hats like it all over Europe.

Ten minutes later he buttoned up the overcoat, shook hands with Rashenko and left Kölnerstrasse 11. On the pavement outside he stopped for an instant, took a deep breath of fresh, cold air and turned to the left.

12

Mr Hodgkin

Taking a route described by Rashenko, Kenton made for the centre of the town.

Carefully suppressing the temptations to turn up his coat collar to conceal his face and to dive down every side-street he passed, he walked quickly past the Parkbad and the Hotel Weinzinger. In the Brücknerplatz he found what he wanted – a travel agency. He went inside.

To his relief, the place was far from empty. At the long counter which ran across one corner of the room, a Swiss couple were asking about the trains to Basle. Next to them a tired-looking Englishwoman was asserting in a loud and penetrating voice that the hotels were better in Cairo. On the left-hand side of the room, sitting in chairs ranged behind a large notice which announced in German, French and English that at twelve o'clock exactly a conducted party would leave by luxury motor-coach for a tour of the Bohemian Forest country, sat a chattering group laden with cameras and binoculars.

He looked round for a map of Austria and found that there was one on the wall behind his head. He concentrated on the area north-east of Linz.

He had decided that his best plan would be to go by train to some point near the Czech frontier, wait for nightfall and, leaving the road, strike off across country, trusting to luck and the darkness to get him past any frontier guards who might be patrolling the unfrequented stretches. He could then rejoin the road on the Czech side, walk to a town, and board a train for Prague.

The map revealed two possible alternatives. Either he could go to the railway terminus at Aigen and try to reach Schwarzbach across the frontier, or there was the route via Garsbach and Summerau on the Austrian side to Budweis and Prague direct. The latter route looked far from promising. For one thing, there was no frontier town marked on the map, which might mean that passports were examined at any point on the journey and that he would have no chance to get off the train. Apart from that, it was a main route out of Austria and the police would probably be scrutinizing all travellers very carefully. The other plan looked better until close inspection showed a number of small black triangles marked on the frontier north of Aigen. That meant that there were high altitudes at that point. It occurred to him that the very fact of the railway's stopping some miles short of the frontier suggested that the country ahead was impracticable for transport.

He was beginning to think that he would have to take a longer route east, when he noticed that due west of Freistadt a single thin line was shown crossing the frontier into Czechoslovakia. It was a road. He looked again and saw that across the empty area surrounding it was the word – *Böhmerwald*.

For a moment he continued to stare at the map. *Böhmerwald* – the Bohemian Forests! And just behind him, sitting waiting, was a party going that way by motor-coach. He glanced at the clock. It was twenty to twelve. He returned to the map. His road went through a place called Neukirchen. He went up to the counter and a man hurried forward.

'I have a few hours only to spare in Linz. Is there perhaps a drive, a tour that one could make?' he asked.

Certainly, there were many. There were the afternoon drives to the Hallstätter excavations, the Bauernberg and Freinberg heights. Or, if *mein Herr* wished, there were trips to the Pöstlingberg and Steyr with many places of educational and artistic interest. There was much baroque.

Kenton nodded carelessly in the direction of the motor-coach party.

'This excursion here, it is good?'

Yes, yes; a drive of never-to-be-forgotten beauty; through

Neukirchen up into the woodlands to the highest point, one thousand metres, from which one could see into the heart of old Bohemia. Unfortunately, if *mein Herr* had only a little time it was not possible. The return was not until the evening.

Kenton explained hurriedly that he did not leave until late that evening, bought a ticket, sat down as quickly and as unobtrusively as he could with the rest of the party, and broke out into a nervous sweat. 'Highest point one thousand metres', 'see into the heart of old Bohemia' – the two phrases were ringing in his head. He forced himself to breathe easily and regularly, and took stock of his travelling companions.

He counted nineteen and, as far as he could see, they were mostly Austrians. In front of him, however, was a rather severe-looking young Frenchman talking in a passionate undertone to a woman next to him. The journalist caught the words '*ta famille*', '*ce vieux salop*', and '*vicieuse*'. Next to them was a man immersed in a newspaper. His back was to Kenton but the journalist saw, with a pang of fear, that he was reading about the Hotel Josef murder. Kenton stared at the floor and wished he had thought to buy a book or a newspaper behind which to hide his face. Out of the corner of his eye he saw that the man beside him was looking at him expectantly and would at any moment start a conversation. Telling himself that he must at all costs act normally and that to appear reticent or unsociable would attract attention to himself, he turned with the remark that it was a fine day for the drive. His neighbour, however, was now deep in conversation with a stout Austrian woman in front of him and did not hear. Feeling rather foolish, Kenton resumed his study of the floor. After a few moments his eyes wandered furtively towards a small table about six feet away from him. On it were arranged eight neat piles of travel booklets. He gazed at them longingly. With one of those to look at he would not look so conspicuous. To get one, however, he would have to stand up, cross six feet of floor, return and sit down again. It needed courage; but at last he stood up and walked to the table. In his overwrought imagination everyone in the room promptly stopped what he or she was doing and stared at him.

Unnerved, he grabbed a booklet from the nearest pile and turned quickly to get back to his seat. The metal buckle on the belt of his overcoat hanging loose at his side promptly swung round and hit the table with a loud report.

Crimson in the face Kenton blundered back to his seat and buried his face in the booklet. It proved to be a list of December sailings from Genoa. Two minutes later, to his profound relief, a man with a long gold-braided coat and a peaked cap came in and announced that the motor-coach had arrived and that those with tickets for the tour might now take their places.

Half the seats in the coach were already filled by a party collected from a big hotel and Kenton, who had manœuvred himself to the tail of the procession, found when he climbed inside that there was only one seat left. He found himself wedged between a rather gawky middle-aged Austrian woman and the newspaper reader, a little thin-faced Austrian man with rimless spectacles and a pair of very sharp blue eyes. He settled himself in his seat and looked out of the nearside window. The next instant his heart nearly stopped beating for he was staring straight into the eyes of a policeman standing on the pavement.

For a moment he lost his head. His first impulse was to scramble out through the offside door and run. Then he saw that, owing to the reflection on the window-glass, the policeman could not see him. He relaxed, wiped his forehead furtively with the back of his hand, and prayed silently that the driver would stop talking to the conductor and get a move on.

'Funny outfits, aren't they?'

Kenton started violently. It was the little thin-faced man beside him and he was talking English with the unmistakable accent of the inner London suburbs.

Forcing himself to keep calm, Kenton turned to the speaker.

'*Bitte?*'

The sharp blue eyes gleamed with amusement through the spectacles.

'Go on! You're not going to tell me you're not a Britisher?'

Kenton laughed feebly.

'I'm sorry. One gets so used to speaking German.' He felt himself blushing. 'Yes, they do look a little odd,' he added hastily.

'Efficient lot, though, the Austrian police,' pursued the other. 'I've been in and out of the country for years now and I reckon they're one of the smartest lots in Europe. Not like the Germans, all red tape and la-di-da. Get their man every time, they tell me. They're all trained in Vienna.'

Desperately Kenton changed the subject.

'How did you know I was English?'

The other winked heavily.

'Spotted you as soon as you walked into the place.' He jerked a thumb at the travel agency. 'You'd never guess how.'

'The clothes?' said Kenton cunningly.

'Yes and no.' He fingered Kenton's overcoat contemptuously. 'That's Continental stuff and Continental cutting. The hat's German. No, it was your jacket lapel, the bit showing under your overcoat collar.'

'My jacket?'

'Yes, it's English.'

Kenton remembered that he had bought the suit in London.

'I don't see how you can tell. I might have got it in Paris or Berlin anywhere.'

The little man shook his head triumphantly.

'No, you couldn't of, friend; and I'll tell you for why. The only stitch of that worsted on the Continent is in my bag of samples at my hotel. I'm the Continental rep. for the firm that makes it – Stockfield, Hatley and Sons of Bradford. It's my day off to-day. Mr Hodgkin's the name.'

'You're very observant,' said Kenton, who was beginning to feel slightly hysterical.

'Get used to looking at stuffs if you're in the trade,' said Mr Hodgkin. He leaned forward in his seat and raised his voice: '*Sie da! Sollen wir den ganzen Tag hier sitzen bleiben, oder wann geht's los?*'

There was a murmur of agreement from the rest of the coach, and the conductor glared across the heads seeking the author of this call for action.

'Hanging about like a couple of old women!' grumbled Mr Hodgkin, 'and then look narky when you tell them so. That's the worst of the Austrians. Nice chaps when you know them, but gossip! my goodness, they'd make a mothers' meeting sound like a party of deaf mutes. Always talking! – politics mostly. I've been in and out of the country for fifteen years now – my ground covers everything west of the Carpathians and we don't do much beyond there; my brother does London and the Home Counties – and believe me, I've never heard such talkers. I was speaking to a chap in Vienna the other day – Keller. He runs a lot of men's shops. Know him?'

'I can't say I do.'

'He's a big buyer. Everybody knows Keller. Still, he was gassing his head off about Hitler and the *Anschlüss*. "The situation in Germany is serious but not hopeless," he says; "the situation in Austria is hopeless but not serious." Have you ever heard such a lot of crack-brained tripe? That's just like them – gas, gas, gas instead of getting down to business.'

To the journalist's relief the coach started and for a few minutes Mr Hodgkin stared out of the window. Kenton made up his mind to change his seat at the first stop they made. If he were to carry out his intention of slipping away from the party near the frontier it was essential, even if it meant being rude, to disembarrass himself of Mr Hodgkin. The man was obviously the sort who would cling like a leech given the slightest encouragement.

'The Czechs now,' resumed Mr Hodgkin suddenly, 'are different. When I say Czechs, of course, I don't mean Slovenes. A Slovene is no more a Czech than my Aunt Muriel. They know what they're doing, the Czechs. Businesslike. No nonsense. Faith, hope and thirty-three and a third on the gross – that's their motto. The Czech police are pretty hot too,' he added inconsequently.

Kenton began to find these references to police efficiency a little disquieting.

'Business good?' he said.

Mr Hodgkin laughed shortly.

'Am I the Queen of Sheba?' he demanded bitterly. 'I tell you, friend, with labour the price it is in Czecho and Hungary it's a marvel we ever see as much as the smell of an oil rag. I'm selling on quality and that's something these Continental chaps don't understand. The old buyers know me and take my stuff because they like the feel of it. But they won't sell it, and they know it. Too pricey. A pal of mine used to travel for a Northampton shoe firm before the war. Bata came along after the war and killed his trade here stone dead. It's the same all round. The only thing you could sell here nowadays is a nice new line in machine-guns, and the Continental boys have got that business pretty well wrapped up too. In one of my reports home I said I reckoned we ought to start making military uniforms to brisk up business. Of course, I was only having them on. A joke like, see? What do you think they wrote back?'

'What?'

'They said they'd started a new factory doing nothing else; but as they were working night and day on Government contracts, they couldn't take any more orders. That makes you laugh, doesn't it? Still,' said Mr Hodgkin thoughtfully, 'I expect you've got troubles enough of your own without mine. May I ask what your line is?'

'Oh, I'm more or less holiday-making.'

'You don't say!' Mr Hodgkin produced a huge meerschaum with a woman's head carved on the bowl and started to fill it from an oilskin pouch. He kept his eyes fixed on his task as he went on. 'You know, until I saw that jacket of yours, I should have put you down as a German. You spoke German as good as a native when you were talking over the counter. That coat, too—'

Kenton's heart missed a beat.

'I've been in a sanatorium in Bavaria for some time,' he said wildly. 'Chest trouble,' he added.

'Too bad,' said Mr Hodgkin sympathetically. 'Hope everything's O.K. now. I knew a chap—' He broke off suddenly and pointed with his pipe stem out of the window. 'See that? That means snow tonight.'

Kenton followed the other's gaze. The coach was running smoothly down a long tree-lined slope. The sun was shining; but far away to the north-east there was a curious leaden look about the sky.

'I shan't mind bed to-night,' said Mr Hodgkin cheerfully. 'Where are you stopping at Linz?'

Kenton remembered just in time that the representative of Stockfield, Hatley and Sons might have overheard his conversation with the agency clerk.

'I'm leaving for Vienna to-night.'

'Ten o'clock train?'

'Yes.'

'It's the best.'

Mr Hodgkin lit his pipe. There was a volley of excited protest from the woman on Kenton's right. Mr Hodgkin glanced at the woman, drew twice at the meerschaum, inhaled, blew the smoke down his nose and tapped the tobacco out carefully on the floor.

'That's the Continent all over,' he said calmly; 'smoke a cigar like a bit of greasy rope and nobody minds. Put on an honest pipe and what do you get?'

Kenton acknowledged the anomaly and there was silence for a time.

Mr Hodgkin, the journalist decided, was typical of that strange species of Englishman – the export travellers. You came across them in the most unexpected places; in remote Far Eastern towns, on local Continental trains, in the smaller hotels in cities all over Europe. They spoke foreign languages fluently, grammatically, but with appalling accents, and were on excellent terms with all the various nationals with whom they came in contact. They drank foreign drinks, ate foreign foods, listened to foreign points of view and remained completely incurious and indomitably English. For them, the journey from Paris to Istanbul was different only from the journey from London to Manchester in that it was longer and punctuated at irregular intervals by baggage examinations. The cities of the earth were so many railway stations, distinguishable only by the language displayed on the advertisements and the kind of coinage expected by the porters. They were mostly bachelors and spent their summer holidays alone at Bognor or Clacton-on-Sea, drinking tea or sitting near the band. It needed no stretch of imagination to picture Mr Hodgkin in those circumstances. There was, perhaps, a married sister living in Clapham or Hendon who wrote to him once a month. Perhaps . . .

Mr Hodgkin interrupted these reflections by nudging Kenton sharply with his elbow.

'We're stopping at Neukirchen for *Mittagessen*. They'll probably try and scoop us into one of these tourist restaurants and charge us the earth. You and I'll slip off on our own, friend. We'll get better grub, and a darn' sight cheaper.'

Kenton thought quickly. Now was his chance to lose the man, to be rude. He surrendered the opportunity weakly.

'That'll be fine.'

'Good. You've got to watch points with these tourist sharks.'

'I suppose so.'

'Rather! I often do these trips. I like a bit of scenery now and then. Though, mind you, I think Devon or the Lake District have got this licked to a frazzle.'

'In a different way, of course.'

'Any way you like it. Look at it!' They were speeding through a majestic valley. 'Pines, nothing but pines. There's nothing but pines from here to Vladivostock. Dull, uninteresting, no variety.'

'You said you liked scenery.'

'And so I do. I always do this trip when I'm in Linz. But it's not because of the drive. It's the last bit that makes it worth it. You get up about a thousand metres – it's nine hundred odd really – and you can see for miles on a clear day. Of course, there's nothing much actually you can *see*, but you get a real kick out of looking all that way. Leastways, I do. I was real sorry when they talked about pulling down the Eiffel Tower.'

Five minutes later the coach stopped in Neukirchen.

As Mr Hodgkin had predicted, the bulk of the party was shepherded into a picturesque restaurant off the square. Kenton followed his companion down a side-street to an unpretentious eating-house behind the church.

Over a meal of *Wicklkraut* and beer, Mr Hodgkin told several old and salacious anecdotes. All were in a Rabelaisian vein and concerned the amorous adventures of commercial travellers.

'It's a treat,' he said, 'to swop yarns with a Britisher. These foreigners' funny stories are always about politics or suchlike. You wouldn't think so the way they go on, but it's a fact.'

Kenton agreed a little absently and got on with his food. It might be many hours before he could safely eat again. It occurred to him, however, that there was a possibility that Mr Hodgkin might solve one very important problem. Over the brandy, he interrupted a long account of cut-throat competition in Jugoslavia by asking if Mr Hodgkin knew Prague.

'Like the back of my hand,' was the prompt reply. 'It's quite a nice city. The lavatories are as clean as the German, which is more than you can say for Italy, even if they do have German plumbing. Mussolini might have a go at them as well as the trains. Not that that trains-running-to-time business isn't all my eye. It's only the tourist trains. The last time I went from Cremona to Rome we were forty minutes late, and packed like sardines with a lot of *caribinieri* going to have medals handed out to them.'

'I've always liked Prague, too,' persisted Kenton; 'I wonder if you know a man named Bastaki.'

'Who?'

'Bastaki.'

Mr Hodgkin turned down the corners of his mouth, and shook his head slowly.

'No. Name seems familiar somehow, but I can't place it. What does he do?'

'I don't know. A friend of mine mentioned him.'

Mr Hodgkin screwed up his eyes, raised his right hand and snapped his fingers several times as if to summon Divine assistance.

'What nationality?' he said suddenly.

Kenton, convinced that Mr Hodgkin could not help him, took a long shot.

'Roumanian.'

A look of amazement spread over Mr Hodgkin's face. Then he tapped the table lightly but triumphantly with his forefinger.

'Got it!'

'You know the man?'

'Got it! I knew I'd heard the name somewhere. Bastaki! He's in Prague.'

Kenton's heart sank.

'Yes, I knew he was in Prague.'

'Bastaki, that's the man!' Mr Hodgkin continued excitedly: 'I suppose your friend isn't Eccles, of Parker, Sons and Kelsey of Oldham?'

'I'm afraid not.'

'Well, that's a pity. You'd like Eccles. I only run across him once in a month of Sundays. He's a nice chap. Parker, Sons and Kelsey do a bit of business over here, but Eccles spends a lot of his time in Oldham. He likes Oldham, though, of course; he's got a nice house just outside. Married. Got two grown-up youngsters. The boy's in the Navy.'

'He knows Bastaki?'

'Of course, that's what I'm telling you. Bastaki's one of his customers in the electrical trade. Eccles is in cotton, of course.'

'But you said Bastaki is in the electrical trade.'

'Yes, that's right – cable-making. Use hundreds of miles of yarn a year for insulation. Braiding, that's what they call it. Eccles sells him the stuff in bobbins – hundreds of miles of it. He's got a factory outside Prague.'

'Who? Eccles?' Kenton was getting confused.

'No, Bastaki. Pots of money, of course, and as fly as they come. Eccles says Bastaki's father owns pretty near half Roumania – industry, not land, of course. Like that bloke de Wendel in France, only not so big. His wife's a Czech or something.'

'Bastaki's wife?'

'That's right. It's a pity you don't know Eccles. He's a nice chap. If you run across him, give him my love and tell him he owes me a couple of francs. He'll know what it's for.' He leered roguishly.

Sensing that some sort of joke had been made, Kenton laughed and promised to pass on the message.

'Well,' continued Mr Hodgkin seriously, 'I suppose we ought to be getting back now. Not that they'll be ready to start.'

Half an hour later the coach left Neukirchen and ran once more into the open country.

Mr Hodgkin seemed, for the moment, to have nothing more to say and, after a second unsuccessful attempt to smoke his pipe, stared gloomily out of the window. Kenton, who had plenty to think about, pretended to doze.

Bastaki was a Roumanian. His father was an important Roumanian industrialist. Saridza was meeting him. In association those facts told their own story. And it was a very familiar story. What the Thyssens and Krupps did for Hitler, the Bastakis and Balterghens could do for Codreanu. For the first time since he had left Rashenko's room he felt that he had been wise to do so. Not even the consciousness that his plans were, to say the least of it, hazy, that, in fact, he had not the remotest idea what he was going to do with his knowledge, could dispel a sense of quiet elation. He reminded himself that he was still well inside Austria, that he had a frontier to cross without showing a passport, and that he had acquired, with his information about Bastaki, the leech-like representative of Stockfield, Hatley and Sons of Bradford. He came to the conclusion that elation was a trifle premature. He must devise some plan of action, something simple yet something ingenious and effective. But it was warm and comfortable in the coach. He had arrears of sleep to make up. He found it difficult to concentrate on the problems of the future, however immediate they might be. Unaccountably, he found himself thinking of Zaleshoff's sister. In his note, Zaleshoff had declared caustically that her maternal instincts had been aroused. He smiled to himself. It was pleasant to think of her. Her hands were lovely. Maternal? That was what Zaleshoff *would* say, of course. A lovely mouth.

The chatter of the other passengers and the hum of the coach seemed to recede slightly. A minute later his head nodded forward on to his chest and he was asleep.

He awoke with a start, Mr Hodgkin's elbow at work on his ribs.

'We're there, friend.'

'Ah yes! I must have dropped off to sleep for a moment.'

'Best part of an hour,' said Mr Hodgkin.

Kenton looked out of the window.

The coach was grinding slowly over the crest of a steep hill. Trees grew almost to the edges of the road. A little way ahead was a small highly coloured timber inn set back from the road in a clearing. The coach stopped outside it.

'This is us, friend.'

They got out shivering. Mr Hodgkin peered at Kenton over his misted spectacles.

'Do you want to follow the others or shall I show you a better spot? I found it two years ago.'

Kenton glanced uncertainly at the rest of the passengers being marshalled by the conductor for the walk to the heights.

'Won't the conductor think we're lost?'

'Fat lot he cares. They've had our money.'

'All right.'

Mr Hodgkin led the way down a path beside the inn. For a hundred yards or so the way was clearly defined, then the path lost itself among the trees.

'Straight ahead,' said Mr Hodgkin.

The inn was now completely out of sight and they were threading their way among the trunks of tall firs growing so closely together that the foliage overhead almost shut out the sunlight. It was very cold and quiet. Except for the faint stirring of the branches above, there was no sound but the crunching of fir cones under their feet. After a little the ground sloped sharply upwards and there was a gleam of light between the trees. A minute later they had left the forest and were standing in a rocky clearing a few yards across. On three sides of it the firs rose like stockades. On the fourth there was nothing but the wooded hills of Bohemia rolling away into the distance, an unbroken wave of green-black monotony.

'There!' said Mr Hodgkin.

'It's a splendid view.'

Mr Hodgkin drew a deep breath and nodded.

'It's fine,' he murmured.

He sighed and gazed out solemnly towards the grey, misty horizon.

Kenton was racking his brains for an idea. It would have been better to have gone with the rest. He might at least have been able to lose himself until they had gone. What could he do now? Run? It seemed the only way. The ground sloping away from the promontory was not very steep and the trees started again a short way down. Even if Hodgkin ran after him, he would lose him among the trees. The man would soon grow tired of searching. But he might report the occurrence to the conductor. If . . .

Then he saw that the little man's shrewd eyes were watching him. He smiled.

'The air's good,' he said.

Mr Hodgkin looked away.

'The frontier is four miles from here,' he said slowly; 'if you start now, you'll reach it by dusk, Mr Kenten.'

For a moment Kenton felt as if a bomb had exploded under him. He knew that there was something he should say, but his brain seemed numb. It seemed to him that he had stood there for hours before he uttered a sound. At last:

'Kent*on*, not Kent*en*,' he said. It was the best he could do.

Mr Hodgkin turned his head. There was the suspicion of a grin on his thin lips.

'Sorry, friend, they've got Kent*en* in the papers.'

'A small point,' said Kenton evenly. He was beginning to recover himself. 'When did you spot me?'

'As soon as you walked into that agency.' He looked grave. 'I tell you, friend, you've had some pretty good luck to-day. You deserved to be copped. You walk into a travel agency two minutes after the police have been in making inquiries about you there, peek right and left like you were a villain on the pictures, and start glaring at a map and mumbling in English. You've got a bit of scrub on your upper lip that looks about a day old and an English tweed jacket showing under an overcoat that doesn't fit you. Then you marches up to the counter and say you've only got an hour or two to spare, but you'll take a trip that lasts eight. You nearly fall over yourself you're in such an almighty hurry to get a back seat; then you grab a Genoa sailing list as though you're pinching the till. You see a policeman and look as if you're going to have a heart attack, tell me you're leaving for Vienna by a train that doesn't run, and start asking questions about one of the best biggest twisters from here to Shanghai. You say you've been in a sanatorium in Bavaria, but you speak German with the best Berlin accent I've heard outside of Berlin for a long time. And, if you'll pardon my mentioning it, there's a stain the size of Lake Geneva on the back of your right sleeve that looks like blood. That Froggy in the coach had his eye on you, and if we hadn't been talking so friendly, he'd have done something about it. While you were having a snooze he told his wife about it, and if she hadn't been having a fit of the sulks because of his nagging her and not told him he was seeing things, you'd have been for the high jump when we stopped. I saw him looking at the reward in the paper, and you know what the French think about money. Yes, friend, you've been pretty lucky.'

Kenton laughed rather shakily.

'It's no laughing matter,' said Mr Hodgkin severely, 'and you aren't clear yet. The frontier's four miles ahead and you have to veer slightly to your right, because the road bends to the right towards the frontier. And when you're actually crossing it, look out for alarm bells. They sometimes put them down for smugglers. If you get through – I said "if", because, mind you, I don't think you will – if you get through, you can pick up a bus at one of the villages on the other side that'll take you to Budweis. There you'll be O.K. for a train. But for goodness' sake, get rid of that coat and hat. They're poison.'

Mr Hodgkin turned away, and began to fill his pipe. There was a pause.

'Have you gone yet?' he asked over his shoulder.

'No,' said Kenton; 'I was waiting to thank you, to say good-bye and to shake hands.'

Mr Hodgkin turned his head grimly.

'Listen, friend,' he said, 'I've done a lot for you to-day. I don't say it's been a hardship, because that'd be lies. I've enjoyed having one of my own countrymen to talk to. But if you think I'm going to shake hands with a cold-blooded murderer, you've got another think coming.'

'Then,' said Kenton angrily, 'do you mind explaining why, if you believe I'm the cold-blooded murderer these asinine police seem to think, you are not giving me up and collecting the reward?'

A curious expression crossed Mr Hodgkin's sharp pinched face.

'Why?' he echoed derisively; 'I'll tell you why, friend. Listen. If this was England I'd hand you over to the nearest copper I could see because that'd be the proper thing to do, guilty or not guilty. Why don't I hand you over now? The answer is, friend, because I'm getting a bit of my own back. Fifteen years I've been trailing about this blasted Continent now, and I've hated every moment of it. I hate their grub, I hate their drinks, I hate their way of going on, and I hate them. They say the British are all stuck up about foreigners, that we're all men and women just the same, that they've got a lot of good points that we haven't. It's all lies, and when you've been away from home as long as I have, you'll know it, too. They're not like us, not at all. People come over here for a fortnight's holiday and see a lot of pretty *chalets* and *châteaux* and *Schlösser* and say what a fine place it is to live in. They don't know what they're talking about. They only see the top coat. They don't see the real differences. They don't see behind the scenes. They don't see them when their blood's up. I've seen them all right. I was in sunny Italy when the Fascisti went for the freemasons in twenty-five. Florence it was. Night after night of it with shooting and beating and screams, till you felt like vomiting. I was in Vienna in thirty-four when they turned the guns on the municipal flats with the women and children inside them. A lot of the men they strung up afterwards had to be lifted on to the gallows because of their wounds. I saw the Paris riots with the *garde mobile* shooting down the crowd like flies and everyone howling *"mort aux vaches"* like lunatics. I saw the Nazis in Frankfurt kick a man to death in his front garden. After the first he never made a sound. I was arrested that night because I'd seen it, but they had to let me go. In Spain, they tell me, they doused men with petrol and set light to them.

'Nice chaps, aren't they? Picturesque, gay, cleverer, more logical than silly us. Good business men they are, too. You can't move your little finger without paying graft. The factory owners treat the work-people nearly as good as pigs. Why not? There're always other poor devils round the corner so desperate for a meal that they'd blackleg for anyone. If a man's sacked, he's blacklisted by every factory owner in the district. Talk to a foreign office worker. He spends half his life scared out of his wits wondering if the man on the stool next to him is trying to pinch his job. The bosses like that. It keeps people from asking for more money, and that means they can turn out more filthy mass-production trash even cheaper than before. They take no pride in the stuff they produce. They don't know what craftsmanship means. They don't care. They're out to make money. I don't blame them for that. We all are. But they don't want to give value for money. They don't think that way. Business for them isn't honest trading. It's just another sort of politics and nearly as crooked. "How much is this cloth?" they ask me. I'll tell them. They'll laugh; and when I tell them to look at the quality they get wild and hold up a piece of fifth-rate muck that I wouldn't use to polish my boots, and tell me it's cheaper. They don't talk the same language as us. I don't mean that they don't speak English, but that their minds are different. They're like animals, and because I hate the sight and sound of them, and because you're a Britisher, I'm telling you to get out now while the going's good. Now for God's sake get out and leave me.'

His thin face was flushed, he was breathing quickly, there were tears glistening behind his spectacles. He looked away.

The journalist watched him for a moment, then turned on his heel and started down the slope towards the trees. When he reached them he stopped and looked back up the hill to the promontory; but Mr Hodgkin had gone.

Sick at heart, Kenton walked on among the trees. The air was heavy with the scent of pines, and the sun filtering through obliquely from the west made patterns of light on the soft brown surface of the hillside. It was, he thought, better than the view from Mr Hodgkin's promontory.

13

Barbed Wire

By nightfall Kenton was within a few yards of the frontier.

It had taken longer than he had expected. With vague memories of reading that persons unused to forests lost their senses of direction and walked in circles, he had made repeated detours to re-establish contact with the road. In this way the four miles had become more like six. The sun had gone down and the light was going when at last he saw, from the edge of the road about a quarter of a mile away, the small white guardhouse and the striped barrier of the frontier post against a dusky and smouldering sky.

He retreated into the forest until he had put about a kilometre between himself and the road, and then began to work his way forward.

He was now in darkness and there was only the upward slope of the ground to guide him. He continued in this way for about twenty minutes, then the ground became level, the pines thinned, and putting out his hand to feel for obstacles ahead, he touched the smooth, cold surface of a sawn-off tree stump. He halted. By the faint early evening light, no longer shut out by the trees, he could distinguish the outline of a clump of bushes. He moved forward and came up against another tree stump. He was in the frontier clearing.

He remained still for a moment and listened. There was not a sound but the faint sighing of the stiffening breeze. Then, far away on his left a pin-point of light flashed. He watched, and a minute later the light appeared again. This time, however, it did not go out but bobbed jerkily from side to side. For a moment or two he was puzzled, then, as the light grew slightly larger and brighter, he realized that someone was coming, and that whoever it was, was flashing a hand-lamp among the bushes. He stepped back hastily into the shadow of the trees and crouched down.

The light came nearer and Kenton could hear the crunch of a man's feet on what was evidently a path. The footsteps grew louder and the light winked through the bushes. The man drew level. He was humming softly. The light swept across the ground once and he was past.

Kenton stood up quickly and peered after him. The man was in uniform, and had a rifle slung over his left shoulder. Of more immediate interest to Kenton was what he could see by the light of the lamp. It depressed him profoundly.

He was about thirty yards from the actual frontier line. From where he stood on the edge of the forest to the path there was roughly twenty yards of half-cleared ground, dotted with tree stumps and squat, scrubby bushes. The path itself was about six feet wide and covered with large grey stone chips and a sprinkling of weeds. Beyond the path the ground sloped up sharply to the most formidable-looking fence Kenton had ever seen.

It was about eight feet high and composed of barbed wires stretched tightly between heavy steel stanchions, grounded into concrete bases at intervals of ten feet. The wires were so close together than it would have been difficult to push so much as a hand between them without the barbs drawing blood; but the designer of the fence had evidently meant to leave nothing to chance, for the horizontal strands had been festooned with so many additional coils of wire that the structure looked more like a bramble thicket than a fence.

Kenton sat on a tree stump to think things over.

One thing was clear. There could be no crawling through the fence. If he had had a pair of heavy wire-cutters, and thick armoured gloves, he might have tackled it with that end in view; but he had neither cutters nor gloves. Besides, he did not want to leave any trace of his passage across the frontier if he could avoid doing so. He had no wish to have the Czech authorities on the look-out for him at the frontier towns. He considered putting his overcoat on top of the fence and endeavouring to climb over, then concluded that this was impossible. He would need several thicknesses of blanket to muffle the wire sufficiently; and, even if he could get across that way, it would be difficult to retrieve his coat once it was entangled in the wire. He toyed wildly with the idea of getting a long branch from somewhere and using it as a pole with which to vault over; but this he soon abandoned. He had never attempted to vault eight feet, even with a proper pole. He would probably break a leg and be impaled on the top of the fence. He shivered miserably. The wind was blowing harder, and it was bitterly cold. He remembered Mr Hodgkin's prophecy of snow. Should he return to Linz? He promptly rejected the suggestion. Even if he could find some means of getting back there, there was the risk of capture. Mr Hodgkin's catalogue of his blunders had shaken his confidence in his ability to avoid arrest. There was nothing for it but to get across the frontier – somehow. It ought not to be so difficult. According to their biographers, men like Lenin and Trotsky, Masaryk and Benes, Mussolini and Bela Kun, to say nothing of their friends, had spent half their political lives 'slipping across' frontiers with prices on their heads and no passports in their pockets. But perhaps the rising generations of frontier officials had read those biographies too.

He glanced in the direction in which the guard had gone, saw that the coast was clear and crossed the path to the fence.

It might, he thought, be possible to climb up one of the stanchions, using the horizontal wires as steps. A few seconds' careful exploration with his fingers showed, however, that the bulk of loose wire made this impossible. There was only one thing to be done. If he could not go through the fence or over it, he must go *under* it. He knelt down and investigated. To his joy, he found that the ground at the foot of the fence consisted for the most part of large stones which had been piled up to form a small embankment. He began to pull them away, and after about five minutes' work, was able to push his hand under the bottom wire. Suddenly he stood up and scurried back to the shelter of the trees. The guard with the light was returning.

Kenton crouched behind a tree until the man had passed. Then he went back to the fence and worked away furiously at the stones and earth. Speed was essential, for as the gap under the wire grew larger the risk of its being seen by any more guards who might patrol the fence increased. There was an additional danger, too, in the shape of the guards on the Czech side. So far there had been no sign of life from the other side of the fence; but he could not rely upon that state of affairs continuing.

Twenty minutes later the gap was wide and deep enough for him to get his head and shoulders through and he was experimenting with this development when he had to dash once more for cover as the light of the returning guard approached.

This time Kenton was thoroughly frightened. The breach in the embankment was now about a yard wide and surrounded by loose stones and earth. The guard must see it. Cursing the man's conscientious prowling, Kenton nursed his grazed and ice-cold fingers anxiously among the trees.

The guard came on steadily. Suddenly, within a yard or two of the breach, he stopped. Kenton heard him emit a grunt. His heart in his mouth, the journalist waited for the shot that would give the alarm. He crouched down, his heart thumping painfully. Then, in the silence, he heard the sound of footsteps approaching from the right. A second or two later someone coughed and said: '*Guten Abend.*'

''*n Abend*,' answered the man on the path.

'*Heute abend wird's schneien.*'

'*Jawohl.*'

'*Ich bin mal wieder schwer erkältet.*'

'*Das tut mir leid – gute Besserung. Bei mir sind's die Füsse.*'

'*Gerade diese Woche muss ich Nachtdienst haben.*'

'*Ich hab's besser. Schultz hat morgen abend diesen Dienst.*'

'*Ich mach mir nichts aus Schultz. Er tut so vornehm.*'

'*Er ist nicht besonders beliebt. Er kommt von Carinthia und ist immer unzufrieden.*'

Kenton listened to this gossip for a few moments, then cautiously raised himself until he could see the speakers. The Austrian guard was standing on the path, his lamp shining through the fence on to the feet of a man in the uniform of a Czech infantryman; and, to Kenton's horror, they were six feet from the gap. Fortunately the Czech guard had extinguished the small torch he carried, but as they talked the Austrian displayed a growing tendency to gesture with the hand holding the flashlamp.

'We have been told,' the Austrian was saying, 'to keep a special look out for the Englishman, Kenten, who murdered that German in Linz.'

'He has been seen?'

'A woman reported that there were two Englishmen on a tourist bus making a tour in this direction. When they got out at the inn, one of them did not return. She has been questioned by the police, and says that she thinks that the one who returned is the murderer. She says he scowled a lot at her and smoked a pipe; but it appears his papers are in order. Of the other, nothing is said but that we must keep a look out for him. The Neukirchen police are fools.'

He waved the hand holding the lamp disdainfully and the beam danced across the ground near the gap. Kenton waited breathlessly for discovery; but the guard went on talking, and at last the Czech announced that he had to report at the guard-house and moved off. The Austrian continued on his way to the right.

The moment they were out of earshot, Kenton went back to his work. Below the stones he struck solid earth and progress was slower; but after another quarter of an hour, and a little feverish experiment, he found that by wriggling forward on his back, and holding the bottom wire away from his face and clothes, he could squeeze through. Having carefully piled the stones by the edge of the hole so that he could refill the breach from the other side, he prepared to go. Two minutes later, dishevelled and very dirty he crawled into Czechoslovakia.

He had just crammed the last of the loose stones back into place when he heard footsteps approaching from the direction of the road. In his excitement he had slackened his watch on the paths and the man was quite close. The intermittent flashing of the light told him that it was the Czech guard – the Austrian kept his lamp switched on the whole time. There was not a moment to lose. He turned and dashed blindly for cover; but he had gone no more than a dozen paces when his foot caught in a tree stump. Desperately he tried to recover his balance, then he stumbled again and went down flat on his face. The next instant his outstretched fingers touched a thick strand of rusty wire. In a flash, he remembered Mr Hodgkin's warning about alarm bells. There was no time now to get up and go on. He lay still, praying feverishly that the good luck which had saved him from blundering against the alarm wire would hold out for the next two minutes.

As the footsteps approached they seemed to accelerate slightly, then slow down. A few yards from where the journalist lay, paralysed with fright, they almost stopped. The guard had evidently heard something of the noise of Kenton's fall. The torch flickered among the tree stumps. Then a man started to cough. It was a heavy bronchial cough and painful, for Kenton heard the man gasp out an oath as the paroxysm subsided. The torch went out and the heavy boots grated once more on the stones. The man went by and his footsteps died away.

Kenton took a deep breath and stood up. Then, holding the rusty wire carefully between his thumb and forefinger, he stepped over it and went on slowly.

Once in the forest again, however, he pushed on as quickly as he could. It would not do, he decided, to return to the road too near the frontier post. Travellers on foot would probably be rare on that part of the road, and it was just possible that he might be stopped and asked to show his passport. Accordingly he set a course which he judged would bring him to the road about a mile from the frontier. But in the darkness and among the trees, he soon lost his bearings, and after an hour's walking, came out on the road less than a hundred yards from the frontier post. Deciding that it must be getting late, he made up his mind to follow the road from the fringe of the forest, and use the trees as cover only if he met with any traffic. But the road was deserted. A clock somewhere was striking eight o'clock when, ten minutes later, having dusted himself down and straightened his tie, he walked into the village of Manfurth.

In the tiny square a ramshackle bus was standing outside the post office with lights on and engine running. Inside sat a peasant woman with a crate of live chickens. On the step, clasping a huge composition suitcase, was a grinning and bashful young labourer bidding good-bye to a hilarious group in the roadway.

Kenton glanced at the destination board. The bus was bound, via Hohenfurth, Silberberg and Kaplitz, for Budweis.

At a quarter to twelve that night the train from Budweis steamed slowly into Prague.

In his empty compartment, Kenton stood up, put his left hand into his pocket so that the sleeve of his overcoat was hidden and went into the corridor.

The train clanked to a standstill. He got down, walked along the platform, gave his ticket up at the barrier, and crossed to the nearest exit.

The station was crowded, and he did not notice the two men until they were level with him. Suddenly his arms were linked forcibly with those on either side of him and he felt the hard ring of a gun barrel pressed under his rib-case. His heart sank.

'Herr Kenton?'

He hesitated, then shrugged his shoulders. They had got him. How, he couldn't think; but since they had got him, it was not much use trying to brazen things out. Might as well bow to the inevitable. He nodded.

'Ja.'

'Gut.'

They led him through the exit and down the steps to a large closed Mercedes with a uniformed chauffeur.

One of the men got in the back. His companion prodded Kenton after him.

'Einsteigen!'

Kenton got in, followed by the man with the revolver and sat in the middle. The blinds were pulled down and the car started. For the first time the journalist began to wonder if he ought not to have asked the men for their warrants. They looked like police, but there was an unusual informality about their behaviour.

He turned suddenly to the man on his left.

'Where are you taking me?' he said in German.

'*Stillschweigen!*'

The revolver was rammed into his side to enforce the instruction.

Kenton relapsed into his seat thinking furiously. If they were not the police then who on earth were they and where were they taking him?

His destination was not, it seemed, in Prague itself. The car was travelling fast and, after ten minutes, twisting and turning and hooting, settled down to a straight run on a road which, from the smoothness of the surface and the banking on the bends, he judged to be a main road out of the city.

He glanced at his captors. Nondescript, clean-shaven men with black mackintoshes and dark grey felt hats, they looked, he excused himself, typical Continental plain-clothes policemen. By way of starting a conversation, he asked if he might smoke. The man with the revolver, who appeared to be in command, grunted permission, but shook his head when offered a cigarette. The other man did not answer at all. Kenton gave it up.

A few minutes later, the car swung to the left and dropped downhill; then it bore to the right again, slowed down and stopped.

For a moment or two no one made any movement to get out. Then the door of the car was opened from outside.

'*Heraussteigen!*'

Kenton climbed out and, flanked by his escort, mounted a broad flight of steps leading to an imposing pair of doors. He had no time to do more than catch a glimpse of the façade of a large, expensive-looking house when the doors were opened by the chauffeur, and he was ushered into a long, narrow and brilliantly lighted hall.

A door at the far end opened, and a man came out and hurried forward beaming. For a moment, Kenton was too surprised to speak. Then he nodded slowly.

'I might have known it,' he said grimly.

'You might indeed,' chuckled Zaleshoff. 'But I expected you by an earlier train. You must be tired. Come on in and have a drink. Tamara's looking forward to seeing you again,' he added, and on his lips was the confidential smile of a match-making dowager.

Kenton walked down the hall in a daze. He was beginning to wonder whether it might not be he who was mad.

14

Manœuvres

Kenton glanced round the room into which he had been led and nodded appreciatively.

'Nice place you have here.'

Zaleshoff looked up from the tray of drinks.

'The man who owns it is a secret admirer of the late lamented Empress Eugenie. That explains the decorations. Frankly, they make me a little uneasy.' He handed Kenton a whisky and soda.

The journalist took it and held it up to the light.

'No knock-out drops, no little-known vegetable poisons, no dopes?' he asked tentatively.

Zaleshoff frowned.

'I've had occasion to notice in you before, Kenton, an irritating habit of facetiousness. If you don't want the drink, say so before I pour out another for myself.'

Kenton put the glass down and sighed.

'Sorry, Andreas, but you really can't blame me. You push off and leave me holding a nasty little baby in the shape of a murder charge; I ask your henchman, Rashenko, for a little help in getting away, and he gives me an overcoat stained with blood, which, I can't help feeling, once belonged to a gentleman named Borovansky – the blood I mean; then you send along a couple of thugs disguised as detectives, to kidnap me. Now you offer me a drink. Why, in Heaven's name, *shouldn't* it be doped?'

The door of the room opened and Tamara came in. Her face lighted up when she saw Kenton. He nodded distantly. She smiled.

'I'm glad you got here safely.'

'Mr Kenton was just explaining,' put in her brother, 'that he suspects me of poisoning his whisky and soda.'

'What nonsense!'

'For goodness' sake,' exploded Kenton angrily, 'let's get down to business and leave this cross-talk until later. Why the devil have you brought me here? Don't bother to embroider it. It's just the plain facts I want, that's all. I'm feeling tired.'

'Now, now,' said Zaleshoff soothingly, 'let's sit down and talk things over. Take your coat off.'

'I'm not stopping.'

'As you please. At any rate, do sit down.'

'You know darn' well it's not as I please. I'm not such a numskull as to think you brought me here for a drink and a chat.'

'Well then, why keep your coat on?'

Kenton glared at the Russian for a moment. Then he mastered his rising temper. He must, he told himself, keep cool. He took off the overcoat. Zaleshoff took it from him and held out the left sleeve for the girl's inspection.

'You see,' he said, 'it doesn't show unless you're behind a man wearing it. Rashenko can hardly be blamed. He could not have seen it.'

'Of course,' put in Kenton sarcastically, 'I'm only the mug who's been wearing the coat. I can hardly expect you to give me any sort of explanation.'

Zaleshoff patted him on the arm.

'Now listen, Mr Kenton. When I left Linz this morning I wrote you a note asking you to wait at Rashenko's room until I could fix things for you. Why didn't you?'

'Because I don't trust you. Why should I? Why should you bother about me? You have your job to do. It's probably very convenient for you to have me accused of murder instead of that nasty-looking employee of yours on the train.'

'Employee? Train?'

'Certainly. Men's hats acquire a personality of their own when they've been worn a bit. You've probably noticed it. My hats always look as if I've picked them out of the garbage bin after I've had them a week. It's the way I pull them on. Your hats, I should say, always look as though you sat on them hard every morning. You probably grip the crown too hard as you put them on.'

'Very interesting, but . . .'

'When Rashenko gave me this hat it seemed vaguely familiar. On the train tonight I did a bit of thinking. Then I remembered where I'd seen it. It was on the head of the man Sachs told me was a Nazi spy. I didn't remember the coat well enough to identify that as well; but putting two and two together it seemed that the owner of the hat was probably the owner of the coat too, and a friend of yours. The coat had a bloodstain on the sleeve, Sachs had been scared out of his wits by the man wearing it, I had found Sachs stabbed. Well, how would that have looked to you?'

Zaleshoff pursed his lips.

'You said, "putting two and two together", Mr Kenton. What did you mean by that?'

'Rashenko got that hat and coat from somewhere in his house. He didn't go out because he was in a dressing-gown.'

'And so you decided to come to Prague?'

'Yes.'

'How did you get here? Did you show your passport?'

'I'm not a fool all the time. I sneaked across the frontier at Manfurth.'

Zaleshoff whistled.

'Manfurth! Whatever made you choose that spot? It's much easier farther south.'

'I couldn't see another road on the map. Besides, the woods gave me plenty of cover.'

'I should say you needed it. Did you say you came *across* the frontier? Do you mean you climbed over it?'

'To be precise, I crawled underneath it.' He explained what he had done.

'There, Tamara!' said Zaleshoff delightedly, 'there's resource for you! Only do remember another time, my dear fellow, that the stretches of frontier that look easiest on the map are always the best guarded.'

'I'm hoping I shan't have to make a practice of it.'

Zaleshoff laughed uproariously.

'You know, Tamara, I like this guy Kenton. He amuses me.'

'Not nearly as much as you amuse me, Andreas,' said Kenton grimly. 'You've a really charming way of edging the conversation away from an awkward subject. Let's get back to the point.'

Zaleshoff sighed.

'Very well.'

'Good. Now, I came to Prague with an object in view. That object was to steal those photographs back from Saridza and do a deal with you. My price for the photographs was going to be your friend with the nasty face, in a parcel, complete with evidence ready for the police.'

'And, always assuming that you could get the photographs – a fatuous assumption – how, pray, were you proposing to get into touch with me?'

'Through the Soviet Embassy.'

There was a pause. It was the girl who broke the silence.

'A little optimistic, weren't you, Mr Kenton?'

'Not so optimistic as you might imagine. This morning I remembered one little piece of information that I'd forgotten to give Andreas here. It was something Saridza said to Mailler. It seemed unimportant at the time. Now, I think, it has become vital.'

'What is it?' snapped Zaleshoff.

Kenton shook his head.

'Nothing doing, Andreas,' he said. 'Being wanted for murder you didn't commit has a curious effect. You become strangely secretive.'

Again there was a pause.

'You realize, Mr Kenton,' said Zaleshoff at last, 'that I could, if I wished, *make* you talk?'

'Now you're being really silly.'

'Not at all. Supposing, only supposing, mind you, that I were able to tell you that I knew who murdered Borovansky. Supposing I told you that I had intended from the start to use that knowledge to free you from suspicion. Supposing I told you that, in view of your pig-headedness, I had decided to hand you over to the police forthwith. What would you say?'

'I'd still say you were silly.'

'Would you? I don't think you realize just how good the police case against you is.'

'I realize it only too well. I say you're being silly because I know that it's far more important to you that you should have a line on Saridza than that you should shield the real murderer or score off me.'

The girl laughed.

'Very good, Mr Kenton! Very good indeed! Now do drink your whisky and soda. It really is quite harmless.'

'And for pity's sake sit down,' added Zaleshoff irritably. 'It's quite impossible to think with you standing about.'

Kenton sat down beside the girl and sipped at his drink cautiously.

'You really have very little to think about, Andreas,' he said. 'Are you going to talk business with me or aren't you? It's very simple.'

Zaleshoff looked at him thoughtfully for a moment.

'You know, Kenton,' he said at last, 'the trouble with you is that you were born a member of one of the ruling races. Your sense of danger is deficient, your conceit is monumental. Or is it, I wonder, that you lack imagination?'

'You mean that I'm in no position to dictate terms?'

'Exactly. Those men who brought you here are both good shots with revolvers. And, what is more, they have no inhibitions to spoil their aim when the target is alive. You could not leave this house without my express permission.'

'I can't think why you got me here.'

'Probably not. Would you be very surprised if I told you that it was largely for your own good?'

'Very surprised; and, if you will forgive my saying so, rather sceptical.'

'Naturally.'

The Russian rose and walked the length of the room and back.

He stopped in front of the journalist's chair and looked down at him aggressively.

'Listen,' he said, 'I don't believe you've got anything at all on Saridza that you haven't told me. I think you're bluffing; but I can't call your bluff. Frankly, I want those photographs badly. If I don't get them – well, there'll be trouble and it won't be only in Roumania. If you've got a speck of information that I haven't got, then I can't risk ignoring it. *Have* you got any information?'

'Yes.'

'I hope so. In any case I'm going to give you what you want. I'm going to tell you who murdered Borovansky and how you're going to get out of the spot you're in. But I tell you this. You're not going to do anything about it until I say so. You're here now and here you'll stay until I'm ready. You'll see why. Then you can tell me what you know – if anything.'

'I know something all right.'

'I doubt it.'

Zaleshoff poured himself out another drink, swallowed it at a gulp and sat down in an armchair.

'When Borovansky left Berlin a friend of mine there put a man named Ramon Ortega, a Spaniard, to follow him and recover the photographs in Austria.'

'Ortega being the owner of my hat and coat,' put in Kenton.

'If you're going to interrupt . . .'

'Sorry.'

'Ortega was told to steal the photographs. He exceeded his instructions. When he got to the Hotel Josef he stabbed Borovansky. He said Borovansky pulled a gun but he was probably lying. Ortega, you see, *liked* stabbing people. He once worked in a slaughter-house in Ceuta. He may have acquired the taste for it there.'

'Sachs did have a gun in a holster under his arm. It was gone when I found him.'

'Ortega took it. What he didn't take was the photographs. You had them. Anyhow, Ortega got out of the back entrance and went to Kölnerstrasse 11. Rashenko arranged to hide him in an empty room on the floor below. The next thing that happened was that the police got on to you. Now that was awkward because, while I'm no sentimentalist, I'm not quite the man you evidently think me. I didn't much like the idea of a man being run for a killing he didn't do. So I persuaded Master Ortega to write and sign a confession.'

'Just asked him kindly if he'd mind signing a life sentence for himself in an Austrian prison, I suppose?' said Kenton unpleasantly.

Zaleshoff bounded to his feet with a roar of anger.

'Tamara,' he snarled, 'tell this reporter, this – this bum scribbler, that when he's ready to listen I'm ready to talk.'

'All right, all right,' said Kenton hastily, 'no offence meant. I was just asking.'

'I'm not asking you to ask,' said Zaleshoff violently, 'just telling you to listen.'

'I'm listening.'

'Well, all right then. Only listen and don't make any more dumb cracks.'

'Sorry.'

'Ortega confessed because he darn' well had to and because it didn't matter a nickel to him either way. He's wanted for murder in Lisbon and I threatened to turn him in for extradition unless he confessed to killing Borovansky. Naturally, I didn't tell him why I wanted the confession. He thought it was because we wanted another screw to turn on him in the future. Besides, what's one conviction more or less to a guy like that? He may be wanted in Spain too, for all I know. Both Portugal and Austria have abolished the death sentence for murder and he couldn't be in two prisons at once, so what the hell? Anyhow, I'd got his confession ready to use if things got hot for you. The difficulty was this. I had work to do. If you were arrested you'd certainly tell your little story and that might be inconvenient at present. If I'd fixed it for Ortega to be taken he'd have spilled *his* story too with a bit added on. When Rashenko telephoned that you'd gone, my first idea was that you'd decided to give yourself up. It was lucky for you you didn't. You'd have been in a nasty jam and made it difficult for me to help you. The police don't like having to do any more thinking once they've got what they've decided is their man. But Rashenko said you were coming to Prague and that as I'd not told him to keep you there by force he'd let you go and given you Ortega's things as well. If he'd thought there was a possibility of your going to the police, he'd have put a bullet in you before he'd have let you go; but he's fairly shrewd when it comes to weighing people up, and he reckoned you were telling the truth about going to Prague. The only thing he didn't spot was the bloodstain on that sleeve. When I told him about it on the telephone he nearly threw a fit. I must say I was a little anxious until you arrived. I suppose you realize that it was that stain on your sleeve that enabled those two men to pick you up at the station?'

'How does Rashenko talk on the telephone if he's dumb?'

'He's got a special signalling arrangement hooked up.'

'Hm! I still don't see why he had to give me Ortega's things.'

Zaleshoff sighed noisily.

'Because, my dear Mr Kenton, it would have been too dangerous to buy them in a shop in a town the size of Linz. The police, you know, are not complete fools.'

'Well, well, and what's the next move? I suppose I'm expected to hang about here until you're ready to tell the Austrian police that I'm innocent.'

'That's right,' said Zaleshoff blandly, 'although, of course, it won't be quite as simple as that. Ortega must be discovered in suitable circumstances. There must be no question of myself or Rashenko becoming involved. In any case, Rashenko will have to move his quarters.'

'Why?'

Zaleshoff did not answer.

'I suppose,' said Kenton, 'that wouldn't be because I know where he lives?'

'Another drink, Mr Kenton?'

'Thanks. You're a cold-blooded devil, aren't you, Andreas? This man Ortega may be a lousy cut-throat, but I don't quite like the idea of handing him over to the police with a confession he wrote to save himself.'

Zaleshoff operated the syphon.

'Very fussy all of a sudden, aren't you? A little while ago you were cracking on about the injustice of their accusing you. Now that there's a fair prospect of your seeing justice done, you don't like it.' He turned to the girl. 'That, Tamara, is a typical piece of Anglo-Saxon thinking.'

The girl helped herself to a cigarette from a box on the tray.

'I don't think Mr Kenton should worry,' she said; 'I think he will find that Ortega will regard the whole matter philosophically when the time comes.'

'That, my dear,' said her brother, 'is not in the best of taste.'

Kenton was about to demand an explanation of this somewhat cryptic remark, when there was a sharp knock at the door. With a word of apology, Zaleshoff got up and went out of the room, closing the door behind him.

'What's happening?' asked Kenton.

'I don't know,' answered Tamara.

Kenton let this obvious untruth pass.

'I have been puzzled,' he said. 'Do you mind explaining exactly how you come to be mixed up in this business? I suppose you could call it a business?'

'Yes, you could call it a business. As for your other question, it is one I ask myself constantly. I never get any reply. One day, soon I hope, for the first time in years my brother and I will take a holiday. For a little while, perhaps, we shall live as normal people away from this imbecile game of snakes and ladders.'

'That sounds as if you don't like it.'

'It's not a question of liking it or not liking it, it's just whether you happen to be a counter or not.'

'And whether you're going up the ladders or down the snakes?'

'No, I don't care about that. My brother does. If he's winning he feels good. If he's losing he's miserable. For me it makes no difference. I just feel that it's another game of snakes and ladders.'

'I don't very much care for these allegorical metaphors. In the end they lead one to all sorts of nonsenses.'

'Nor do I, but it saves thinking. My brother calls that sort of thing "*Wagon-lit* philosophy", because people always seem to get that way in trains.'

'They do. I've had some. A man I met once in the slip-coach for Athens kept me awake all night explaining the universe in terms of a game of poker he'd played the night before. Needless to say, he'd been winning.'

She laughed, but before she could reply, the door burst open and Zaleshoff came back into the room.

His manner had changed. The rather hearty mien of a few minutes ago had been replaced by an elaborate air of carelessness which Kenton failed to interpret. He glanced at the girl but she was gazing disinterestedly into the fire.

'Sorry to have been so long,' said Zaleshoff; 'I had a little matter of business to attend to.'

'Kidnapping somebody or just bumping them off?'

The Russian ignored the sally and sat down on the edge of a chair.

'Now, Mr Kenton,' he said genially, 'let us, as you are so fond of putting it, get back to the point. I've set your mind at rest on the unfortunate subject of Borovansky's killing. Supposing you fulfil your part of the bargain by giving me that precious piece of information you talked about?'

He spoke easily, almost indifferently; but behind that ease and indifference there was, Kenton felt, something very much akin to a boiler a few seconds before it is to burst. Clearly, something important had happened while he had been alone with Tamara.

'Well?' said Zaleshoff.

Kenton nodded.

'All right; but on one condition.'

'More conditions, Mr Kenton?'

'A very simple one. I want a chance to be in at the death. I have a particular wish to see Saridza's face when the photographs are removed.'

'You mean *if* the photographs are removed.'

'I mean *when*.'

'We won't argue the point. I see little prospect of meeting Saridza.'

'I don't see how you're going to get the photographs without meeting him.'

'Perhaps you don't. But I'm waiting for your information.'

'Very well then, here it is.' Kenton leaned forward impressively. 'When I told you that Saridza said he was going to Prague, I forgot one thing – that he said he was going to meet a man named Bastaki. In the coach to the frontier I met an English commercial traveller named Hodgkin. I found out from him that not only is Bastaki a Roumanian but also that his father is one of the biggest industrialists in Roumania. Bastaki himself has an electric-cable works just outside Prague and this man Hodgkin described him as one of the biggest twisters from here to Shanghai. Now if that isn't a useful piece of information, I'll eat Ortega's overcoat.'

Zaleshoff rose slowly to his feet and walked to the window. For a moment or two he stood looking at the pattern on the heavy curtains. Then he turned round.

'Mr Kenton,' he said solemnly, 'words fail me. I have done myself a grave wrong. I should, without a doubt, have handed you over to the police in Linz. I have expended a considerable amount of both time and breath on you in the hope that you had the merest scrap of information to give me, and what do I get?'

'Don't you believe me?'

Zaleshoff clapped his hands to his forehead and closed his eyes as if praying for strength.

'Certainly I believe you, Mr Kenton. Certainly!' His voice rose, then, suddenly, the words came tumbling furiously from his lips. 'I believe you, my dear friend, because I was given exactly the same information over the telephone three minutes ago. I can even, though the fact will no doubt come as a great surprise to you, add something to it. Saridza met Bastaki at the cable works offices exactly one hour ago. With Saridza were the photographs. Half an hour later, while you were trying to decide whether I was doping your drink or not, Bastaki left for the station and caught the twelve-twenty train. Saridza has gone with Mailler to Bastaki's house on the other side of Prague. Half an hour ago, Mr Kenton, those photographs were within reach. Thanks to you, they are now on their way to Bucharest.' He paused and drew a deep breath. 'Well, what have you to say to that, Mr Wise-Guy Kenton?'

Kenton looked at the carpet.

'Nothing much.'

Zaleshoff laughed unpleasantly.

'Nothing! That's splendid. At least we shall retain our sanity.'

'I said nothing *much*.'

Zaleshoff snorted impatiently and started pacing the room furiously.

'Tamara,' he said suddenly, 'telephone the police and tell them that you have had a necklace stolen, a diamond necklace. Say it was snatched from your neck by a man who held up your car in the Altstadt. Give Bastaki's description. It's in the files. Say that your chauffeur chased the man into the station and that he caught the twelve-twenty going to Bucharest. Tell them to hold him at Brünn. No, that won't do. Make up your own story. Make it sound good, but arrange it so that Bastaki is held at the frontier long enough for us to get at him. Tell Serge to get the small car ready and to put on his uniform. You'll have to interview the police. Grigori will get out the Mercedes for me. Whatever you do, hurry!'

The girl started for the door.

'Don't go for a minute,' said Kenton.

The girl paused.

'What is it now?' snapped Zaleshoff.

'I shouldn't bother about Bastaki.'

'What do you mean? Go, Tamara.'

'Bastaki hasn't got the photographs.'

'What?'

Kenton leaned back in his chair.

'You know, Monsieur Zaleshoff,' he said in malicious parody of the Russian's manner, 'your great weakness is that you get too close to your job.'

'If you've got anything to say, say it and be quick about it.'

'Certainly, only keep your hair on. You jump to conclusions. If I'd told you about Bastaki the moment I got here you wouldn't have had time to do anything if, as you say, the meeting with Saridza broke up half an hour ago.'

'This is a waste of time.'

'Wait a minute. I say you jump to conclusions. Bastaki meets Saridza who has the photographs. Bastaki afterwards leaves for the station and catches a train. You're so obsessed by the bogey of those photographs getting to Bucharest that you immediately assume that Bastaki must be taking them there. He's not.'

'How do you know?'

'Because I've frequently caught the twelve-twenty from Prague myself. It's a very convenient train, but it doesn't go to Bucharest. It goes to Berlin.'

'Berlin?'

'Exactly. And if you had half the gumption I thought you had, you'd know why Bastaki is going to Berlin after meeting Saridza.'

'Well, why *is* he going there?'

'Do you remember that very clear exposition you gave me of Saridza's relations with the Roumanian Fascists?'

'I do.'

'Then you will remember pointing out that one of Codreanu's principal aims was a German alliance.'

Zaleshoff nodded.

'Has it occurred to you to wonder just why Bastaki comes into the picture at all? Why Saridza comes to Prague instead of going straight to Bucharest?'

'It hasn't.'

'It should have done so. Bastaki is a comparatively insignificant person. The fact that his father is a big Roumanian industrialist is misleading. Why doesn't Saridza deal with the father, who is, presumably, a financially interested party? Where does Bastaki junior come in? Those, Andreas, were the questions I asked myself while I was waiting at Budweis for a train this evening. Accordingly, as I had time to spare, I amused myself by getting on to a

Prague news agency, pretending I was their Vienna correspondent, who happens to be a friend of mine, and making a few inquiries about the Bastakis. I uncovered something juicy. Bastaki's wife is a Czech – that's why he works here – but she is a German Czech, and, believe it or not, her brother is Schirmer, the Nazi Under-Secretary at the German Foreign Ministry. Now do you see why Bastaki goes to Berlin after seeing Saridza? Bastaki's job was to inspect the photographs, assure himself of their authenticity and run off to brother-in-law Schirmer to tell him the glad news. Codreanu is no fool. He's making sure of his support before he makes a move. Meanwhile Saridza sits tight until Bastaki returns with the official blessing. Balterghen is no fool, either. He's not moving to help Codreanu until he's quite sure he's going to get his money's worth. I should say you could rely on Saridza's sitting on the photographs in Bastaki's house a clear thirty-six hours – that is, until Bastaki returns. You might, of course, telephone your little friend in Berlin to delay Bastaki, but I wouldn't recommend it. You might fail and then the fat would be in the fire. Saridza would be off like a shot out of a gun.'

Zaleshoff ceased his pacing and looked at the ceiling. Kenton squirted some soda-water into a glass and drank it. Suddenly he felt the Russian's hand on his shoulder.

'I think, Mr Kenton,' said Zaleshoff, 'that I must be getting old. Or perhaps it is that I haven't been to sleep these three nights. I am sorry, my friend, that I insulted you.'

'That's all right.'

'But why,' interposed the girl, 'didn't you tell us all this before, Mr Kenton?'

'Because,' snorted her brother angrily, 'I didn't give him a chance to tell us.' He turned to Kenton mildly. 'Thirty-six hours is your estimate?'

'Perhaps a little longer. I was allowing reasonable time for him to get to Berlin, see Schirmer and get back again to Prague.'

Deep in thought, Zaleshoff walked to the door. Then he turned round.

'Is there anything that I can do for you, my friend? Anything with which I can reward you? That is,' he added hastily, 'apart from the matter of Ortega.'

'Yes, there is,' said Kenton promptly. 'I should like a hot bath and a comfortable bed.'

The Russian turned to his sister.

'You know, Tamara,' he said. 'I like this guy Kenton. He's reasonable.'

Forty minutes later, for the first time in three days, Kenton went to bed.

For a minute or two he lay on his back, relaxing his muscles and enjoying the soothing ache of his tired body. Then he reached out and switched off the light. As he did so there was a slight creak from the passage outside and a soft *click* as his door was carefully locked. Grinning to himself in the darkness, he turned over on his side. As the warmth of sleep began to steal over him, he heard the faint sound of a car starting in front of the house. Then he slept.

Frau Bastaki was a silent, middle-aged woman with untidy, greying hair and a parched, unhealthy complexion. She sat stiffly in a high-backed chair and stared at her clasped hands. It was obvious that she found her husband's guests as uncongenial as they found her. At half-past two, seeing that they had both finished their brandies and determined not to offer them more, she rose and suggested that she should show them to their rooms.

The man who called himself Colonel Robinson stood up and bowed slightly.

'Come, Mailler,' he said in English, 'the woman is anxious to get rid of us.'

Captain Mailler muttered a monosyllabic and ungallant description of his hostess, drained his glass again and followed them.

A few minutes later the two men nodded a casual good night to one another and went in to their adjoining rooms.

Saridza made no immediate effort to get undressed but went to one of his suitcases and got out a box of capsules, a small bottle and a collapsible tumbler. He swallowed a capsule, half filled the tumbler with water, added a small quantity of liquid from the bottle and drank the mixture. In an hour's time he would be able to sleep. He switched out the light, wrapped a blanket round his shoulders, and sat down by the window.

For half an hour he sat there motionless in the darkness. Outside, wind-driven clouds raced across the risen moon. Then came a gap in the clouds and for a few seconds the moonlight shone clearly on the gardens. Suddenly he leaned forward in his chair and wiped the slight mist from the window. Then he got up and went to the communicating door.

Captain Mailler was already in bed when Saridza entered.

'Hallo, chief, not in bed yet?'

'Go down quietly to the room next to the one in which we were sitting and switch on the lights. Look as though you've come down for a cigarette. That's all. There is someone outside on the terrace. I wish to see who it is.'

'I don't see . . .'

'The curtains are not drawn in that room. I want to get the light on his face. No, don't take a gun; just do as I tell you.'

He went back to the window and stood looking down at the terrace below. A minute later, light flooded suddenly across the terrace and a short, thick-set figure moved quickly into the shadows.

When Captain Mailler returned, he found Saridza getting undressed for bed.

'Spot him, chief?'

'Yes, it is Zaleshoff, the man who took the journalist.'

'My God! I'll soon get the little swine.' He started for the door.

'Come back, Mailler, and get to bed.'

'But damn it . . .'

'Do as I tell you.'

The Captain retreated rather sullenly to his own room. At the door he paused.

'I'd like to get my fingers on that little swine.'

Saridza glanced at his employee's face and smiled faintly.

'I think you will have an opportunity of doing so. Good night, Mailler.'

'G'night.'

Saridza got into bed wearily. That stuff took a long time to work, but when it did, *Gott sei dank*, it worked well.

15

Plan and Execution

Kenton was awakened by the unlocking of his bedroom door. There was a pause, then a discreet knock. He said '*Herein!*' and a man entered carrying a tray. Kenton recognized the leader of the previous night's kidnapping party.

The man said '*Guten Tag, Kamerad*', put the tray on a table by the bed and drew back the curtains. Then, after going into the bathroom attached to the room and turning on the water, he withdrew with a friendly nod.

Kenton ate his breakfast and went into the bathroom. A razor, a toothbrush, a brush and comb and towels were laid out ready for use.

When he returned to the bedroom he found that in his absence a suit of clothes together with clean underwear and a shirt had been left for him on the bed. The suit was a rather Alpinesque green tweed but, to his relief, proved a reasonably good fit. He finished his dressing and made his way down to the room into which he had been led the night before.

He found Zaleshoff sitting in front of a roaring fire drinking tea and reading a newspaper.

As he entered, the Russian put down the paper and surveyed him critically.

'Quite good,' he said at last, 'quite good. I'm glad you kept the moustache. You'll find a pair of clear glass spectacles in one of the pockets. Put them on.'

Kenton did so and examined the result in a large gilt mirror on the wall.

'A little theatrical perhaps?' he suggested.

'That's only because you're not used to yourself that way. You ask Tamara; she'll be down in a minute. Have a good night?'

'Very good, thanks. Your chief kidnapper is an excellent valet. He called me "comrade".'

'Grigori is a mechanic in Prague when he isn't working for the man who owns this house – or me.'

'I still say he's a good valet. I hope you feel better after your night's rest.'

Zaleshoff chuckled.

'You heard me go out then? I went to reconnoitre Bastaki's house. You see, I take your deductions seriously. It's about six kilometres from here and stands in its own grounds.'

'That tells me nothing. Where is "here" exactly? I've looked out of every window I could find and all I can see is trees.'

'Oh, we're quite near Prague.'

'So I gathered when I was driven here. Well, well, I suppose it doesn't much matter. What are you going to do? Launch a mass attack on Bastaki's house, shoot Saridza and Mailler and pinch the photographs?'

Zaleshoff winced.

'Nothing so crude, I hope.' He waved the newspaper. 'By the way, you're in the news again this morning. They've arrested you in Vienna.'

'They've done what?'

'Arrested you. The Austrian police are always working that trick. They announce an arrest, the wanted man comes out of hiding laughing up his sleeve and walks into their arms.'

'Supposing Ortega sees it?'

'He won't. Rashenko has looked after that.'

'I'm glad to hear it. Returning to Saridza, I should be very interested to know what you are really going to do about those photographs.'

Zaleshoff poured himself out some more tea.

'I was going to talk to you about that.' He examined a slice of lemon thoughtfully. 'How would you like to assist in their recovery?'

'Very much. But what can I do?'

'Various things,' was the evasive answer; 'you see, I shall want more men than I have here even if Tamara drives the car.'

Kenton grinned at the Russian.

'When you say exactly what you mean without beating about three or four bushes first,' he said, 'I shall know there's something wrong. The trouble is, I suppose, that you can't leave anyone here to keep an eye on me?'

'Nonsense, my dear fellow; you said last night that you wanted to be in at the death. Here's your chance.'

Kenton sighed.

'Have it your own way. What do I do?'

'Carry an unloaded automatic and come with me.'

'That doesn't sound very useful.'

'It will be. You see, although we believe that Saridza has the photographs we do not know exactly where they are. Does he carry them on him or are they hidden in his room? We must have freedom to search. It is impossible if we have to watch people at the same time.'

It sounded a rather feeble explanation to Kenton, but he let it go. Saridza would be sure to carry the photographs on him. Still, if Zaleshoff was afraid to leave him in the house alone, all the better. It would be pleasant to renew his acquaintance with Colonel Robinson and Captain Mailler.

'What's the plan of campaign?' he said.

Zaleshoff produced a rough sketch-map of a house from his pocket and talked for ten minutes.

'It's quite simple,' he concluded; 'all you have to do is to follow instructions. Serge will take the garage, Peter will keep a look-out at the gate, Grigori, you and I will look after the inside.'

'Supposing Saridza has his bunch of thugs there?'

'He hasn't. There are only he and Mailler there apart from three maidservants and Frau Bastaki. Grigori will look after the women. You and I will attend to the real business.'

'I don't see how I can attend to anything with an unloaded automatic.'

'There must be no shooting. You are already wanted by the Austrian police for murder. It would be unfortunate if you really did kill somebody. Automatics are tricky things if you're not used to them and an unloaded one looks just as dangerous as a loaded one.'

'All right, when do we start?'

'About ten o'clock, I think. I don't want to wait till they're in bed. We'll leave here at about a quarter to ten.'

At that moment Tamara came in.

'I was just explaining to-night's programme to Mr Kenton,' said Zaleshoff. 'He is disappointed because I say his automatic must not be loaded. I tell him he might kill somebody.'

'Mr Kenton looks capable of it in that outfit,' said Tamara. She herself, Kenton, noted, was looking extremely attractive in a blouse and skirt.

'Your brother said that you would approve of the disguise.'

She smiled.

'If Saridza's wearing dark glasses he may have to look twice before he recognizes you.'

'That doesn't sound so good.'

'You needn't worry,' said Zaleshoff; 'Saridza won't get into touch with the police. He'd have too much explaining to do.'

Kenton was silent for a moment.

'I wonder,' he said at last, 'what Saridza will say when he loses his photographs.'

Zaleshoff looked at his watch.

'Nine hours from now,' he remarked, 'we should be hearing the answer to that question. Come, Tamara, we have work to do.'

Left to himself, Kenton lit a cigarette and wandered over to a book-case in the corner of the room. Most of the volumes in it were in Russian. Poking dismally among them in the hope of finding one printed in a language he could read easily, he came across an odd volume of Florio's *Montaigne*. He carried it to the light and opened it at random. Half-way down the page a sentence caught his eye.

'As for military enterprises, no man is so blinde but seeth what share

fortune hath in them: even in our counsels and deliberations, some chance or good lucke must needs be joyned to them, for whatsoever our wisdome can affect is no great matter. The sharper and quicker it is, more weaknesse findes it in selfe, and so much the more doth it distrust it selfe.'

He shut the book with a sigh and put it back in the case. Then he walked slowly to the fire and stood watching the flames hissing from the side of a soft, tarry coal. If only Herr Sachs had chosen a different compartment.

A little after nine-thirty that evening, Zaleshoff inspected the magazine of a large Luger automatic, made sure the breech was empty and handed it to Kenton.

The journalist slipped it into the pocket of the leather raincoat with which he had been provided and felt better. It might be unloaded, but it supplied what he had so far missed – a touch of the dramatic.

During that day he had had plenty of opportunities of letting his imagination get to work. He had pictured the scene – the grim, purposeful assembly in the hall, the final instructions from Zaleshoff, the silent, tense atmosphere as zero hour approached – and the fact that the real thing did not conform with his picture in the slightest, was upsetting him.

They might, he thought, have been setting out on a picnic. Tamara produced, with some pride, a Thermos flask full of hot coffee, Zaleshoff could not make up his mind whether he should wear a scarf or not, the two men, Serge and Grigori, wrangled over their places in the car. Kenton, whose nerves were by this time thoroughly on edge, was on the point of losing his temper with all of them when Zaleshoff, looking at his watch, announced that they would leave immediately.

Any hopes that Kenton had entertained of surveying the neighbourhood in which Zaleshoff's headquarters were situated, were dashed. The girl climbed into the driving-seat and drew the blinds over the partition behind her. Grigori repeated the process with the remaining windows. Kenton was placed beside Zaleshoff in the back seat facing Grigori and Serge. The third man, Peter, sat in front with the girl.

'Not taking any chances, are you, Andreas?'

Zaleshoff chuckled but did not answer, and started talking in Russian to Grigori.

The car turned to the right on to the main road, but, after running for a short distance along it, swung left on to a secondary road with a poor surface. For fifteen minutes or more the Mercedes leapt and slithered among the pot-holes, then it slowed down, the engine was switched off, and it coasted to a standstill.

'Quiet now,' said Zaleshoff.

They got out.

The Mercedes had come to rest with its lights out across the entrance to a small, dark lane. By the faint light from the sky, Kenton could see that there were trees all round them. The dim, pale shape of the road along which they had come curved away to the left and was lost in the shadows. It was very cold. As he turned up his coat collar someone brushed against his elbow.

'*Vorwärts*,' said Zaleshoff, 'the others have gone ahead.'

As they moved into the blackness of the lane he saw the glow of the girl's cigarette through the windscreen of the car and fancied that it moved in a valedictory gesture. Then the trees shut out the sky and they were walking forward blindly. Zaleshoff's hand found the journalist's arm.

'Careful just here.'

A few seconds later they left the intense blackness of the trees, the ground rose sharply and Kenton heard a faint ripple of water. The next moment he was walking on something very hard, and his footsteps seemed to ring. He strained his eyes, and saw that they were crossing an iron bridge over a stream.

On the farther bank, the lane bore to the left, and for a minute or two he was able to see his way fairly easily. Then a dark mass loomed up and Zaleshoff slowed down.

'Those are the gates by the trees. The others will be waiting for us.'

As he spoke there was a slight sound of a foot grating on a stone and the shadows ahead seemed to move. Someone whispered. A moment later Kenton was alone. He walked forward a few paces, then stopped and put his hand out. It encountered brickwork. He was by one of the gate-posts. Then Zaleshoff rejoined him. With him was Grigori.

'Forward now and be silent.'

From the plan which Zaleshoff had shown him, Kenton knew that the house was reached by a semi-circular drive that enclosed a stretch of grass dotted with trees and shrubs. Zaleshoff's route ran across this to a point beyond the end of the drive and slightly to the left of the house. It had looked very simple on the plan, but they had gone no more than a few yards from the gate before Kenton had lost his bearings. He abandoned any attempt to recover them and concentrated his attention on following the two dim figures ahead. At last they stopped and he drew level with them.

'There's only a ring of trees now between us and the garden,' whispered Zaleshoff. 'In a moment you will see the house. But we must give Serge time to reach the garage.'

For five minutes the three stood there motionless. The grass was damp and Kenton's feet were getting numb when Zaleshoff at last signalled them on. A second or two later they emerged from the trees.

The house was built on rising ground and the garden was terraced up to a long stone balcony on to which three pairs of french windows opened from the ground-floor rooms. On the right of the balcony, jutting forward to meet the drive sweeping round from the gates, was a small wing containing the main entrance. With the exception of the light showing through chinks in the curtains of the two balcony rooms farthest from the entrance, the house was in darkness.

Zaleshoff murmured something in Russian to Grigori and the man moved silently away.

'He's gone round the back to deal with the kitchen. We'll give him a minute, then go for the balcony.'

They waited, then started to move up under cover of a neatly pruned hedge. A minute or two later they stood on a stone path in front and slightly below the balcony.

'Now, on your toes,' whispered Zaleshoff.

They crept along the path. A few paces brought them to a gap in the balustrade, and three stone steps leading up. Another five seconds and they were in the shadow of the wall. Zaleshoff began to edge slowly towards the first of the lighted windows. His heart beating wildly, Kenton followed.

A foot from the window, Zaleshoff stopped. Kenton leaned forward. The faint murmur of a man's voice came through the window. Zaleshoff listened intently.

'Polish,' he muttered over his shoulder.

He listened for a moment or two longer, then turned round and gently propelled Kenton back along the wall.

'It's too muffled to hear what he's saying,' he whispered; 'Saridza doesn't speak Polish, but I suppose he must be there. This way.'

He moved along the balcony to the unlighted window and Kenton saw him take something that looked like an engraver's tool from his pocket. He inserted the tool carefully in the jamb of the window and pressed. Immediately, the windows swung open.

Zaleshoff stood back quickly.

For a moment or two he remained motionless.

'Good work,' murmured Kenton.

The Russian turned his head.

'They weren't fastened,' he said. 'I don't like the look of that.' Then he shrugged his shoulders. 'Come on.'

They stepped into the dark room. Kenton felt a thick carpet beneath his feet and his outstretched hand touched a small table. He experienced a sudden desire to retreat. For some reason that he could not fathom, a phrase was running through his mind. 'Breaking and entering' – the dusty legal cliché creaked and rattled with rhythmic persistence. At that moment, as his fingers moved over the polished surface of the table, everything was abandoned to the desire for flight; he must get out, away from that soft carpet and polished table that belonged to somebody else, away from the warm, faintly scented darkness of the room into the lighted streets of a town with people hurrying by. He took a step forward.

'Zaleshoff . . .' he whispered.

The Russian gripped his arm.

'Mind that chair. Have you got your gun ready?'

Kenton's hand went to his side pocket. The gun caught in the lining as he pulled it out. His hands were hot and slippery. He fumbled with the smooth, cold metal and cursed under his breath. Zaleshoff already had the door open and was peering into the dark hall. Kenton hesitated, then followed him.

They were in a large hall. Zaleshoff shut the door carefully behind them and moved to the left. A few feet away there was a door with a thin strip of light showing beneath it. Again they could hear the murmur of a man's voice. Kenton saw Zaleshoff lean against the door-post and turn the handle of the door slowly. The blood racing in his head, he raised the hand holding the automatic. Suddenly, Zaleshoff's arm moved. The door flew open and the light from a chandelier flooded into the hall, dazzling him. A split second later Zaleshoff was in the room.

A fire blazed merrily in the grate. The scent of a cigar hung in the air. On one side was a large radiogram. As Kenton entered the room the voice speaking in Polish ceased and a faint hum came from the loudspeaker. But the journalist barely noticed these things for he was staring stupidly at the sole occupant of the room. It was the man Serge. He was lying on the floor, his mouth open and his eyes glazed. Sticking from his back between the shoulder blades was the handle of a knife.

Zaleshoff was the first to move. He stooped quickly and gripped the dead man's wrist. Just as suddenly, he let it go and stood up.

'Quick,' he muttered huskily, 'something has gone wrong. We must get out of here.'

He started for the window. Kenton put one foot forward to follow him. He got no farther.

'Keep perfectly still and drop your guns.'

There was a second's icy silence. Then he loosened his grip on the automatic, and it thudded to the carpet. The blood had drained from his head and there was a singing in his ears. He saw Zaleshoff's revolver fall to the floor, but did not hear it.

'Turn round.'

The sharp order sounded as though it were coming through layers of cotton wool. He turned slowly.

In the doorway, a yellow smile on his lips and a heavy revolver in his hand, stood Saridza.

16

Civilian Casualty

Saridza motioned them away from the windows with the barrel of his revolver.

'Get away from those guns and put your hands behind your head,' he ordered. 'That's better.'

For a moment there was silence. Saridza released the hammer of the revolver slowly and leaned across the back of a chair.

'This,' he continued, 'is a pleasant reunion. Comrade Zaleshoff; I hope you won't spoil it by making any foolish attempt to escape.'

Zaleshoff shook his head.

'No. Saridza has a reputation for accurate revolver shooting,' he added to Kenton.

Saridza beamed.

'What a memory you have, Zaleshoff! I wonder if you remember our last meeting in New York. It was New York, wasn't it?'

'That's right, in nineteen thirty.'

Kenton listened as if in a dream. The two might have been business acquaintances talking over old times.

'What has happened,' Saridza was saying, 'to that man of yours in New York? What was his name? Something beginning with R, I think. Ah yes, Rogojin, that was it. Where is he now?'

'In Moscow.'

'How extraordinary! I must be getting confused. I thought he was now your Basle agent. Another man of the same name perhaps.' He grinned and his eyes flickered towards the journalist. 'And Mr Kenton, isn't it? I am a little surprised to see you here. You see, I really believed your story about meeting Borovansky on the train

– a cruel deceit. However, Mailler will be glad to know that the Austrian police were unsuccessful after all. He is very anxious to see you again, and you too, Comrade Zaleshoff. You must excuse him for a moment. He is attending to a friend of yours whom he found wandering in the servants' quarters. There seem to be quite a lot of people wandering about Frau Bastaki's house tonight. This poor fellow here on the floor Mailler found tampering with the cars in the garage. The body was brought here by way of a little surprise for you. Mailler's idea. A trifle macabre perhaps, but then Mailler's tastes incline that way. The idea appealed to me for a different reason. You know the old Mosaic conception – an eye for an eye? I am glad to know that Borovansky's soul can now rest in peace, avenged.'

'You still talk as much as ever,' said Zaleshoff.

The smile on Saridza's lips faded a little.

'Yes, Zaleshoff, I still talk. I still act also. That fact has probably not escaped you.'

'It has not. I am curious to know how you knew I was calling.'

'I have insomnia to thank for that.'

'You mean you saw me last night. That was when Mailler switched on the light, I suppose. I thought I was quick enough.'

'Not quite. I could have shot you easily but I thought you might come again and bring your friends. I took the precaution of installing a small garrison and of sending Frau Bastaki and the maids into Prague. I was right, although I did not count on this young man's presence. You seem strangely silent, Mr Kenton. Is it the moustache or the glasses that worry you? The last time we met you had quite a lot to say for yourself.'

At that moment there was a crackle of speech from the radiogram and a second or two later, with a roll of drums and a flourish, an orchestra burst into a noisy rendering of 'The Blue Danube' waltz.

Zaleshoff laughed.

Saridza backed to the instrument, touched a switch and the noise ceased abruptly.

'A curious touch of the grotesque,' he commented seriously. 'A dead man on the floor, two condemned men with their hands behind their heads and a Strauss waltz for a funeral march – what could be more entertaining? By the way, our little jest with the loudspeaker was my idea. You responded magnificently. It is a pity, however, that you had to come so early. That lecture from Cracow was the best we could do. It was about the folk dances of Galicia. Half an hour later you would have had Doctor Goebbels speaking from Leipzig. What I should have liked, of course, would have been the Moscow station. But a sense of humour can be a dangerous thing. It would have been embarrassing if they had struck up the Internationale. Your suspicions might have been aroused.'

Kenton barely heard what was being said. Serge was dead. The mechanic, Grigori, might be dead too. What had happened to the other two, the man at the gate and Tamara? Even as these thoughts flashed through his mind there came the distant sound of three shots fired in quick succession. There was a pause, then one isolated shot that seemed louder than the others.

He glanced out of the corner of his eyes at Zaleshoff. The Russian's face was quite expressionless. Kenton looked at Saridza. The man was still smiling but there was a tautness in his expression that showed that he was listening intently. For fully a minute there was dead silence in the room.

Then Zaleshoff cleared his throat.

'How unfortunate if Captain Mailler has been shot,' he remarked.

'Unlikely, I think.'

'I shouldn't be too sure, Saridza. My sister is a swell shot and she has a good cover in the car.'

Kenton jumped. What on earth was the man saying?

'You surely don't think we came here unprepared for emergencies,' went on Zaleshoff calmly.

Kenton coughed warningly, but the Russian took no notice.

'Of course it may be the man I left at the gate. Mailler and his party may have been outflanked.'

The journalist glared fiercely at his fellow prisoner. Then he saw something that made him turn his head quickly and look straight ahead. Zaleshoff was working his way almost imperceptibly towards one corner of the mantelpiece, and the fingers of his hands held behind his head were outstretched to grasp a small brass vase. Kenton held his breath.

But at that moment there was the sound of footsteps in the hall and Mailler walked into the room.

The ex-Black-and-Tan glanced quickly at the two prisoners.

'Get away from that mantelpiece, quick,' he snapped suddenly.

Zaleshoff stepped forward a pace and Kenton's heart sank.

'Well, chief,' said Mailler, 'you've got the swine all right. There's another wired up in the kitchen. I had to bash him a bit.'

'What was that shooting?'

'There were a couple more of them with a car. Took a few pot shots at the sky and cleared off in a hurry. I tried to get their petrol tank, but it was too dark.'

Saridza grunted angrily.

'You ought to have stopped them, Mailler. They may come back. We shall have to get these men away. Hold them here. I will make arrangements.'

Mailler raised a heavy Colt revolver until it was level with his chest.

'O.K.'

Saridza went out of the room. Mailler surveyed Kenton and Zaleshoff through narrowed eyes. The journalist saw that he had been recognized.

'Quite a nice little bag,' said Mailler softly. He raised his voice. '*Heinrichs, komm her.*'

A tall thin man with a disfiguring birth-mark down one side of his face came into the room. He stumbled over the legs of the dead Serge and kicked them viciously out of the way.

'Keep them covered with your gun and see that they don't shift too near that mantelpiece,' ordered Mailler in German.

'*Jawohl, Herr Kapitän.*'

The man took up his position and thumbed back the hammer of his revolver.

Mailler thrust his hands into the pockets of his trench coat and stared at the prisoners for a moment. Kenton noticed that there was a long thin bloodstain down the front of the coat. Suddenly the Captain raised his revolver and walked towards Zaleshoff. A foot from him he stopped.

'So you're the dirty little Red, are you?'

Zaleshoff looked at him steadily.

'I'm pleased to meet you again, Captain. You see, I've found out a little about you. Your real name is Hollinder. What is more, you are wanted in New Orleans for the murder of a coloured woman named Robins.'

Mailler drew back his gloved fist and drove it straight into the Russian's face. Zaleshoff staggered back. The other raised the hand holding the revolver and crashed it across the side of the Russian's head. Zaleshoff pitched forward on his face and lay still.

Mailler turned to Kenton.

'You get yours in a minute, old man.'

He fumbled in his pocket, produced a length of thick copper wire and a pair of pliers and proceeded to lash Zaleshoff's wrists together behind his back. He tightened the wire with a violent twist of the pliers and snipped off the loose ends.

'Now you. Lower your hands – slowly – and put them behind you.'

Kenton obeyed and the wire bit into his flesh. For a second or two he tried to keep his wrists turned so that he would be able to slacken the wire afterwards, but a twist of the pliers promptly defeated this aim. The pain was agonizing and he flinched.

Mailler laughed.

'Bit tight, old man? That's all right; your wrist'll go numb in a minute. Sit down.'

He pushed Kenton backwards and put out his foot. Kenton tripped over it and fell heavily. His ankles were lashed together with the wire and Mailler was giving it a final twist when Saridza came back into the room wearing an overcoat and hat. He glanced at the insensible Zaleshoff.

'What is this, Mailler?'

'The swine got cheeky.'

Saridza frowned and looked down at Kenton.

'I regret,' he said rapidly, 'that we must soon part company again. *Partir est mourir un peu*; but I am afraid that it is you and your companions in misfortune who are going to do all the dying. You are going for a little ride. Mailler, get them in the car. We shall take them to the cable works. I don't think the man in the kitchen will live very long in any case, but he may as well go with them.' He looked thoughtfully at the corpse on the floor. 'This prank of yours, Mailler, has made rather a mess on the carpet. That must be put right before Bastaki returns in the morning. The lake at the back of the house and plenty of weights will take care of this offal. Hurry now.'

'Righto, chief.'

He went out of the room and came back a few moments later with a pale-faced, vicious-looking young man whom he addressed as 'Berg'. Under Mailler's direction, Heinrichs and the newcomer carried the body of Serge from the room.

Saridza watched the operation in silence. When they had gone, he walked across the room and looked down at the journalist.

'You, my friend,' he said, 'are a fool.'

'For the first time, I find myself agreeing with you,' retorted Kenton.

'And yet,' went on the other, 'I am not entirely satisfied to see you die. Within limits you appear to be intelligent. You are a capable journalist. You possess a quality which, as a business man, I value highly – a sense of loyalty. I find it very rare. Loyalty can be secured by coercion, it can also be bought; but I place very little reliance on loyalties of that calibre. I could use your services, Mr Kenton.'

'Are you offering me a job?'

'I am. I do not ask you to betray this man Zaleshoff. He no longer counts. I offer you an alternative to death. If you agree to my proposition, you will remain here instead of going with these other two.'

'What is your proposition?'

'A very simple one. You would continue in your work as before, but under my direction. From time to time you would be given special items of news to be reported. That is all. In return I would pay you a retaining fee of fifty thousand French francs a year. Actually you would make more. As my protégé you would find avenues open to you that would remain closed to plain Mr Kenton.'

'That sounds very attractive.'

'I am glad you think so. But please don't think that by seeming to agree to my suggestion you could interfere any further in this present affair. Your liberty would not be restored to you for several weeks.'

'Until Codreanu is in control, the German alliance cemented and the oil concessions revised in favour of Pan-Eurasian Petroleum?'

'You are even more intelligent than I had hoped. Yes, until matters have been straightened out in Bucharest.'

'And is that all?'

'Not quite. You see, you might also be thinking that if you agree now you may save your skin and be able to retract later. That would not do. I shall require proof of your intentions.'

'What sort?'

'In the kitchen is the man captured by Mailler. On the floor beside you is his employer, Zaleshoff. By this time to-morrow, both these men will be dead. In an uncertain world nothing can be more certain than that. Supposing, therefore, that we were to ask you to shoot them for us? It would be very simple. Just two shots with Mailler's assistants as witnesses and everything would be over. You would merely be anticipating the inevitable. Now, what do you say?'

It is difficult to be dignified when one is lying on the floor trussed like a hen, but Kenton managed it somehow.

'I'd say,' he said deliberately, 'that you ought to be in a home for homicidal maniacs.'

Saridza's lips tightened over his yellow teeth.

'You don't think, Mr Kenton, that anything might cause you to change your mind?'

'No, I don't.'

Saridza sighed.

'That is the first time,' he said, 'that I have seen a man commit suicide by saying three words.' He turned as Mailler came back into the room. 'Hurry now; we have no time to lose. Get these two into the car.'

Kenton was carried across the hall and put on the floor in the back of a car which was standing in the drive with the engine running. A few minutes later, Zaleshoff, still unconscious, was tumbled on to the floor beside him. Then Mailler and Berg reappeared carrying Grigori. Kenton saw by the light from the hall that the mechanic's face was covered with blood. The man groaned faintly as he was dumped on the seat. His breathing was stertorous.

A minute later Saridza came out.

'Take Berg with you,' Kenton heard him say. 'Heinrichs and I will follow in the other car. I will leave you two to deal with the watchman. He must not be harmed, but remember, there must be no question of his identifying you.'

Mailler grunted acknowledgement, the door on the driving side slammed and they jerked forward.

The car roared down the pot-holed road along which they had come earlier that evening, at break-neck speed. Bound and helpless, Kenton was buffeted about unmercifully. To make matters worse Grigori's limp body slid forward on the seat until it was all the journalist could do to prevent it rolling on top of himself and Zaleshoff.

After about twenty minutes of this, the car pulled up and the two men in front got out. Kenton heard their feet crunch away along a road and a murmur of voices ahead. An instant later there was a strangled cry and the sound of a scuffle. It lasted only a moment or two, and there was silence for a while. Then Kenton heard the creak and clang of heavy gates being opened. They must, he decided, be at the cable works. The cry had come from the watchman. Presently Mailler and Berg returned to the car, climbed in and sat in silence. Then another car sounded on the road behind them, they jerked forward once more and turned slowly to the left. A few yards farther on they stopped. There was a slamming of doors and footsteps died away. A few minutes later Berg and

Heinrichs came back, lifted him out and carried him down a concrete path to a wooden door set in a brick wall. The door was sprung and Berg held it open while Heinrichs dragged the journalist through.

In spite of the dim light, Kenton could see by the roof that he was in a very long narrow factory building. There was a strong smell of raw rubber and bitumen. He made out the shapes of a long row of curious machines looking in the gloom like huge crouching insects. In the far corner of the shop, light was coming from a small bay partly separated from the main shop by a corrugated iron partition. It was towards this bay that he was carried.

A single lamp in a steel reflector suspended from one of the roof trusses illuminated the bay. Beneath the lamp, in the centre of a concrete floor covered with chalky dust, stood Saridza and Mailler. Kenton's bearers dropped him on the concrete.

'Leave him and go back for the other two men,' ordered Saridza in German.

The two retraced their steps. Saridza and Mailler started talking in low tones. Kenton rolled over to his left side and looked round him.

The bay was about eight yards wide and twice as long. It was devoid of machinery. Two narrow-gauge rail tracks sunk into the concrete about three yards apart, ran the length of the shop. At one end they stopped below an overhead travelling crane mounted on a gantry running at right-angles into the main shop. At the other end of the bay they ran right up to two round convex iron doors, each about six feet in diameter and hung on massive hinges. On one of the tracks stood three squat trolleys. Two of them carried large metal drums of cable.

Mailler disappeared into the darkness of the main shop and Saridza walked over to Kenton.

'Puzzled, Mr Kenton?'

'Very.'

'Let me explain. It is hardly worth while waiting for the other two. You will have plenty of time to tell them all about it. You see, I have decided to change my plans. I did intend to bring you here, shoot you and leave you. But you will be spared that unpleasantness. Do you know what to-day is?'

'No.'

'It is Saturday; or, rather, it was Saturday until a short while ago. Nobody will come here again until Monday morning. The watchman lives on the premises, but he will not intrude until someone arrives to release him. By that time I shall be many hundreds of miles away. Convenient as it is for shooting, however, this factory offers other amenities. Mailler suggests that we make use of them. Instead of shots, which might, I admit, be heard in some workmen's houses just beyond the railway siding at the back, there will be silence.'

He indicated the two iron doors. 'Do you know what those are?'

'They look like a pair of safe-deposits.'

'They are vulcanizing tanks. The drums of rubber-covered cable are pushed inside on those trucks two at a time, the steam is turned on and an hour or so later the trucks are pulled out with the cable on them all ready for braiding. It is an interesting process.'

'I take it that you intend to roast us to death.'

'Dear me, no. There is no steam available just now. No, you will just be left there to think. The doors seal almost hermetically.'

'You mean you're going to shut us up to suffocate?'

'Believe me, Mr Kenton, I regret the necessity for this almost as much as you do. You are a journalist and naturally inquisitive. It is your misfortunte that you stumbled on an affair that is not yet ready for the attention of the world at large. Later, perhaps, when Codreanu is strutting at the head of the Roumanian Government, your presence would have been acceptable. But you have heard and seen too much. The journalist must report only what has happened, not what is about to happen. I am, I admit, sorry for you. Men like Zaleshoff know what they are doing and the risks they run. You, so to speak, are a civilian casualty. However, don't let me depress you unduly. There are worse ways of dying than by asphyxia. You will just drift off to sleep. A little hardship at first, perhaps; but in the later stages, I believe, everything becomes quite peaceful.'

Suddenly Kenton lost his head. He strove madly to release his wrists. His head swam. He knew that he was shouting at the top of his voice at Saridza; but he did not know what he was saying. For a time he was only partly conscious. He realized dimly that Zaleshoff had been put on the floor beside him and that the Russian's eyes were open, looking at him. Then his brain cleared and he found that he was shivering violently. Feet grated on the floor beside him and somebody laughed. Then he saw that Mailler had undone the wheel-nut that fastened one of the doors and was opening the tank. The iron door was obviously very heavy and it opened slowly. At last, however, the black interior was visible and Mailler walked towards him.

Kenton's arms were seized by one of the men standing by and he was dragged across the concrete. A moment or two later he was lying across the rails inside the tank. He heard Saridza mutter something to Mailler. The latter grunted.

'He's pegged out all right,' Kenton heard him add.

The dead body of Grigori was thrust in. It crouched grotesquely against the curved wall of the tank. Zaleshoff came last. Then the door began to close.

Kenton watched the shrinking crescent of light in silence and without emotion. He was feeling sick. The light narrowed to a thread. Then it disappeared. In the darkness, Kenton listened to the faint squeak of the wheel-nut being tightened from the other side of the door.

17

Time to Kill

For a time Kenton kept his eyes open, but soon the absolute darkness seemed to press unbearably on his pupils. He shut his eyes and lay listening to Zaleshoff's breathing.

The tank was still warm from its use earlier that day. The atmosphere reeked of hot rubber. It would not, he thought, be long before unconsciousness put an end to his fear and misery. Meanwhile there was time to be endured, seconds, minutes, perhaps hours of it; time in which his brain would go on working and his body feeling. It was that, he decided, which he feared. The actual business of dying seemed, by comparison, unimportant. Whether his soul went fluttering on its way to the fires of Purgatory or whether his being succumbed without passion to the laws of biochemistry, did not, at the moment, matter. There was time to be killed. Cornelius de Witt, he remembered, being tortured to death, had passed the time by repeating the Regulus Ode of Horace. He began to repeat to himself some odd scraps of verse of which he was fond – a sonnet of Donne's, a piece of Wilfred Owen's, part of 'Kubla Khan', a speech from Marlowe's 'Tamburlaine' – but after a time he found himself repeating the same line over and over again and gave it up. Poetry concerned itself with the love of life and the fear of death rather than with the prospects of immortality. It was curious, he reflected, how little comfort it brought to physical adversity. Perhaps de Witt had been seeking merely to hurry his executioners. Perhaps . . .

'Kenton!'

The word was spoken in a whisper, but it rang in the confined space.

'Is that you, Zaleshoff?'

'Yes.'

'Have you just woken up?'

'No; I came round as they picked me out of a car.'

Kenton was silent for a moment. Then:

'You know where we are, then?'

'Yes. I'm sorry. It was my fault.'

'How do you feel?'

'Not so good. I've been trying to persuade a pneumatic drill in my head to lay off; but it just keeps on drilling.'

'Did you hear what Saridza told me?'

'No, but I heard what you told Saridza. You were yelling at him like a crazy man when I arrived.'

Kenton decided to break the news.

Zaleshoff grunted.

'This is a vulcanizing tank.'

'I guessed that.'

'It's pretty well airtight.'

'I guessed that too. What's the diameter of the door?'

'I don't know. About two metres, I suppose.'

'And how far back does this go?'

'Saridza said it took two trucks of cable. About four metres, I should say. Why?'

Zaleshoff muttered to himself for a moment.

'That means,' he went on, 'that we've got about twelve and a half cubic metres of air in here. Allowing for the volume of our bodies, say eleven. Is Grigori alive?'

'I don't think so.'

'That gives us five and a half cubic metres each. With a bit of luck and if this tank cools fairly quickly that might keep us alive for as long as seven hours if we keep still and don't talk. The workers should be here by then.'

Kenton checked the reply that rose to his lips.

'Is there any chance,' he said, 'of Tamara or your other man, Peter, looking for us here?'

'Tamara will if she knows we're here; but she won't think of looking in this hole. Besides, she's got her work to do. You heard those three shots?'

'Yes.'

'That was Tamara's signal that she was making her getaway. She'll be keeping tabs on Saridza and getting in touch with our people in Prague. What puzzles me is why Saridza didn't shoot us. He must be getting tender-hearted.'

Kenton took a deep breath:

'I wish he had shot us. You see, Andreas, there will be no workers here for another thirty hours. It's Sunday.'

For a minute there was not a sound but the ticking of the watch on Zaleshoff's wrist. Then the Russian laughed softly.

'I see,' he said; 'that means we shall have to do some thinking.'

'Such as?'

But Zaleshoff did not answer. For a long time neither spoke. Kenton felt that it was getting hotter. He began to sweat profusely and found that he was breathing a little faster than usual. He guessed that the amount of oxygen in the tank had begun to diminish. He lay perfectly still, trying unsuccessfully to keep his breathing deep and regular.

'Are you sure,' said Zaleshoff after a time, 'that Saridza said this held *two* trucks?'

'Yes, why?'

'The air's getting bad already. We can't have been in here more than an hour.'

'It seems like more.'

'It would. Isn't there a watchman?'

'Slugged by Mailler.'

'We must do something. Have you got anything we can knock on that door with? If Tamara comes or if the watchman got free we might be able to attract attention.'

Kenton felt that this was rather a slender chance but it provided something to think about.

'I haven't got anything. What about Grigori?'

'They might possibly have left his gun. Have you got any matches?'

'In my pocket, but I can't get at them.'

'Roll over beside me.'

Kenton did as he was told. He felt Zaleshoff's manacled hands fumbling at his coat pocket. A moment or two later, Zaleshoff grunted that he had the box.

'We can't afford to waste oxygen on matches,' he said; 'I'm going to strike a match and put it out after three seconds. In that time you must see where Grigori is lying and where his right side pocket is. He kept his gun there. Then lever yourself across with your back to him and feel for the gun.'

The stalk of the first match broke.

'Fingers numb,' muttered Zaleshoff.

A second later a match flared, lit up the black side of the tank and went out. Kenton began to wriggle his way towards the body. It took him several minutes to get into position. The exertion made him pant for breath and the sweat ran into his eyes, but at last he rolled over and his knuckles pressed against the dead man's coat. The pocket was empty. He rolled over again and lay still striving to regain his breath.

'No?' said Zaleshoff.

'No. But I can tell you why the air's going quickly.'

'Why?'

'There's a truck with a drum of cable on it in with us.'

'Is the core of the drum hollow?'

'I didn't notice.'

'If it is it'll take up nearly a third of the volume with the cable itself and the truck. It looks as though we've only got about four and a half hours to go now.'

'Four and a half too many.'

'Maybe you're right.'

They were silent. Kenton's head was beginning to ache. He tried to sleep but in spite of the lassitude he could feel stealing over his body, sleep would not come. He wished that his heart would not pump so rapidly in his head. Perhaps if he raised himself to a sitting position on the rails and leaned against the curved side of the tank the blood would drain from his head. But he found that he could not summon sufficient energy to make this move. Again and again he counted up to ten, mentally resolving that as he came to eleven he would make the effort to sit up; but each time it was only in his imagination that he moved. His body remained where it was. There was a faint singing in his ears. It was curiously like the whine of a mosquito. Suddenly he gave a convulsive start. He had been dozing. He knew now that he did not want to go to sleep, that he must keep awake at all costs. Someone might come. No sooner had the thought crossed his mind than, following it, came the bitter reflection that of all human follies the most pitiful was the hope that sprang eternal, the refusal to accept the inevitable even when the footsteps of the executioner were ringing in the corridor outside. Someone might come. Something, the impossible, might happen. The age of miracles . . . a stitch in time . . . amazing escape. His eyes filled with tears.

'Zaleshoff,' he said at last, 'do you think we could untie each other's hands?'

There was no reply.

'Zaleshoff!' he cried sharply.

'All right, I was thinking. Did you happen to notice how the door was fastened?'

'I thought you'd gone to sleep. Yes, there's a kind of lug with a slot in it. A long thick bolt with a wheel-nut on it goes into the slot, then the nut is done up.'

'Is the lug part of the door or bolted on to it?'

'Part of the door, I think. Why? You can't touch it from this side.'

'What about the hinges?'

'They're about four inches thick.'

'Part of the door?'

'I don't know. What are you getting at?'

'A little while ago we were looking for something to bang on the door with. We've got it.'

'What do you mean?'

'That truck of cable. It's on rails. One of them is sticking into the small of my back; that's what reminded me of it. If we get behind the truck we'll have about a six-foot run to the door. Is the drum full of cable?'

'Yes.'

'Then it probably weighs nearly half a ton with the truck. If we could get a bit of momentum on it, it would give the door a bad shaking.'

'And make plenty of noise. Yes, I see.'

'It might do something more than make a noise. I've been feeling the surface of that door. There's not much pressure inside a vulcanizing tank and no need for anything like boiler-plating. It's made of cast iron. That's why I asked you if the lug is cast as a part of the door.'

'I don't understand.'

'Cast iron is brittle.'

Kenton's heart missed a beat. For the first time there was a minute scrap of justification for hoping. He repressed his rising spirits firmly.

'But we can't do anything with our hands and feet tied.'

'No, that's the first thing to tackle. We can try undoing each other's hands as you suggested but I don't think it'll do much good with wire. My fingers are paralysed.'

'So are mine, but we can try.'

They rolled over and manœuvred until they were back to back with their arms touching. Kenton felt his hands pressing against something, but his fingers were numb and he could not tell whether he was touching Zaleshoff's wrists or the rail below them.

'It's no use,' he said after a minute or two. 'There's not a scrap of feeling in my fingers.'

'Same here,' said Zaleshoff; 'the only thing we can do is to file a wire through on the edge of the rail. The inside edge is quite sharp.'

'We'll never do it.'

'We've got to try.'

Kenton heaved himself into a sitting position and found that by turning sideways, he could get his hands on either side of the rail. It was impossible in that position, however, to get any pressure on the rail. He was forced to lie alongside the rail on the short steel cross-pieces that functioned as sleepers. He started on the strand nearest his hands.

The two men worked in silence. For a time the rail edge scratched from side to side across the inch of wire between Kenton's wrists; but eventually it made a nick in the copper and he found the going easier. But even so, the exertion in the rapidly fouling air and the cramped position soon left him gasping for breath and bathed in sweat. At last he lay still, his aching head resting against the warm side of the tank.

'Keep at it,' panted Zaleshoff.

'All right.'

Setting his teeth, Kenton attacked the wire again. He made no effort now to conserve his strength. Bruising his wrists and arms and cutting his fingers, he hacked desperately at the wire. His entire consciousness became centred in a small cross-section of hard copper wire. Another twenty strokes would cut it through. The twenty became forty, eighty, a hundred. He started counting from one again. But still the wire held while the time went on and the supply of oxygen became smaller and smaller. He was nearly sobbing with exhaustion when, suddenly, Zaleshoff let out a hoarse cry of triumph.

'Made it!'

Kenton put out his last ounce of strength. Two minutes later the wire gave and the tension on his wrists slackened. He rolled on to his back and stretched out his fingers luxuriously. He began massaging his fingers to restore the circulation. They started to ache. The ache became excruciating pins and needles as the blood flowed back into his hands. He reached down, freed his ankles and then, very gingerly, stood up. A hand touched his coat.

'O.K.?' said Zaleshoff.

'More or less.'

'Now for the truck.'

'What about Grigori?'

'We'll have to get him out of the way.'

'There's a space below the rail sleepers.'

They felt their way to the body and dragged it to the centre of the track. Then they slid it forward and downward, feet first, between two of the cross-pieces. As they eased the head down Zaleshoff murmured some words in Russian.

'He was a good Soviet citizen,' he added, 'and also of the Greek Church.' He was silent for a moment. 'Come on,' he said at last.

They squeezed their way past the truck and found that there was a foot to spare between the cable drum and the end of the tank.

By this time the air had become almost insufferably hot and foul. Before attempting to do anything further, they stripped themselves to the waist.

'Now,' panted Zaleshoff, 'we push together. Take care not to put your foot between the sleepers.'

They heaved at the truck. It squeaked forward a few inches.

'Again!'

The truck gathered speed. The next moment there was a loud crash as it hit the door. They stumbled after it and tried the door; but it was firm.

'Back with it.'

They lugged the truck back into position and tried again; but still the door held. After the eighth attempt Kenton sank to his knees exhausted. His head was swimming and there was a pain in his chest; he wanted to retch and his arms and legs felt as if they did not belong to his body.

'It's no use,' he managed to gasp out, 'we're finished.'

He could hear the Russian struggling to get his breath.

'Must go on,' Zaleshoff muttered at last; 'but rest first.'

Kenton abandoned himself to the desperate fight to get enough oxygen into his lungs. A great weight seemed to be pressing down on him, crushing him, forcing his head down lower and lower . . .

A stinging slap on the face brought him round with a jerk.

'Kenton!'

'Yes?'

'Come on, get up.'

He crawled slowly to his feet and lurched forward against the side of the truck.

'Back with it, Kenton . . . for God's sake push!'

Scarcely knowing what he was doing, the journalist put his shoulder to the truck and stumbled forward. The truck rolled ponderously to the end of the tank.

'Get behind it!'

Fighting for breath, Kenton dragged himself round the side.

'I . . .' he began.

Zaleshoff shook him.

'Quick . . . Kenton,' he gasped, 'last chance . . . then sleep . . . quick!'

Through the roaring of the blood in his head, Kenton heard the other's voice. With a tremendous effort, he straightened himself and gripped the end of the truck. He felt the Russian's body slide against his.

'Now!'

The truck began to move. A sob broke from the Russian's lips. Kenton flung himself forward. The truck screeched over the rails and smashed into the door. At the moment of impact there was a sound like the crack of a whip. Zaleshoff cried out. Dimly, Kenton heard him scrambling towards the door. Then he became conscious of being dragged forward over the rails. A moment later he realized that he was breathing cold air.

For a quarter of an hour neither said a word. It was Zaleshoff who eventually broke the silence.

'We'd better get our clothes on,' he said, 'or we shall catch pneumonia.'

They groped their way back into the tank, secured their clothes, carried them to the air, and dressed.

The sky outside was beginning to lighten and the glass in the roof had become dark blue. Zaleshoff struck a match and looked at his watch.

'It says ten to five, but it's smashed,' he said. 'We must have been in that filthy hole over four hours.'

'Is that all?'

'Wasn't it enough?'

'Quite, thank you. But I thought it must be about six.'

'We shouldn't have lasted that long. There must have been quite a lot of rubber fumes in there. How do you feel?'

'Apart from a head that feels as if it's falling in half and a pulse that's still working overtime, not too bad. I've got you to thank for that, Andreas.'

'For what?'

'For saving my life – I shouldn't have been able to do anything about it without you.'

'You wouldn't have been in there if I hadn't been so dumb. How do your legs feel?'

'A bit wobbly.'

'Good enough to get going on? We've got to get out of here.'

'I'm ready.'

'Then we'll start.'

'What about Grigori?'

'He stays where he is.'

'What'll happen when he's found?'

'Much the same as if we'd been found with him. The police will be called in.'

'Oughtn't we to do something about telling them?'

'So that you can be arrested? Besides, I'd be held for questioning and I still have to get those photographs. Bastaki is due in an hour or two.'

'All right.'

They went into the main shop.

The door through which they had been carried in was locked. Zaleshoff produced the 'engraver's tool' from his pocket and attacked the lock. A few minutes later he straightened his back.

'I can't do anything with it.'

'How did they unlock it?'

'Probably took the keys off the watchman.'

'What about a window?'

'I don't think there are any, but we'll look.'

A careful search proved him right. In the course of it, they came upon three more doors. One was padlocked on the outside; the locks of the remaining two would not yield to the Russian's attempts to pick them. He swore impatiently.

'This tool's no good for this sort of lock,' he said.

'There must be some form of ventilation in the place,' said Kenton.

'Probably in the roof.'

'Well, why don't we go out that way?'

'How?'

'I noticed an overhead crane at the end of that vulcanizing room. They must be able to get up to do things to it, if it goes wrong.'

'That's an idea.'

Zaleshoff would not allow the lights to be switched on, and Kenton used up the best part of a box of matches before they found a steel ladder, bracketed against one of the stanchions supporting the gantry. Telling Kenton to stay where he was, Zaleshoff climbed up to the top of the ladder and crawled along the gantry. The journalist watched him moving among the girders, a vague black shape against the smokey blue of the lightening sky. A minute later he called out that he was coming down.

'There is a window,' he reported; 'it's in the unglazed part of the roof and it's opened from down here. We shall have to move the crane along until it's just below the window before we can reach it.'

Further search revealed an ironclad switchboard. Adjacent to it was the crane control-box. The Russian grasped one of the switches and pulled. There was a flash and the handle of the switch flew back with a bang.

'Hell!' said Zaleshoff.

'That's a starter for one of the motors,' said Kenton, 'you have to pull them over gradually. But we don't want to start the whole shop up. Let me have a look.'

Zaleshoff lit one of their few remaining matches and Kenton explored the board.

'Do you know anything about it?' said the Russian sceptically.

'Not much, but if there's a switch joined by a cable to that control-box, I think we ought to try that first. Here we are!'

He pulled down a switch and went to the control-box. A second later there was a whirring noise from overhead and the rumble of wheels.

'Hold on,' said Zaleshoff; 'I'll tell you when it's below the window.'

After a considerable amount of manœuvring, Zaleshoff called out that the crane was in position, and Kenton switched off the current. He found the Russian working at the winding gear that opened the skylight.

'It only opens about eighteen inches,' he reported; 'it'll be a tight fit.'

He led the way back to the steel ladder and started to climb. Kenton followed. The ladder came to an end two feet from the top of the stanchion. By holding on to a roof truss, Kenton was able to steady himself while he got to his feet on top of the gantry.

'Be careful,' said Zaleshoff, 'it's greasy.'

The gantry was about eight inches wide. The rail, along which ran the wheels of the hoist platform, occupied about four inches in the centre, thus leaving two narrow ledges on either side of it.

Kenton edged forward cautiously to where Zaleshoff was standing by the hoist platform.

'I should go on all fours here, Kenton.'

He himself crawled out along the two transverse girders to the steel casing which enclosed the hoisting gear, clambered on top of it and stood up. A few seconds later, Kenton stood beside him. About eight feet above their heads was the open skylight.

'You go first,' said Zaleshoff. 'You can take off from that joist there.'

Kenton grasped the joist, jumped and hauled himself up. For a moment he hung suspended in mid-air, then he got his foot in the crutch of two intersecting steel angles and shifted his hold to the window frame. A few seconds later he was lying face downwards on a sloping galvanized iron roof. A cold drizzle of rain caressed the back of his head.

There was a scuffling noise from below and Zaleshoff was lying beside him.

The sky was now grey and Kenton could see the jagged outlines of the rest of the cable works beyond a tall metal chimney at the end of the roof on which they lay. With the exception of the sound of a train rumbling past in the distance, and the thin patter of rain on the roof, there was silence. Then Zaleshoff moved beside him. His voice, when he spoke, sounded curiously remote in the open air.

'Let yourself slide down about half a metre. There's a ridge you can catch your foot in.'

Kenton did as he was told.

Zaleshoff commenced to work his way along the ridge to the end of the roof. A few minutes later they lowered themselves down a drain-pipe to a cinder path running between the walls of two factory buildings.

'This way,' said Zaleshoff.

They walked to the end of the path. There the Russian stopped.

'We shall have to go carefully now.'

They stepped out of the shelter of the wall and found themselves in a large yard. Facing them were the main gates – steel frames filled in with rusty plating and surmounted by spikes. They were shut. Beside them was a small brick building with a window looking on to the yard.

Skirting the yard they crept up to the door of the building. Zaleshoff held up his hands for silence. They waited for about a minute; then a faint moan came from the interior.

'The watchman,' whispered Zaleshoff.

They stayed where they were for a few minutes. Then, hearing no further signs of life from inside the building, they crept round it to the gates. They were locked. Kenton glanced up at the spikes, then looked at Zaleshoff. The Russian shrugged his shoulders.

'The fates are against us,' he said, 'come on.'

They retraced their steps to the point at which they had descended from the roof. Zaleshoff pointed to a space between the buildings a few yards farther on.

'We'll try that.'

For a short way the cinders continued; but beyond a narrow door in the left wall it was overgrown with grass and weeds. The end of it was heavily shadowed, and for a minute Kenton thought they were in a cul-de-sac. Zaleshoff gave a sudden crow of delight, and ran forward. Kenton caught him up.

'What is it?'

'A private railroad siding. Look!'

As they emerged from the passage Kenton saw what had shut out the light. Close to the end walls of the factory was a squat embankment, carrying a single rail-track. On it was a train of empty goods trucks.

'I don't see where this is going to get us,' he said.

'The siding has got to leave the factory somewhere,' Zaleshoff explained irritably.

Kenton followed him up the embankment and along the side of the track to the end of the trucks. In the gloom, he could see the wet rails curving away from the factory towards a high corrugated iron fence some distance away.

'There must be a gate that shuts across the track when it's not in use,' said Zaleshoff.

They crossed the rails and started towards the fence across what was evidently the works refuse dump. Loose coils of wire caught round their feet, they sank ankle-deep into ash and cinders. Then there was a sharp drop, and they walked on through wet grass towards the point at which the siding curved round to the fence. They were walking in silence. The grass deadened the sound of their footsteps. Suddenly, from ahead, came the creak of rusty hinges. The two stopped dead.

'Stay here,' muttered Zaleshoff, 'I'll see what this is.'

Kenton saw that the Russian had picked up a short length of lead-covered cable, about an inch thick, from the refuse heaps, and that he was weighing it ominously in his hand as he went on ahead.

He dissolved into the shadows by the fence and for a minute or two the journalist could see nothing. Suddenly he heard a quick rustle of feet on the grass and a cry. He dashed forward. He saw two figures locked together and swaying from side to side.

He stopped short. One of them was Zaleshoff. The other was Tamara.

18

Smedoff

When the man Peter had come running out of the darkness with Mailler, Heinrichs and Berg at his heels, Tamara had very nearly lost her head. That she did not do so was due, as she afterwards explained, less to her presence of mind than to the fact that her right foot was resting on the electric starter of the Mercedes. In her agitation she pressed it. The roar of the engine startled her. Thereafter she acted with decision. Almost before Peter was on the running-board she had the car in gear and the wheel locked round to get the Mercedes clear of the lane. As she accelerated, her hand dropped to a pocket in the door, came out again with an automatic and fired the three signal shots out of the window of the car. Mailler's answering shot smacked into the rear offside door panel by Peter's legs.

A kilometre down the road she switched on the light and stopped the car.

Peter climbed in beside her.

'What happened?' she asked in Russian.

'They came upon me in the dark. I heard their footsteps and thought it was Andreas Prokovitch and the Englishman returned. Then, a few paces from me, two of them spoke, and I knew that they were enemies. I made to go. They did not see me, but in the darkness I stumbled and they heard.'

'How did you know they were enemies?'

'I heard what they said. One said "Who will shoot them?" The other laughed and said: "We will play cards for the job."'

Tamara tapped the steering-wheel thoughtfully with the automatic.

'You, Peter,' she said at last, 'must go back and keep watch from the road to see if they leave. I will come back as soon as I can.'

The man got out.

'You will not be long, Tamara Prokovna? If they leave I can do nothing.'

'I will not be long.'

Tamara drove to her brother's headquarters, dialled a Prague number, and had a short telephone conversation, as a result of which two nondescript-looking men, each with a photograph of Petre Bastaki in his pocket, and very precise instructions concerning the original of it, spent the night near the Berlin arrival platform in the station at Prague. Then she went to a cupboard, got out a pair of Colt revolvers and a box of ammunition, and went back to the car. Five minutes after she had rejoined Peter near the end of the lane, she saw the two cars leave for the cable works. She followed at a discreet distance and waited for half an hour a short way beyond the works entrance. When the four men left, she trailed them back to the Bastakis' house. While she had been gone, Peter had been joined by the reinforcements from Prague which she had asked for – a small man with a very large motor-cycle who announced that he was from Comrade Smedoff. To this man she gave careful instructions, then turned the Mercedes and headed once more for the cable works.

She spent an hour trying unsuccessfully to find some way of getting inside. Finally she abandoned the attempt, and drove towards the city until she found a telephone booth. She talked and listened for five minutes. Then she hung up, went back to the car and drove to a quiet road near the cable works. There she sat, drinking coffee from the Thermos flask and smoking until the first pale streaks of dawn appeared in the sky. Then she started out once more to reach her brother.

The reunion of Zaleshoff and Tamara was affectionate but hurried. Zaleshoff gave a brief and, Kenton thought, grossly understated account of their night's adventure and demanded anxiously to know what had been done in his absence.

'Saridza went back to the Bastakis' place after leaving you here,' said Tamara. 'I put one of Smedoff's men on to him after that. Saridza and Mailler left a short while after for the Hotel Amerika in Prague. There were two men with them, but they went off by themselves. I also put two of Smedoff's men at the station to pick up Bastaki if he came back before we were ready. I thought maybe that would delay Saridza.'

'Good; but we must get Smedoff to countermand those instructions now. I don't want to interfere with Bastaki if I can help it. How do we get out of this place?'

'There's a piece of waste ground at the back. I would have got to you before, but it was too dark to see anything and I couldn't afford to take risks with you out of the running. Smedoff has only four men, including Peter, and they are where I told you. Otherwise I would have got help to you. Where are Grigori and Serge?'

Zaleshoff told her.

She was silent for a moment. Kenton saw the stony look which he had seen before in her brother's face come into hers. Then she said: 'Your wrists and hands are bleeding, Andreas, and so are Mr Kenton's.'

'We can see to them as we go.'

She led them through the gates over the siding, across a desolate, muddy patch of ground to a broken-down wood fence. Kenton saw the outlines of a row of small buildings and a group of gasometers in the middle distance. Then they were walking up a narrow, rutted road between tracts of scrubby waste land traversed by power lines and telegraph wires.

'Where to now?' said Kenton when they reached the car.

'First to a telephone and then home,' replied Zaleshoff.

He spent about thirty seconds in the telephone box, then he came back to the car.

'Our plans are changed,' he said abruptly as he got in again; 'we will go to Smedoff's. Mr Kenton,' he added as the car started, 'I should like you to exercise the greatest discretion over anything you may see or hear during the next hour or so.'

'All right.'

'What has happened, Andreas?' said the girl over her shoulder.

'Bastaki arrived at the Hotel Amerika ten minutes ago.'

'But the men at the station . . . ?'

'He came by air.'

During the drive into Prague, Zaleshoff ignored the journalist and sat frowning fiercely at the floor of the car. He refused a cigarette with an impatient grunt.

It was now daylight and the Mercedes swung through the deserted streets of the city at racing speed. In the Altstadt, Tamara slowed and turned into the network of clean, silent streets of office buildings. The Mercedes stopped outside a narrow building belonging ostensibly, at all events, to a firm of wood veneer manufacturers. The door to the offices was open.

They alighted from the car and went through the door along a stone corridor to a lift. They got inside and Zaleshoff pressed the button marked 'Basement'. To Kenton's surprise the lift rose slowly to the sixth floor and stopped. Zaleshoff opened a door on the opposite side to that by which they had entered and they walked on to a bare landing. For a moment Kenton could see no signs of any outlet. Then he noticed a flush door set in the wall at one end of the landing.

'Wait here,' said Zaleshoff.

He went to the door, pushed it open and walked straight in. The door swung to behind him.

'What is this place?' said Kenton.

'A friend's apartment,' was the reply.

Kenton digested this tasteless piece of information in silence. Then Zaleshoff returned and beckoned to them.

'How would you like a bath and some coffee, Kenton?'

'Very much.'

'Good.'

He waved them inside.

Kenton found himself in a small carpeted hall with three doors facing him.

'Bedroom, parlour, bathroom,' said Zaleshoff, pointing to each in turn. 'Tamara, you can have the bedroom and make do with a wash. Mr Kenton is very, very dirty. So am I. You take the bathroom first, Kenton, and be quick. The coffee will be ready in a minute.'

Kenton went into the bathroom.

The first thing he saw was a large *papier-mâché* plaque of Lenin's head in bas-relief. It hung in the centre of the wall over the bath. He shut the door and looked at the rest of the room. One corner was filled with bottles and tins of bath salts in a bewildering variety of colours and perfumes. A shelf above was loaded with face creams, skin foods, lotions, astringents and cosmetics. All looked as if they were used frequently. There were no signs of shaving tackle. The owner was clearly a woman living alone. He gave it up and got on with his bathing.

The vulcanizing tank had covered his body with rust. The crane had added a thick coating of black grease to his face and hands. By the time he had removed the worst of the dirt, Zaleshoff was banging at the door.

He dressed hurriedly and went into the 'parlour'.

It was a small room furnished with steel chairs with red seats, a glass-topped steel table and a divan covered with black American cloth. Over a chromium-plated electric fireplace hung a reproduction of a Juan Gris still-life. On the opposite wall was a faded brown photograph of Rosa Luxemburg in a rococo gilt frame. The general effect was, to say the least of it, bizarre.

Seated at the table drinking coffee were Zaleshoff and Tamara. Facing them was one of the fattest women Kenton had ever seen. She was talking in Russian to Tamara.

Zaleshoff waved to him to sit down.

'Have some coffee. This' – he indicated the fat woman – 'is Smedoff.'

The woman glanced at him, nodded and resumed her conversation with Tamara. Zaleshoff went into the bathroom. The journalist sipped his coffee and stared fascinated at Madame Smedoff.

She might have been anything from sixty to ninety years old. The flesh of her face, which quivered as she talked, was a mass of tiny wrinkles partly filled in by the thick coating of white powder that clung like a fungus to the mask beneath it. Her hair was short, henna'd and dressed in innumerable curls that stood out stiffly round her head, so that with her back to the light she looked like a rather disreputable chrysanthemum. Her mouth was very carefully painted to correct an obtrusive lower lip. Two feverish dabs of rouge, a little too high on the cheeks, plucked and pencilled eyebrows and dark blue eye-shadow completed the work. There was not a vestige of character left in the features. She wore a black silk dress with long sleeves from the ends of which protruded two small well-shaped hands. On the third finger of the left hand was a large soap-stone ring. Round her shoulders was, of all things, a red tartan shawl. She adjusted it repeatedly as she talked.

Suddenly she broke off in the middle of her conversation with Tamara and fixed Kenton with a piercing stare. Then, to his amazement, the blue eyelids fluttered coquettishly and an arch smile twisted her lips.

'I have heard of you, Mr Kenton,' she said in English. 'You remind me very much of de Maupassant. You have the same mouth.'

'That is impossible, Madame Smedoff.'

'What do you mean?'

'It is impossible that you should remember. You can have been no more than a young child when de Maupassant died.'

Madame Smedoff looked surprised, then preened herself, giggled and turned to the girl.

'You say he is an Englishman, Tamara Prokovna? I cannot believe it. He is as insincere as a Frenchman, and as grave as a German. It is droll.' Her body shook with silent laughter.

Feeling rather foolish, Kenton buttered himself a piece of bread. The fat woman resumed her conversation with Tamara; but now from time to time she cast roguish glances in his direction, and after a while he kept his eyes on the tray in front of him. He was relieved when Zaleshoff returned to the room.

In spite, however, of Madame Smedoff's distracting presence he did a certain amount of thinking. Almost imperceptibly, he realized, he had come to regard himself as an ally of Zaleshoff and an opponent of Saridza. The fact that this alignment of sympathies had been brought about largely by Saridza's brutal tactics was beside the point. Where exactly did he stand? He was wanted by the Austrian police for the murder of Sachs. His presence in Czechoslovakia was both illegal and precarious. He had lost a considerable amount of sleep and his nervous system had probably suffered incalculable damage. This Russian, Zaleshoff, had it in his power to put him out of danger so far as the Austrian police were concerned. He would not do so. He, Kenton, was virtually a prisoner awaiting the pleasure, through their representative, of the Soviet Government. The thought irritated him. He must be firm with Zaleshoff – present an ultimatum. Zaleshoff must arrange for the immediate delivery of the man Ortega, or he, Kenton, would . . . would what? Give himself up? Out of the question. Get away to England? He had been over all that before. There was nothing he could do except, he concluded bitterly, write to the *Times* about it. He munched his breakfast gloomily. The sight of Zaleshoff, pink and businesslike from the bath, intensified his sense of frustration. The fellow wasn't even good at his job! Here was that thug Saridza making ready to leave for Bucharest at any moment while the champion of the forces of democracy was passing the time taking baths and drinking coffee with a preposterous old harridan who ought to be . . .

'Well, Andreas,' he said with a trace of acerbity in his voice, 'what do we do now?'

'That,' said Madame Smedoff, wheeling round suddenly, and breaking into English, 'is what I want to know. What, Andreas Prokovitch, have you decided?'

Zaleshoff lit a cigarette.

'I haven't decided.'

The fat woman snorted and turned on Kenton.

'You, young man. You appear to have some sense. What do you think?'

'I think you're wasting time here. Saridza may be getting away.'

'There's no train to Bucharest until four this afternoon. There's no plane to Bucharest until to-morrow morning. There is one man watching Saridza's car and another on the second floor of the hotel watching his room.'

'I didn't know that.'

'Didn't you hear what we were talking about?'

'He doesn't speak Russian,' said Tamara.

Madame Smedoff emitted a little screech of laughter.

'Then the poor boy doesn't know what a wicked old woman I am!' She wriggled her huge body kittenishly.

'Olga!' snapped Zaleshoff.

She waved the interruption aside. Her eyes gleamed shrewdly at Kenton.

'Listen, Mr Kenton,' she said; 'this man Zaleshoff is all very good in his way, but he has no sense of strategy. He talks a lot, no one is better at talking; but as for strategy, as distinct from tactics, mark you, he has no sense of it. I have. When you came into this room you looked at me. I knew what you thought. In spite of her age, you said to yourself, this woman has charm, she is attractive, she has appeal, she is to be preferred to inexperienced girls.'

'Huh!' said Zaleshoff.

'Didn't you think that?' persisted the fat woman.

'Yes,' said Kenton.

Madame Smedoff turned triumphantly to the others.

'You see. I have manœuvred him into a false position immediately. He is forced to lie. If,' she went on contemplatively, 'I had decided to take advantage of that position it would have been difficult for him.'

Kenton felt his face turning a bright red.

'The point,' she resumed briskly, 'is this. There is no substitute for good strategy. Your attempt, Andreas Prokovitch, on the Bastaki house was doomed to failure.'

'It failed because of a piece of darn' bad luck,' said Zaleshoff vigorously.

'Doomed to failure,' insisted Madame Smedoff. 'The strategy was at fault. It was crude. Now again you make the same mistake. You would go to the Hotel Amerika and wave pistols at these men, club them, bind them, search for the photographs. I tell you, my friend, that even if you are successful in your violence you will not find the photographs.'

'Why not?'

Madame Smedoff rearranged her shawl.

'Because they are not there.'

'Ridiculous, they must be there.'

'They are not there. You take Saridza for a fool. He is not. Up to a point you were right. When he met Bastaki at the cable works the photographs were with him. Good. But you forget one thing. That same night, he saw you. He knew what you wanted. It is obvious that he would put the photographs in a place of safety. But where? That we must find out and quickly. I think Saridza will travel by car this morning.'

'Why?'

'The four o'clock train is a bad one. It is necessary to change at Budapest, there is long to wait, and there are many stops between there and Bucharest. Also Saridza rarely travels by train.'

'Prague is a large place and the photographs are small.'

'Then we must wait for Saridza to leave and follow him. You ought to be able to do something between here and the Hungarian frontier.'

Zaleshoff thrust out his jaw.

'I don't like the sound of it.'

'Neither do I,' said Madame Smedoff complacently; 'but perhaps you can suggest where we may find the photographs. It is now half-past eight. Bastaki has left and gone back with his wife to his home. Saridza will be starting soon.'

'It is absurd, Olga, and you know it. He might have left the photographs in the hotel safe or at the luggage office at the station – anywhere.'

'If I might make a suggestion?' put in Kenton apologetically.

'Well, young man?'

'If I were in Saridza's place, knowing that further attempts might be made to recover the photographs, I should have a copy made by re-photographing the original prints and put it somewhere safe.'

Madame Smedoff heaved herself out of her chair, went over to Kenton and patted him on the head.

'There, Andreas Prokovitch, you see he has intelligence. A copy, of course. We should have thought of that.' She beamed at Kenton. 'And how do you suggest we find out which photographer he went to?'

'He wouldn't go to an ordinary photographer. The man might think it queer stuff and make an extra print. I don't know whether you've seen those mobilization orders, Andreas. They're stamped on every page with your Government seal. Very official and authentic, they look.'

'That,' said Zaleshoff impatiently, 'is the trouble.'

'So if Saridza wanted to safeguard himself he'd go somewhere where he'd got a pull with the operator. My bet is that those photographs and a duplicate set of prints are now waiting in a newspaper office for Saridza to collect when he's ready. He'll collect one set, of course, and leave the other in the safe. It's easy.'

'But why a newspaper office?'

'It's got a photographic studio. It's well protected. There are people there day and night. It's the ideal place.'

'So,' said Zaleshoff ironically, 'the photographs are in a newspaper office. That is a great help. There can't be more than fifty newspaper offices in Prague.'

Madame Smedoff grunted irritably.

'Use your brains, Andreas Prokovitch. Saridza would not leave them with any paper. I have an idea.'

She flung an arch look at Kenton and waddled out of the room.

Zaleshoff sighed loudly and made a gesture of despair.

'Always,' he said, 'that old woman makes me feel like ten cents.'

'How old is she?'

'God knows! Getting on for eighty, I should say. She was a friend of Clara Zetkin, and she knew Lenin in London. Once she mentioned quite casually that she'd met Marx, and said she'd felt sorry for Frau Marx. Marx died in the early eighties so that must make Olga well over seventy. She never forgets a fact or a face, speaks nine languages and has translated the *Jobelin* of François Villon into modern Parisian argot. There were only fifty copies of it printed and they're worth a thousand dollars apiece to-day.'

'What does she do her face up like that for?'

'She used to have looks. Then she got into a jam while she was organizing a strike somewhere Galicia way and a woman threw vitriol in her face. It didn't do much damage, but it scarred her a bit. That's why she puts so much make-up on. She used to do it very well they tell me. She's got a bit careless about it the last few years.'

Madame Smedoff came back into the room with a grin of triumph on her lips.

'The *Prager Morgenblatt* is the paper.'

'How do you know?'

'I looked through the lists of shareholders of the German language papers. Twenty-five per cent of the Ordinary shares of the *Prager Morgenblatt* are in the name of Elsa Schirmer, that is Frau Bastaki. She's probably her brother's nominee. In any case, she would have quite a lot of influence in the *Morgenblatt* offices and Saridza would know it.'

Zaleshoff got to his feet.

'Tamara, we will go immediately. Kenton, you may come if you wish. Olga, I think this is a waste of time. Please see that Saridza does not get away without our knowing.'

As they hurried from the room, Kenton glanced back.

Madame Smedoff had sunk back into her chair, her dead white mask stretched into a broad grin, her hair glinting redly. Her eyes met Kenton's and she chuckled. Then, very deliberately, she winked.

19

Morgenblatt

The offices of the *Prager Morgenblatt* were situated on the corner of a narrow side street, running parallel to the main road from the Karlsbrücke. Tamara pulled the Mercedes up behind a lorry unloading paper. From the windows above came the clicking and clatter of Linotype machines. Zaleshoff and Kenton got out of the car and walked along to the main entrance, a narrow doorway in the side of the building.

It had been arranged that Kenton, who, knowing something of newspaper offices, might be able to present a more circumstantial front than the Russian, should make the first move. Inside the entrance, a doorkeeper sat in a small glass office. Followed by Zaleshoff, Kenton approached him.

'A packet for Colonel Robinson was to be ready for him this morning. I have come to collect it on the Colonel's behalf.'

The man shook his head slowly.

'I know nothing of it. The packet was to be called for, you say?'

'Colonel Robinson was unable to come himself.'

'I know nothing of it.'

'Let's go,' muttered Zaleshoff; 'we're wasting our time.'

'It is curious,' persisted Kenton; 'the matter was arranged.' His hand on the pigeon-hole in front of the man's face opened slightly and a bank-note rustled.

'If you could perhaps tell me with whom the matter was arranged, *mein Herr*, I will make inquiries.'

Kenton took a chance.

'With the *Herr Redakteur*.'

'Ah! One moment, *mein Herr.*'

The man picked up a telephone and pressed a switch.

'*Entschuldigen, Herr Director.* Two gentlemen have called on behalf of Colonel Robinson. They desire a packet as was arranged.' There was a pause. '*Ja, Herr Direktor.*' He hung up the receiver and turned to them. 'Please to wait a few minutes, the packet will be ready.'

'*Danke.*' Kenton opened his hand and the note fluttered to the doorkeeper's table.

'*Danke schön, mein Herr.*'

'Well,' murmured Kenton triumphantly, 'what do you know about that? A Managing Editor isn't in his office at nine o'clock on a Sunday morning for nothing.'

'I don't like it,' replied the Russian gloomily; 'it's too easy; and, besides, you're forgetting that other print, aren't you?'

'We'll say we've been told to fetch the copy as well. Or Saridza may have intended to leave the extra prints somewhere else. In that case he'll give us both. I don't suppose Saridza's told the man much anyway.'

'It may be a trap.'

'Don't forget we're supposed to be languishing in that tank.'

'Well, I don't like it.'

They waited for about ten minutes, then the doorkeeper's telephone buzzed and the man picked up the receiver and listened. Kenton saw a curious expression cross the man's face and his eyes flickered towards them. Then he said: '*Ja, Herr Direktor,*' and replaced the receiver.

'The *Herr Redakteur* will see you. The packet is in his office. This way.'

There was no lift, and the man led the way up a flight of narrow stone stairs to the fifth floor and along a glass-partitioned corridor to a door at the end of it. They passed through into a small outer office with a secretary's desk in it. On the far side was an imposing pair of tall mahogany double doors. Their guide knocked on them and threw them open. The two walked in.

It was a large cedar-panelled room with a window occupying nearly the whole of one wall. To the right was a smaller door. The man who sat behind the massive desk was a large, square-headed young German with thick pebble glasses which magnified grotesquely the pale blue eyes behind them.

'Be seated, gentlemen.'

They remained standing.

'We have very little time,' said Zaleshoff; 'we understand that the photographs are now ready. We may add that the Colonel has instructed us to take the copy prints also.'

The pale blue eyes moved from one to the other.

'That is understood. Everything will be ready for you in a short time now.'

'We shall, of course, wish to examine the photographs to see that all is in order. Perhaps we can commence now with the originals?'

'Please be patient. I have given instructions for the photographs to be got ready immediately.'

'Very well.'

There was silence in the room. The German sat motionless behind his desk. Kenton wandered across to the window and looked down into the street below. He could see the Mercedes parked behind the lorry. Suddenly a closed car dashed round the corner and pulled up in front of the building with a squeal of brakes. A second later the doors of the car were flung open and uniformed figures got out and ran along the pavement. Kenton turned with a start.

'Zaleshoff!'

'What?'

'Here, quick! It's the police!'

The Russian dashed to the window, looked down and swore.

They swung round.

The German was pointing a small revolver at them.

'Put your hands up and don't move.'

They obeyed. The German's pale eyes gleamed.

'I took the precaution,' he said slowly, 'of telephoning Colonel Robinson before inviting you in here. He advised me to call the police. The doorkeeper will show them up in a moment. The evidence of Soviet perfidy is now on its way by special messenger. Roumania will soon be convinced, in common with the rest of the world, of the reality of the Jew-Communist menace.'

'And the copies of the evidence?'

The German hesitated, then shrugged his shoulders.

'As you will have no further interest in this matter, I may tell you. They are in the safe in the wall behind me. When the time comes the evidence will be given to the German nation.'

Kenton glanced at Zaleshoff. The Russian was standing slightly in front of him, his arms half raised above his head, his attitude that of the man who recognizes defeat when he sees it.

'Keep your eyes on his face, Kenton,' he murmured in English.

'Silence!'

There was a murmur of voices from the corridor beyond the outer office and the sound of hurrying footsteps.

'Stop, Kenton!' shouted Zaleshoff warningly in German.

The trick succeeded. The journalist saw the German start and jerk the gun in his direction. Then Zaleshoff sprang.

The revolver went off and plaster showered from the ceiling as the two rolled to the floor.

'Lock the door, quick!' gasped Zaleshoff.

Kenton dashed to the double door. The key was on the other side of the lock. He pulled one side of the door open and snatched the key as the leading policeman came through the open door opposite. The man shouted and charged across the room. Kenton slammed the door and leaned against it, feverishly trying to get the key into the lock. As he succeeded the handle was wrenched from his fingers and the door was thrust open a few inches. The toe of a boot appeared in the gap. Kenton brought his heel down hard on the boot. There was a shout of pain and the boot disappeared. For a second the pressure on the door relaxed. He threw his weight against the panels and turned the key. The lock clicked home.

He turned in time to see Zaleshoff bring the butt of the German's revolver down hard on its owner's head. The man fell forward on his face. Outside the door, pandemonium had broken loose. The door was quivering under the onslaught. Orders were being shouted.

'Stand away from the door,' said Zaleshoff. 'They'll start shooting the lock away in a minute.'

Even as he spoke the thumping at the door ceased and a bullet crashed through the woodwork by the lock. The Russian rummaged in the German's pockets, then rose to his feet with a bunch of keys in his hand. He went to the small safe recessed in the wall and began to try the keys one by one. He glanced round as another shot rang out.

'See where that other door leads to.'

Kenton was already at the small door and opened it. Inside was a small lavatory. His heart sank. Above the wash basin, however, was a narrow frosted-glass window. He flung it open and looked out. A few feet below was a flat leaded roof with two square glass roof lights, like cucumber frames, built in to it. He dashed back into the room.

'There's a window we can get through on to the roof.'

'Good.'

A volley of shots tore through the lock. Then shoulders were put to the door. It shook violently and there was a loud splitting noise. By this time Zaleshoff had the safe open and was scattering the contents right and left. Kenton stood by the small door in an agony of impatience.

'For God's sake hurry, Zaleshoff.'

'O.K., you go on.'

The journalist hesitated. Then above the din outside he heard a cry of satisfaction from the Russian. The next moment there was a tinkle of breaking glass and he saw that Zaleshoff had thrown a packet of whole plate negatives on to the carpet and that he was pounding them to dust with his heel. At the same instant there was a crash from the door.

'Look out!'

But almost before the cry had left Kenton's mouth, Zaleshoff was across the room and through the door. Kenton slammed it and put the catch up.

'Have you got the prints?'

Zaleshoff held up a large paper envelope, tore it in half and crammed the pieces in his pocket.

'Through the window with you!'

Already the lavatory door was being subjected to a furious battering, and a bullet tore through the thin woodwork and flattened against the opposite wall.

Kenton landed on the roof on all fours. A second later Zaleshoff dropped beside him. The journalist started across the roof between the two skylights. Zaleshoff caught his arm.

'Keep close to the wall or they'll spot us from the windows.'

But their way of escape had evidently already been anticipated for the onslaughts on the door above had ceased.

'There must be a way off this darn' roof,' muttered Zaleshoff. 'We'll try this way.'

Keeping close to the brickwork they followed the wall along. The roof was shaped like a very thick letter E and was bounded on every side by the fifth storey walls. Suddenly they rounded a corner in the centre of the E and found themselves facing a door set in the brickwork. At that moment there was a shout and Kenton saw that they had been seen from a window on the far side of the roof. As they leaped for cover a volley of shots spattered the wall beside them. Zaleshoff tried the door. It was locked.

'They're coming round to where they can get a shot at us,' said Kenton.

Zaleshoff pulled a revolver from his pocket and fired three rounds into the lock. It held. The Russian stood back, then jumped forward and rammed his foot square on the lock. The door flew open and they tumbled down a flight of iron stairs. A few yards from the foot of them was a pair of swing doors from which came the clatter of Linotype machines. The place reeked of printing ink and hot oil.

'Through here,' snapped Zaleshoff; 'don't run, walk quickly.'

They pushed through the swing door and marched in. Above their heads was one of the glass skylights, but the racket of the machines had evidently drowned the noise of the shots, for the men were working as if nothing had happened. It was a long narrow room and they had to pass down the entire length of it to reach the door on the far side. They were about half-way through when a man, who looked like the foreman, looked up from a table piled with galley proofs, frowned and moved to intercept them. Zaleshoff made for him instantly.

'Have you seen two men run through here?'

'*Nein*.' The man looked at them suspiciously.

'We are police. Two criminals have escaped and are in the building. If you see them stop them at once. Is there any way they can get out except by the main entrance?'

'*Jawohl, Herr Kapitän*. There is the fire-escape.'

'Where is that?'

'There is a door, *Herr Kapitän*, between this room and the engraving section. I will show you.'

He started towards the door.

'It is unnecessary,' said Zaleshoff brusquely; 'we shall find it for ourselves. A man must be posted there immediately. Keep alert and report instantly if you see these men.'

'*Jawohl, Herr Kapitän*.'

The man hurried off importantly to tell his subordinates. As he did so the police burst in through the swing doors and shouted something. The foreman looked round uncertainly.

'Run for it,' snapped Zaleshoff.

They dashed through the door leading to the fire exit. To the left were two flights of stairs, one up, one down. Facing the stairs was the fire-exit door. Ahead was the entrance to the engraving plant. As Zaleshoff wrenched the fire door open a man came out of the engraving section. Kenton saw the startled look on the man's face as he caught a glimpse of the police uniforms behind them and anticipated the attempt to stop them getting past. He lashed out with his fist. The man stepped back quickly to avoid the blow and slipped on the smooth stone floor. It was enough. The next moment the two were clattering down the fire-escape. A bullet rang on the steel stairs above their heads, but by the time they were two flights down they were well under cover.

At the foot of the stairs they found themselves in a concrete yard between the back of the *Prager Morgenblatt* building and the side of a building in the adjacent street. Kenton glanced up and saw that three of the policemen were half-way down the fire-escape. They dashed for the road. They were about six yards from the end of the yard when a policeman turned the corner in front of them. The man hesitated for a fraction of a second and his hand went to the holster at his belt. Zaleshoff hurled himself forward and his fist caught the man on the side of the head. The policeman staggered back against the wall and raised his gun. Kenton caught his arm as the gun exploded. The bullet hit the concrete and ricocheted off with a quick whine. Zaleshoff wrenched the gun away. The man began to get to his feet.

'Run for the car,' shouted Zaleshoff.

Kenton ran.

A few yards up the street was the Mercedes. As they sprinted towards it, Tamara reversed to get clear of the lorry in front. By the time they had reached the car she had the near-side door open. As they tumbled in a bullet zipped through the safety glass of the back window and buried itself in the upholstery of the front seat.

'Keep down,' cried Zaleshoff.

The Mercedes shot forward and swung round, its tyres slithering over the wet asphalt, into the street leading to the Karlsbrücke. Tamara changed into second gear, rammed the accelerator down and cut in the supercharger. There was a whining roar from the exhaust and the big saloon flew up the street like a shot from a gun.

'To the Hotel Amerika, quickly!' said Zaleshoff.

The girl made a skid turn into the main road and they roared across the bridge over the Moldau. Zaleshoff drew the two halves of the envelope of prints from his pocket and tore them into minute pieces which he scattered out of the window as they went.

Kenton began to get his breath back.

'Not a bad guess of mine, was it?' he said.

Zaleshoff allowed the last of the fragments to trickle through his fingers.

'No,' he said grimly, 'it wasn't. But what we heard makes it all the more necessary to get the original prints. You heard what he said?'

'What who said?'

'That German. The Nazis are going to use those photographs as a jumping-off spot for another anti-Soviet drive. Roumania won't be the only country to hear about it. I'm not taking any more chances, Kenton. We've got to have those photographs. Strategy or no strategy, I'm going straight out to bust Saridza wide open.'

Kenton laughed. He was feeling a little shaky.

'What's the matter?'

'I was wondering what Saridza will say when he sees us.'

'You'll soon find out.' He leaned over to the girl. 'Turn down a quiet street and run slowly for a minute.'

'What's the trouble?' said Kenton.

Zaleshoff did not reply, but turned back the carpet and pried up one of the floorboards. The car slowed. Kenton saw the Russian catch hold of a mud-caked wire running beneath the floorboards and give it a sharp pull. Something clattered to the road and the car accelerated again.

'What on earth is that?'

Zaleshoff replaced the floorboard.

'It's an old Chicago custom. I've shed the Austrian number-plates. There's a Belgian registration showing now. Have you got the Belgian papers, Tamara?'

'Yes, Andreas.'

'Throw the others down a drain when we stop. Here, Kenton, you'd better have this with you if you want to hear what Saridza's got to say.' He pulled a revolver, similar to the one he himself carried, from a pocket in the door and handed it to the journalist. 'Take care. This one's loaded.'

Kenton took the gun gingerly.

'That is, of course,' added Zaleshoff with a faint smile, 'if your professional instincts are still functioning.'

Kenton slipped the revolver into his pocket.

'Andreas Prokovitch,' he said wearily, 'you are one of the three most infuriating men I have ever met.'

'Who are the other two?'

'Saridza and Captain Mailler.'

Two minutes later they drew up in front of the Hotel Amerika garage. A man came out of a doorway opposite the entrance and walked across to the car. Zaleshoff leaned out of the window. There was a quick muttered conversation, then Zaleshoff withdrew his head and sat back, a grim look on his face.

'The map, Tamara.'

The girl passed a thick folded map over in silence.

'What is it?' said Kenton.

'Saridza and Mailler left in their car five minutes ago. Mailler was driving. Tamara, take the Brünn road; and for the love of Mike step on it!'

20

The East Road

A quarter of an hour later they were speeding through the outskirts of the city along the Brünn road.

Zaleshoff sat hunched up in his corner, his face expressionless. To Kenton's questions he replied with grunts. At last, he leaned forward and instructed the girl to stop at the next village.

'Why stop?' said Kenton.

Zaleshoff turned his head slightly. He spoke as if the journalist had invited his comments on the weather.

'We've got a man following Saridza's car on a motor-cycle. He won't go more than twenty kilometres outside the city. When he stops he should telephone Smedoff. I want to get his report to make sure we're on the right road.'

'I see.'

Three minutes later they pulled up outside a small post office. The Russian got out leisurely and went inside. In two minutes he came out again and got back into the car and slammed the door.

'We're wrong,' he announced. 'They must have realized from that call from the *Morgenblatt* offices that they were only one jump ahead. They've taken the road due east to the German frontier at Nachod. They aim to get out of Czechoslovakia as quickly as they can and go down through Cracow to Bucharest.'

For a minute or two he pored over the map, then folded it up.

'Make for Nimburg, Tamara. Smedoff is getting a check there. We shall have to try and catch them between there and Nachod. Have you got plenty of gas?'

'Plenty.'

'Then let's go.'

The Mercedes leaped forward. A minute later, Kenton saw the speedometer needle edge past the hundred-kilometre mark.

After half an hour's going they swung left and sped on in a north-easterly direction. Tamara drove with the skill and assurance of a road-racing professional and the Mercedes flew up and down the hills with scarcely any variation in speed. Zaleshoff stared out of the window and smoked Kenton's cigarettes. The journalist tried to go to sleep but, in spite of his physical exhaustion, his eyes would not remain closed. Every time Tamara slowed for a corner his right foot moved, pressing down an imaginary accelerator to drive the car on faster, faster. It was, he told himself, merely the crude excitement of the chase. But he knew that there was more to it than that. Separated by miles of road were two cars. In the first one were fifteen pieces of chemically-coated paper more dangerous than the most powerful high explosive, the deadliest poison gas; fifteen pieces of paper with a message of fear and suspicion and hatred for millions of peasants who believed that their God was good and just and that their destinies were in His keeping. If the first car were permitted to reach its destination, that message would be delivered. All that stood in the way of it doing so was a pitiful band of three – a worried Russian, a girl, a tired journalist with a severe headache and a gun that he didn't know how to use. He smiled grimly. 'Stood in the way' was not a particularly happy description of their position. Overhauling a fast car with a good start was not an easy task, even for a supercharged Mercedes with a good driver.

The early morning drizzle had now given way to a steady downpour that beat on the windows, obscuring the low hills through which they were racing. It took them forty minutes to reach Nimburg. Tamara slowed as they entered the town. Zaleshoff leaned forward.

'Stop outside the *Spielhaus*.'

Tamara drove on for a minute or two and then pulled up. Zaleshoff got out.

Kenton wiped the mist from the window and saw the Russian walk over to a man standing on the pavement under an umbrella. The man was fingering ostentatiously a piece of red ribbon in his buttonhole. Zaleshoff raised his hat politely and the owner of the buttonhole said something and pointed in the direction in which the car was facing. To an onlooker it would have seemed as if a motorist were asking a bystander for directions. Zaleshoff raised his hat again and walked back to the car.

'Quick, Tamara,' he said as he got in, 'they passed through here eight minutes ago. That means we're about twelve kilometres behind them. It's only two hours from here to the frontier. We shall have to go fast to pick up that lead.'

The car shot forward again. As they left the town behind them, the speedometer crept steadily round to the hundred-and-forty kilometre mark and stayed there. Kenton had never been driven so fast in his life before. There was little traffic on the road and for this mercy he was thankful, for Tamara's estimates of the space required for the safe passage of the Mercedes seemed to be based on a scale marked in centimetres. The road, though straight and good, was narrow and slippery from the rain. The girl seemed unaware of these limitations.

'Have you been in many smashes with your sister driving?' said Kenton after one specially hair-raising moment.

'She's never had an accident in her life.'

But Kenton thought the tone of the assurance a little too emphatic to be altogether convincing.

Twice they were held up by level crossings. Once, on the outskirts of a small town named Königgratz, they were stopped by a police patrol. Zaleshoff pulled the blind down over the bullet-holed rear window and showed the Belgian registration papers. The man examined them, handed them back and waved the car on with apologies and the information that he had been told to stop all cars with foreign registrations, as a gang of international thieves had that morning broken into a newspaper office in Prague. Somewhat overwhelmed by the narrowness of their escape, they drove on.

After the first and, for Kenton, interminable hour, Zaleshoff began to peer ahead through the segment of windscreen cleared by the electric wiper.

They were passing through hilly country dotted here and there with tiny white villages clustering round church spires. Now, the rain no longer beat on the windows but the clouds were very low and the car kept running into patches of thin, drenching mist. The girl was forced to slow down a little. Then, on a clear straight stretch of road, about a quarter of a mile ahead, they saw the black saloon car.

Almost immediately it ran into mist, but the sight was enough to send a thrill of excitement surging through Kenton's veins.

'Overtake it until you're about fifty metres behind it, then follow for a bit,' ordered Zaleshoff. 'Get down, Kenton. We can't afford to risk their seeing us.'

The two crouched on the floor. A minute or so later the Mercedes slowed and Kenton could hear the faint hum of the other car. Tamara spoke over her shoulder.

'They're doing about ninety kilometres an hour.'

Zaleshoff raised his head cautiously until he could see over Tamara's shoulder.

'Wait until you're round the corner,' Kenton heard him murmur, 'then pass them and get about a hundred metres ahead.'

Tamara accelerated and sounded the horn. Zaleshoff bent down again. His heart thumping against his ribs, Kenton listened to the noise of the car in front coming nearer.

Suddenly Tamara spoke.

'They're accelerating.'

'Crowd them in on the next corner.'

Kenton heard the supercharger whine and felt the car leap forward. A moment later it swerved violently. The roar of the other car grew suddenly. There was a sharp crash and the Mercedes rocked and swerved again.

'Caught them with a fender,' said Tamara.

'Pull up quickly and back across the road.'

There was a shriek of brakes, and Kenton was hurled forward against the back of the driving-seat. He felt the car skidding wildly. Then gears crunched and the Mercedes lurched backwards. The motor stalled. There was a moment's silence, then Kenton heard the roar of an exhaust.

'They're turning round,' cried Tamara.

'Quick, Kenton! Out!'

Zaleshoff scrambled on to the road. Hauling the revolver out of his pocket, Kenton followed him. Twenty-five yards away was the black car reversing to turn round. There was a spit of flame from one of the side windows and a bullet hit the body of the Mercedes a foot from Kenton's head. Out of the corner of his eye he saw Zaleshoff raise his gun deliberately. The Russian fired. The next instant there was a stream of flame from the petrol tank in the rear of the black car.

'Quick!' cried Zaleshoff. 'Off the road!'

The road was built on a low embankment fringed on either side with birch trees. The two jumped down the side of the embankment and, keeping their heads low, ran along the gully at the bottom towards the blazing car. Already flames were leaping eighteen feet into the air, and the blazing petrol was pouring all over the road like liquid fire. Zaleshoff stopped and raised his head cautiously. A shot rang out above the roar of the flames and a bullet hit the edge of the road two feet away. Zaleshoff ducked down again.

'They've taken cover down off the other side of the road. We've got to do something quickly. If anyone comes along we're done. Get back to the car and get across the road behind it. You'll be able to take pot shots at them from there. It doesn't matter whether you hit them or not – you won't at that distance – but I want to keep them busy so that I can get at them from this side.'

'All right.'

Kenton ran back along the gully and got into position behind the car. Through the space between the spare wheels and the back of the body he could see Mailler and Saridza crouching beside a pile of stones below the road level. Tamara got out of the driving-seat and stood beside him. He rested the revolver on the spare-wheel casing, squinted along the barrel and squeezed the trigger. The gun kicked and he saw Mailler duck his head.

'Have you ever fired a revolver before?' said the girl.

'No, why?'

'You nearly hit your man.'

His ears still singing from the report, Kenton tried again; but the smoke from the burning wreckage of the car obscured his target. At his third shot he had the satisfaction of seeing Mailler peer round uncertainly looking for the source of the danger. The next moment the girl gave a little cry.

'What is it?'

'Look!'

Then he saw that Zaleshoff had left the shelter of the embankment and was crawling across the road.

'He's crazy! He'll get killed!'

As he spoke he saw the Russian's arm shoot out and a stab of flame from his gun. Mailler's hands went to his head. Almost at the same moment Saridza fired and Zaleshoff fell forward. The next instant Saridza turned and vanished among the trees.

Kenton dashed along the road. When he got to Zaleshoff, the Russian was trying to get to his feet, his hand clasped to his side, his face contorted with pain. Kenton went to help him. The wounded man waved him away.

'Saridza,' he gasped. 'He's got away.'

'All right,' said Kenton. He turned to the girl as she came running up, her face white.

'Get back to the car. He may try to get away with it.'

'Do what he says, Tamara.'

The girl turned and ran back. Revolver in hand Kenton plunged down the embankment and threaded his way among the trees. Then he stopped and listened. For a moment or two there was not a sound but dripping of water from the branches. Then he heard a slight movement ahead and to the left. He made his way carefully in the direction of the sound. Suddenly a twig snapped beneath his foot. A second afterwards a gun crashed and a bullet whipped through the undergrowth. He bent double and crept forward. The man ahead fired again. Kenton halted. Then, through a gap between the trees, he saw Saridza. The man was peering about him like a hunted animal. Kenton raised his gun. At that moment Saridza saw him. His arm jerked up. The revolver in his hand clicked twice, but no shot came. Kenton saw panic seize him. Saridza dropped the revolver and put his hands up.

'I surrender,' he said quickly.

His finger quivering on the trigger, the journalist walked forward into the clearing. His eyes met those of the other man and he knew that he could not shoot.

Saridza licked his lips.

'What are you going to do?'

'I haven't decided. I'm trying to think of a single reason why I shouldn't shoot you as dead as you would have shot me a minute ago.'

'You were armed.'

'If our positions were reversed, you would tell me that to run out of ammunition was part of the fortune of war – that is, if you bothered to do any explaining.'

Saridza regarded him warily.

'I know you want the photographs. Let me go free and you shall have them. That is a fair bargain.'

'You are not in a position to bargain. I could take the photographs off your dead body. I know what you are thinking at the moment. You are thinking that the longer you can keep me talking the less likely I am to shoot you down in cold blood. You forget that I cannot afford to let you go alive. Mailler may be dead. You would go to the police.'

He had expected protestations. To his surprise a look of genuine amusement came into Saridza's eyes.

'You must have a very poor opinion of your friend Zaleshoff if you think that he would allow himself to be caught like that. He would have dozens of witnesses to prove that he and you never left Prague today.'

Kenton raised his revolver until it was pointing at the man's chest.

'I don't think we need prolong this interview.'

The amusement faded from Saridza's eyes. His face went a yellow grey.

'I'll give you half a minute to get those photographs from your pocket and throw them on the ground where I can pick them up. Which pocket are they in?'

'The right-hand one, inside my coat.'

'Put your left hand in slowly and take them out. Keep the other hand up. I hope your nerves are good because if your hand jerks a fraction of an inch I shall fire.'

Saridza obeyed. A packet fell at Kenton's feet. Keeping his eyes fixed on the man in front of him, Kenton stooped and picked it up. He eased the prints out of the packet and counted them.

'There are only ten here. Where are the other five?'

Saridza hesitated. Kenton thumbed back the hammer of the revolver.

'In the left-hand pocket.'

A few seconds later another envelope was lying on the ground. Kenton counted the remaining prints carefully and put them in his pocket with the others.

'All right, walk back four paces.'

Saridza did so. Kenton stepped forward and picked up the revolver the man had dropped. They faced each other.

'May I ask you a question, Mr Kenton?'

'Yes?'

'Who released you from that tank?'

'No one. We released ourselves.'

'I bow to your ingenuity. May one ask how?'

'I'm afraid I haven't got time to go into that now. Turn round.'

The other obeyed.

Kenton reversed the revolver he had picked up and held it by the barrel like a club. He walked up behind Saridza.

'Just a moment, Mr Kenton.'

'What is it?'

'Before you knock me insensible I should like to remind you of an offer I made to you last night.'

'Well?'

'That offer is still open but I would, if you cared to reconsider your decision, double the retaining fee. A letter addressed to me care of Mr Balterghen of the Pan-Eurasian Petroleum Company, London, will always find me. That's all.'

Kenton stood back.

'Turn round, Saridza.'

The man turned. Kenton regarded him grimly.

'The Anglo-Saxon sense of humour, Saridza, is one of the most emasculating influences known to mankind. I am the unfortunate possessor of such a sense of humour. You can go. Go on. Clear out. But I warn you. If you show your face within the next twenty-four hours I shall shoot you on sight.'

Saridza turned without a word and walked off among the trees. He did not look back.

Kenton made his way back to the road.

Zaleshoff had crawled to the side of the road and was lying in the mud attempting to staunch the wound in his side with a blood-soaked handkerchief. His face was white and drawn, his eyes searched the journalist's face anxiously as Kenton clambered up the embankment.

'You failed?'

Kenton took the two envelopes from his pocket and scattered the contents on the ground by the wounded man. Zaleshoff examined them feverishly. Then he looked up.

'I heard shots. You killed him?'

Kenton shook his head. The Russian was silent for a moment.

'It is a pity,' he said at last, 'but I am glad you did not. It would have worried you.'

Kenton glanced at the body of Mailler lying at the bottom of the embankment.

'What about him?'

'Dead. Have you got a match?'

Kenton went down on one knee, crumpled the photographs together and set light to them. When they were burned, he scattered the ashes with his foot.

It was late in the afternoon and the light was going when Madame Smedoff waddled into her parlour. Kenton sat up on the divan on which he had been dozing.

'How is he?'

Madame Smedoff rolled down the sleeves of her black silk dress and rearranged her shawl.

'He has a little fever but the wound is not dangerous. The bullet passed right through the side, just below the rib-case. In a fortnight he will be able to get up.'

'Oughtn't we to get a doctor?'

She fluttered her eyelids at him and smiled impishly.

'I am a doctor, Mr Kenton. I was trained at the Sorbonne.'

'I beg your pardon.'

'Don't be a silly boy. Go in and see Andreas Prokovitch. He needs sleep badly, but says he must see you.' She looked at him solemnly. 'He is embarrassed. He asked me to thank you for what you did for him today. He does not wish you to think him ungrateful.' She patted his arm.

Kenton smiled and went into the bedroom.

Tamara was sitting beside the bed. Her eyes were shining in a way Kenton had not seen before.

Zaleshoff greeted him weakly.

'Look at Tamara,' he added, 'she is happy. For years I have not seen her look so happy. And all because I say we will go to Moscow for a holiday. It is incredible.'

His eyelids drooped wearily.

Kenton saw that there were tears in the girl's eyes.

'No more snakes and ladders for a bit?'

She smiled.

'What are you talking about?' muttered Zaleshoff. 'Did she tell you, Kenton, that Ortega was arrested this morning?'

'Yes, how did you work it?'

'He was found by the railway track, dead.'

'Dead!'

'He died the night after he killed Borovansky. The confession was found by his body with the gun that killed him. He committed suicide.'

'I'm ready to make allowances for a sick man, Andreas, but you don't expect me to believe that, do you?'

'He committed suicide just as surely as if he had fired the gun himself. Just before we got you back to the Kölnerstrasse, he tried to escape from Rashenko. That *is* suicide.'

'Then where has he been all this time?'

'In the empty room below Rashenko as I told you. Rashenko owns the whole of that house. The woman who lives downstairs is his cousin.'

'And do you mean to say that you let the police go on hunting me when you could have cleared the thing up as you have now?'

'I told you to stay with Rashenko. When you turned up in Prague I asked for instructions. I was told to keep you with me in case you communicated with the newspapers or the English authorities. I did so.'

Kenton swallowed hard.

'Well, Zaleshoff,' he said at last, 'when I classed you with Saridza and Mailler as my pet banes, I did them a gross injustice. You beat them with plenty to spare.'

Zaleshoff opened his eyes. His gaze flickered from Kenton to his sister. Then a slow smile spread over his face, and he closed his eyes again.

'You know, Tamara,' he murmured drowsily, 'I like this guy Kenton. He amuses me.'

Two days later Kenton boarded the Berlin train at Prague.

A lot of sleep, numerous baths and new clothes (supplied by an adamantly insistent Zaleshoff) had done much towards repairing the ravages of the previous few days. An invitation, issued by Zaleshoff through Tamara, and ultimately received via Madame Smedoff, to visit Moscow in two months' time had induced an optimistic outlook. He was feeling good.

The train was fairly crowded. He shared a compartment with three men. One of them he judged to be Hungarian. The other two were Czechs. From their conversation, Kenton gathered that all three were commercial travellers. He began to read the newspaper he had bought on the station.

The train drew slowly out of the station. He put the paper down and felt in his pocket for a cigarette. The Hungarian caught his eye.

'Pardon, *mein Herr,*' he said, 'we are about to play a game of poker-dice – one *pfennig* is the maximum stake. We are three. Would you care to play also?'

Kenton hesitated. Then he smiled regretfully and shook his head.

'Thank you, *mein Herr.* It is good of you. I am afraid I don't play.'

JOURNEY INTO FEAR

Eric Ambler

It is 1940 and Mr Graham, a quietly spoken engineer and arms expert, has just finished high-level talks with the Turkish government. And now somebody wants him dead. The previous night three shots were fired at him as he stepped into his hotel room, so, terrified, he escapes in secret on a passenger steamer from Istanbul. As he journeys home – alongside, among others, an entrancing French dancer, an unkempt trader, a mysterious German doctor and a small, brutal man in a crumpled suit – he enters a nightmarish world where friend and foe are indistinguishable. Graham can try to run, but he may not be able to hide for much longer . . .

'One of the best stories you'll ever read' *New Yorker*

THE MASK OF DIMITRIOS

Eric Ambler

English crime novelist Charles Latimer is travelling in Istanbul when he makes the acquaintance of Turkish police inspector Colonel Haki. It is from him that he first hears of the mysterious Dimitrios – an infamous master criminal, long wanted by the law, whose body has just been fished out of the Bosphorus. Fascinated by the story, Latimer decides to retrace Dimitrios' steps across Europe to gather material for a new book. But, as he gradually discovers more about his subject's shadowy history, fascination tips over into obsession. And, in entering Dimitrios' criminal underworld, Latimer realizes that his own life may be on the line.

'Not le Carré, not Deighton, not Ludlum have surpassed the intelligence, authenticity or engrossing storytelling that established *The Mask of Dimitrios* as the best of its kind' *The Times*

IN COLD BLOOD

Truman Capote

Controversial and compelling, *In Cold Blood* reconstructs the murder in 1959 of a Kansas farmer, his wife and children. Truman Capote's comprehensive study of the killings and subsequent investigation explores the circumstances surrounding this terrible crime and the effect it had on those involved. At the centre of his study are the amoral young killers Perry Smith and Dick Hickock, who, vividly drawn by Capote, are shown to be reprehensible, yet entirely and frighteningly human.

The book that made Capote's name, *In Cold Blood* is a seminal work of modern prose, a remarkable synthesis of journalistic skill and powerfully evocative narrative.

'The American dream turning into the American nightmare ... a remarkable book' Tony Tanner, *Spectator*